You Reap What You Sow

By: Jerome D. Dickson

ISBN-13:978-1717391094
ISBN-10:1717391095

Cover Design: Crystell Publications

Book Productions: Crystell Publications
You're The Publisher, We're Your Legs
We Help You Self Publish Your Book
(405) 414-3991

Published in the USA

DEDICATION

To: My Daughter, Zamora A. Dickson: As I Pray to God for forgiveness, I beg it from you. My child, know that I am not what I once was, and that I am now a man, a better man for having held you. My course was written in Galatians 6:7 NJV, "Be not deceived, God is not mocked - for whatsoever a man soweth, that shall he also reap." God's words are truth. Zamora. I will love you for a thousand lifetimes, and in each one of them, I will love you even more...

    Love You, Baby Girl

    To forgive is something that a lot of people have a very hard time doing, but also some people don't know how to forgive because they don't know the meaning of it. To Forgive is to renounce anger of resentment against someone, as a result of something that happened in their life. It's sometimes hard to forgive someone that you don't know, even someone you don't like or care for. But more so, someone you hate. A lot of people feel like forgiveness is for the weak. As we get older, we find it a lot easier to forgive, it becomes natural. I hear a lot of people say it takes a real man, or a real woman, to forgive. If a child says, "I'm sorry" Is he, or she, asking for forgiveness? Most people say if I were you, I would not forgive him, or her; Also in the same breath, a lot of times those same people that said I would not forgive him, or her, are the very same people that ask others to forgive them. They want forgiveness, but don't want to forgive. Why ask for forgiveness, but do the same thing again? When you forgive, forgive them from your heart.

    For all those I have hurt Mentally, Psychologically, and Emotionally, I would like to truly say I'm sorry and ask for forgiveness.

ACKNOWLEDGMENTS

To all those that never gave up on me and believed in me when I did not believe in myself...

To my mother, Phyllis Wells: If there was one word to describe you, it would be, "Love". Even when I did the unthinkable and disrespected you time and time again, it never stopped you from showing the love you have for me. I Love You, Mom.

To my father, Marvin Wells: I thank God every day for putting you in my mother's life. It takes a real man like you to put up with me, my three sisters, and my mother. Only a real man like you can put up with three kids who are not yours. You not once left us on our own and you always did your best to give us advice in any situation. I thank God for that. Love you, Dad.

To my cousin, Travis Johnson: Even though I was your older cousin you would look up to me, not realizing I was looking up to you. If there was anyone I would give the respect to call authentic, that one person would be you. You define the word Authentic. There were plenty of times I did things in them streets that I was in the wrong for and you would give me advice. Even when I thought I was right and it seemed like I was not listening, in the back of my mind I was. Keep being that authentic person you always have been. Love you, Cousin.

To the mother of my child, Natasha Joseph: I thank you for putting up with me throughout these years. I know I put you through a lot, but still, you are by my side like you said you would be. I truly do Love you and thank you. Love you.

To my grandma, Mary Weaver: You are one strong woman that's been through a lot and always tried to hide it from the family. But all that did was show us you are a strong woman and you're not going to let anyone get over on you. Grandma, you might now see it but you showed me that a real woman would not let anyone or anything stop her from being that woman. If I ever find that right woman, I would want her to be like you. Love you, Grandma.

To my sister, Rodesha Wells: At first, I thought I was going to have problems with you when you got older because you had an attitude problem and your mouth was a litlle crazy. But I guess you just needed the right man to come in your life to straighten that out. I thank God for showing you that if no one got your back, he does. I thank you for believing in yourself even when people like me had doubts about you. Love you, sis and keep being the respectable woman you are. Love you, sis.

To my son, Quannell Mitchell: I never realized how much you looked up to me until I was not around you. Quannell, I know you are still mad at me for leaving you and your mother out there all alone. There is not much I can say except that I'm sorry. Forgive me and hopefully one day you will understand why I left. Love you, Son.

To my sister, Ja'Quesha Dean: I'm so proud of you. There was not a doubt in my mind that you would become the successful young lady you are today. I know I was hard on you growing up but it was out of love. I would have been a fool if I would have let them street thugs ruin your life or hurt you. Everything I taught you paid off. You are a bright young successful lady. I would say I am sorry, but I'm not because I know I did it all out of love. I'm proud of you. Love you, sis.

To my friend/brother, Cyhien J Barnes, Jr "Cash": I miss you like crazy. I don't think there has been one day that I have not thought about you. October 31, 2011, your life was taken from you. Still to this day it kills me on the inside but I know you're in a better place. A lot of people say they were your friend, but when asked what was your favorite color, car, kind of music, book, or food, they would not know. But that doesn't mean anything because they could know all those things and still not be your friend. I know one thing: As you look down from heaven you realized your real true friends. Love you, Bro "Cash" Rest In Peace, Cyhie J. Barnes.

To my aunt, Narobia Harris: I truly thank you for everything you did and do for me. Even though you are my aunt, a lot of times you were more like a mother. No matter what I did you always put a roof over my head and food in my stomach. I will always remember those things and I will always remember that I love you and thank you.

To my uncle, James "Squalla" Wright: There is a 60% chance that you are not in Heaven and a 40% chance you are. Wherever you are at, I know you are looking out for me. I learned a lot from you when it came to the streets. If I had not listened to you, I would have been in jail a long time ago. Just when I thought I had it all figured out, look where I ended up! Squalla, I thank you for trying to guide me as long as you did. No matter where you are, I love you, Uncle.

To my sister, Keyona Harris: So many good memories that we shared. I could not ask God for a more loving sister. KJV Proverbs 16:16 – "How much better is it to get wisdom than gold and to get understanding rather to be chosen than silver." But how much better is it to have a loving sister like you. Love you, Lu-Lu.

Prologue

Boom!!!

"U.S. Marshals don't move!" they say pointing their guns directly at me and my girl as we lay in bed. Still unsure of what is going on, I lay there until I can get a look at their faces. One of the officers turned the light on in the bedroom, and then, six heavily armed marshal's surround me and my girl. I attempt to get a glance at their faces, but the barrel to one of the marshal's .45s, and the sound of his deep voice had me puzzled. He asked if I was Jerome Dickson.

That's when my life forever changed. Let me go back to the beginning of My Life Story....

You Reap What You Sow

CHAPTER 1

Damn, that shit is loud, I want to sleep again, but I got to get up. Looking out of the window, I notice it's nice out and the sun is shining. Let me turn this movie off, I been in this house all day watching, *Set It Off. What time is it?* I think to myself, as I'm run to my mother and stepdad's bedroom to look at the clock. *It's 1:55 in the afternoon, I got to get ready. Besides, it's Friday, and I need to get my haircut.*

I knew if I got in the shower, I would go right to sleep. Opening my new shoe box to get a look at them, I tell myself, *this shit is nice.* I slid on my dark blue Levi's and put on my T-shirt. When I pulled out my new shoes to put them on, I forgot they still had that brown paper on the inside. I took it out and slid my feet into them. *Damn, these feel good,* I thought, making my way downstairs to the kitchen to get something to eat. Immediately, I noticed a $20 dollar bill on the freezer with a note. I open the note and quickly realize that it's a letter from my mother. She was letting me know that she'd be back around eight or nine that morning. She had gone to Connecticut to visit my stepdad's mother and that there is food in the refrigerator. She also wanted me to know that she'd left $15 for my haircut, and $5 for something to eat, while I was out of the house. I ran back upstairs to go get some cologne from my stepdad's bathroom. My heart was racing cause I knew I was not supposed to be in his things. I ran back downstairs as if they were coming in the house, went out the back door, and locked it. The cool air hit my skin, it felt like 75° degrees outside. There was a beautiful blue sky, and as I made my way down the block, I could smell the aroma of hamburgers and the best smelling smoked sausage comin off the grill. Kids outside were running around, playing as the ice cream truck made its rounds. Down the block, the music comin from the ice cream truck struck the kids' ears, so they looked around for their parents or family members to accommodate their desire for ice cream.

One of the kids went by the name, "Poo". As our paths crossed, she stopped me to ask a question.

"Rome do you have some money for me, so I can get something from the ice cream truck?" As I thought about it, part of me wanted to say yes, but I instead I said no. That was due to me only havin $15 for my haircut and $5 for food. However, in my heart, I really wanted to say yes. Besides, I knew I could have asked my cousin, Tank to loan me $5 to replace the money I would have given, "Poo". Actually, it would not have sat right with me, knowing that I hadn't looked out for the other kids in my hood. Nonetheless, I walked down the block feelin like I was getting closer to the aroma comin from the grill. I glanced down and noticed a shoe print on my new Retro 13s. I stopped and immediately used my right thumb as an eraser.

As a teenager living in the ghetto, I had to keep my appearance up to par. Being only 16 years of age, and being one of few in my area with the new white, baby blue and gray Retro 13s that retailed for $165, I had to keep them clean. Besides, it would be awhile until I could get a new pair from my stepfather. I was still lost as to how that shoe print got on my new shoes. *It had to be Poo she the only one that I came across.* All day, my mind was running a 100 miles an hour. I was thinking about all the things I wanted to do, yet, after hearing an adult male on his phone discussin how he had to be somewhere at 3:00 p.m, and it was ten minutes to 3:00 p.m. I walked at a swift pace down the block to make it to my destination.

However, before I arrived, I came across an old associate from elementary school. "Rome Rome!" He called out my name to get my attention. "Is everything ok," he asked, due to my fast pace. For some reason, he thought something was about to happen. I stopped and held a brief conversation for two mins just to specify to him why I was moving at the rapid pace I was.

"Man, everything is fine. I'm just trying to make it to the barbershop before it closes." Glancing out of my peripheral, something got my attention. "Talk to you later," I said, as we went in our own directions. Still stuck on if I had seen someone or not, reappearing out of the blue, from the side of a house was a beautiful face. *Damn*, I thought as she looked directly into my eyes and gave me a light grin. As we crossed paths for a brief moment, our spirits merged. I glanced over my shoulder to observe her butt, not realizing she was observing my physique as well. That's when our eyes made contact for a second time, and we both just smiled and continued on in our separate directions. That was the first time I'd laid eyes on Butterfly.

Still stuck on her beautiful face, I slowly began to come back to reality, after hearing the sound of tunes coming from a tinted out, dark blue, Toyota. And coincidentally, it just so happened to be my cousin, Tank. *Perfect timing. That's my ride to the barbershop, and considering he's a working man, and he needs his free time, I'm hoping he can make time to drop me off.*

As he rolled down his window, I made my way to his car. I could see that he was checking out my Retro 13s. He called me over to his car. Tunes still beating, he turned it down.

"Where you headed?"

"To the barber shop," I replied.

My cousin was not much of a talker, so he nodded his head and turned his tunes back up. Halfway to the barber shop, my cousin gave me the impression that something was wrong. He was very tense, highly nervous, and not the same cousin I knew. Before I could ask if everything was alright, he looked at me as if he was going to say something, but before he could I asked him.

"Cousin, are you ok?" I asked, watching as he turned his music down to a much lower volume.

"Yes. Everything is just fine." I wanted to see if he was going to say something else, so when we were a few minutes from the barbershop, he looked at me again and asked, "Why don't you consider going back to Connecticut?"

"I'd pondered on it… but I didn't have a lot of memories in Connecticut, due to my mother moving to York, PA when I was five years old. So, no, I have not considered moving back to Connecticut. What made you ask?"

He replied, "Things have not been the same with me and my girl. She's thinking about moving back to Puerto Rico because she thinks I had my ex-girl at the house."

Now knowing my cousin, he's always been a player, and knowing that, I believe he did have his ex-girl at his house. Judging by the look on his face, I did not want to put him down anymore.

"Cousin just tell her you love her and you wouldn't disrespect her like that."

A smile appeared on his face, "Thanks for the advice cousin, I needed that," he said as we pulled up to the barbershop. I was about to get out of the vehicle, but he stopped me.

"Them Retro 13s is nice. How much you pay for them?"

"$165. My stepdad got them for me when he went back to Connecticut."

"You have some money?" he asked me.

"Yes, $15 for my haircut and $5 for some food." He put his hand out and asked for the $20. "Cuz, this is all the money I have."

He went in his armrest and pulls out an $100 bill. "I was

going to give you $80, but I don't have any change so let me get the $20, and I'm going to give you this $100."

Now knowing my cousin, it's always a lesson to be learned. Yet, when it came to things like this, I was very indecisive; especially when it came to taking the $100 from my cousin. But the more I thought about it, I was not going to let him change his mind about giving me the cash, so I gave him the $20, and he gave me the $100.

I got out of the car, and before I could cross the street, my cousin called me.

"Rome, Rome come here. I want you to know that money is not for you to be giving it away. Save as much as you can. Love you, cousin."

The way he said that was like it would be the last time I'd ever see him. He rolled his window up, cranked his tunes back up, and drove off.

CHAPTER 2

I finally got to the barbershop. There weren't a lot of people in there. I walked up to my barber to let him know I was there. He told me I would be next in line, and that I shouldn't go anywhere. I sat down to wait for my haircut, but the only thing on my mind was my cousin. *How can a player like him let one girl get him all discombobulated? He got money, nice cars, big house, good job, and can get any girl he wants. I just hoping he don't do something crazy over her.*

My thoughts were disturbed when I heard a familiar voice from the right of me. It was my homeboy, Woodz. I knew I recognized that voice, I just didn't see him when I first walked into the barbershop. Woodz got up out of the barber chair and walked over the mirror to check out his haircut. He nodded his head in a way that lets the barber know he did a good job, and then he finally noticed me with a smile on his face from ear-to-ear.

"How long have you been in here?" my homeboy asked.
"For like 5 minutes. Are you getting your haircut?

"Yes, I'm up next, I'll wait for you. Besides, I got something to discuss with you."

"Rome Rome, come on and take a seat," my barber said. "How are things going, and what are you getting today?"

"1A," with the grinned. Once he started my hair, I went into a daze from all the things that were going on, from my mother going to Connecticut and not asking me if I wanted to go, to not giving Poo that cash for some ice cream, to seeing that beautiful girl, down to the things my cousin was asking me, and finally, on to Woodz and the things he wanted to discuss with me.

After I heard my barber, and then the guy next to me having a very deep discussion about women that are beautiful without an education, my barber asked the guy next to me would he date a woman that looked beautiful without an education. He also wanted to know would he date a woman that looked unattractive with an education. Woodz and my barber and a couple of people waited on him to answer the question as the guy thought about it. I thought about it myself, *would I talk to a woman that is beautiful without an education?* Before I could think things all the way through, the guy next to me started talking.

"I'd date the beautiful one without an education," he said. My barber then chimed in, "Why not the unattractive one with the education?"

"Because she unattractive, too plain; and besides that, if I got the one that's beautiful, I could get her to enroll in school and get her education."

My barber argued the point that he would talk to the one

that was unattractive, because she would work hard in life to become somebody, and the women who are beautiful are always looking for a handout in life. Now with me only being 16 years old, I noticed a lot of beautiful women that seemed to always get a handout based on their looks. As they were talking something ironic happened. My barber paused in mid-sentence as the door to the barbershop opened. Out of nowhere, a woman walked in with two little boys. Everyone in the barbershop stopped as if time stood still on its own, and it felt like the woman and her two 'Boys were the only ones moving.

She smiled, and then asked in a very polite tone, "Hi, can someone assist me? My two boys need their hair cut."

By her accent and the sound of her voice you knew she was from out of town. The way she looked and carried herself, the only word to describe her was gorgeous. She had smoky dark skin, curly long black hair down to the top of her ass, and stood about 5'8". Before she could get to someone the barber beside me called her. "Sweetheart," he said.

She made her way toward him. "How long have you been cutting hair?" she asked.

"About four or five years."

"Okay, how much are you going to charge me for my two boys' hair?"

"For you, it's free," he said.

"Thanks but, no thanks. Here is $40 for my kids' hair," she said in a respectful tone. "I would appreciate it if you didn't call me sweetheart. Call me Ms. Santiago."

She gazed over at me. "Nice haircut. Where are you

from.

"Connecticut," I answered. She was having more of a conversation with me than anyone in the barbershop. I, on the other hand was lost for words. The only thing I could do was nod my head. She asked me where I'd gotten my Retro 13s and I told her.

"I just bought some pink ones from New York, that's where I heard of them," she said. "I wanted to get some for my boys but they ran out of their sizes."

My barber cut in on the conversation. "Are you from New York?" he asked.

"No," she answered. She turned back to me. "Men here don't have manners or respect. He could have said excuse me before just started butting in on the conversation."

The barber beside me must have heard her. "Excuse me," he said. "How would you like your son's haircut?"

She looked at me as if I knew how she wanted her son's hair. "Can you assist me with this decision?"

Give him a 1A with the grin, 'round the back and ice picks down as long as you can get them."

"Thank you," she said while going in her Burberry bag to get something. She pulled out her phone. "Seven missed calls," she whispered under her breath. "I'll be back." She made her way toward the door. Her youngest boy had fallen asleep in the chair. She stopped to take her summer jacket off and cover her son with it. She gave him a kiss on the forehead and went out the door.

My barber handed me the mirror to look at his work. "Youngin," he said. "She was all over you. If you were older, you could have pulled her."

I smiled, but not about what he'd said but at how good of a job he'd done on my haircut. My self-esteem was a little low when I'd first come outside, due to me not having a haircut. Feeling like no one could tell me shit, I went in my pocket and felt the keys to the crib. My heart dropped. I couldn't find the $100 bill I came in with. It came to me. It was in my third pocket, I pulled it out, unfolded it and gave it to my barber. He went in his pocket to get change, pulled out a wad of cash and handed me. Four $20 bills and a $5 dollar bill.

"Woodz, you ready?" I asked.

We stepped outside. The sun was shining at an all-time high but there was a cool breeze at the same time.

"Woodz what do you have to talk to me about?"

"You remember the girl, Angel, that stays up the block from me? She's having a party tonight and wants me to tell some people about it. So you're invited. It's around nine p.m. and it's at her house. Are you going to come?"

"I don't know. My mother and father are coming back from Connecticut around that time. You know how my mother feels about me being out around the block. Bad shit is always going on. But I'll see... Look, Woodz. That shit is nice," I said pointing at an all-white Mercedes Benz with some 22" rims on it. Someone beeped the horn as we passed it. The tint was so dark all I could see was my own reflection.

The window rolled down. It was Ms. Santiago from the barbershop. "Come here, sweetie." She motioned for me to come to her car.

"Is my son still asleep?" she asked.

"Yes, Ms. Santiago," I said.

"Thank you," she said. "Let me get back in there. If my son gets up and doesn't see me, he's going to have a fit. I'm not going to hold you up, handsome. With your pearly white teeth," she said. As she got out of the car, something caught my eye, besides her thong peeking out. She had nickel plated .25 pistol on the right side of her hip. She put her car keys on the hood of the car and fixed her attire before looking across at me.

I nodded. "Bye, Ms. Santiago," I said.

"Rome, Come on!" Woodz said. "You been in that woman's face all day."

"No, she's been in my face all day."

Now, Woodz had been my homeboy for some time. I knew him, and the way he was talking was like he was jealous she was giving me some attention.

"Woodz, you seen that?"

"Seen what, Rome?"

"She had a nickel plated .25 pistol on her"

"No, I didn't see that. But I did see that fat ass!" he said, looking back to get one more look at her before she entered back into the barber shop.

Hearing the sirens of cop cars getting closer made my heart drop. I hoped it wasn't my cousin. I looked back to see the cops on the ass of a two-door, black Lexus. The Lexus was giving the cops a run for their money. They flew by doing about eighty or one hundred miles an hour.

All Woodz and I could do was smile. We liked the fact that the black Lexus was getting low on the cops. It had always amazed me when someone got over on the cops.

I hope the cops don't catch that person, I thought to myself.

I felt a pain in my stomach. I didn't know if it was because I hadn't eaten a thing all day.

"Woodz, you eat?"

"No, why?"

"Because I haven't eaten all day. My stomach is on empty. What time is it?"

"5:10."

"I've got to get something to eat, like now."

Woodz decided to go to his mother's house so we could get something to eat and get dressed for Angel's party.

Cop cars came from every direction. We turned the corner and the street was full of cops. The black Lexus's driver's side door was open but no one was in the car. The cops had their guns out, running around like chickens with their heads cut off.

We stopped to look but Woodz's mother ran up the block, yelling at Woodz and me to come to her. She embraced us with a hug and kiss.

"Come in the house until the cops leave," she said. "Whatever the guy did, the cops want to find him bad."

She spoke like the cops hadn't gotten him. That was always a good thing in my eyes.

I was so hungry that my stomach was in pain. I must have had the look of hunger in my eyes. Woodz's mother sat a plate right in front of me. I ate that food so fast, it was hard to breathe. By the time Woodz came back into the kitchen, I was done.

After my meal, all I could think about was getting some

sleep. But with all the people in and out of Woodz's house, it was difficult to get any rest.

It always seemed like a holiday at Woodz's house. There was lots of food and lots of people. I couldn't let my Friday go by, by sleeping all day. And with my mother and father not comin' back until that night, I had to have some fun.

I usually didn't get time to have fun like a lot of kids. Like Woodz, he could be out until one in the a.m. on a school night. Me on the other hand, I had to be in by nine on school nights and ten on weekends. I knew it was because my parents wanted the best for me. Not to say my homeboy's parents didn't want the best for him, but I felt like one in the morning was late for any kid.

As kids, we don't realize how much our parents care for us until we get older, and have kids ourselves. We think our parents don't want us to have fun. In all reality, they want us to have fun, be happy and do the right things in life. As kids, the decisions we make sometimes aren't good for our futures.

Seein' all the people in and out of Woodz's house, I knew nothing good was going to come out of being in there. I got up to walk to the stairs and Poo was on her way down.

"Rome, you want me to get my brother for you?" She asked.

"Yes, Poo!"

One thing I could say about Poo was being around that environment didn't stop her from being a very respectful and very understanding young lady. When it came to her mother or father telling her she couldn't have something or go somewhere, she didn't talk back.

If I had a little girl, I would've wanted her to be just like Poo. Didn't talk back to her mother or father, or anyone for that matter.

As kids, we don't know why our parents say no to the things we want to have or want to do. We think it's because they don't care but little do we know it's for the best. How is it that a little kid like Poo could be positive in a negative environment? It's so hard for adults or young adults to stay positive in a negative environment because they don't want to be positive. People can choose to be positive in any environment. It's all up to that person.

Poo came back downstairs to let me know her brother said he was coming. I heard a knock at the door and Poo ran to open it. She found police officers standing in the doorway. She looked as if she'd done something wrong.

"Are your parents around?" one officer asked.

"Yes," she said.

"Can we talk to them?" the officer asked.

Ms. Mary came to the door. "Yes, can I help you?"

One of the officers talked while the other officer looked around.

"We got a report that a suspect ran into your house. We want to know if we can look around?"

"No, officer you may not take a look in my house. That happened like two hours ago. You know that guy did not run into my house."

"Well Ms. Mary, if we find out you are hiding the guy we are looking for, you can be charged for hiding a fugitive! Thank you for your time."

Ms. Mary slammed the door in the cop's face.

Woodz finally came downstairs.

"Why were the cops at the door?"

"They were looking for the guy from earlier today that was driving that black Lexus."

Woodz's mother really didn't want us to go out.

"Y'all be safe out there today. The cops have been messing with everyone all day." Woodz's mother handed us a bottle of water before we left the house.

As soon as we got outside, two cop cars rode right by us looking at us as if they were going to jump out the car.

"We need to go to my house so I can jump in the shower. This hair got me itching and I want to see if my mother and father called," I said.

"I'll go with you. But before we go to your house, I need to stop by my cousin's house to get my phone. She put it on the charger for me while I went to the barber shop."

"Okay, but don't be long. I want to jump in the shower before it gets too late."

"Come on, Rome. Hurry up, there's my grandma. Let me see if she can give us a ride to your house." Woodz ran up to the car to talk to his grandma, Mrs. Fish. "Rome, come on. She's going to give us a ride."

Mrs. Fish was very down to earth and would do anything for anyone, at any given time. She always made sure to have something to eat and she loved to cook while playing her old school music.

"Are you staying at my house this weekend?" Mrs. Fish asked Woodz. "If you're not, call me to let me know so I can lock my door."

We got to my house and Woodz got out to get in the passenger seat of his grandma's car.

"Rome, I'll be back. I'm going to go get my phone from my cousin's house," Woodz said.

"Okay, I'll leave the back door unlocked."

CHAPTER 3

I walked in my house. It was always a good feeling to be in my mother and father's house. My mother always kept the house clean, smelling good and in order. I hadn't talked to her all day. I had to call to see if everything was okay with them before I got in the shower. I looked on the phone and saw that my mother had been calling all day to see if I was okay. Before I could turn the phone on, it rang. I almost dropped it. What a coincidence, it was my mother. I knew she was going to be upset with me for not calling her all day.

"Hello," I said.

"Hi, son. Why haven't you called me?"

"Because I went to get my haircut and I just got back to the house. How is grandma doing?"

"She's doing good son. She misses you and wants to see you the next time we come to Connecticut."

"Tell grandma don't forget to send me that photo we took at her house." I heard someone in the background calling out my name. "Mom, who is that calling out my name?"

"Your sister."

"Put her on the phone so I can ask her something," I said.

My sister was being smart, because she was out of town and I was home all by myself, looking over the house for my mother and father. But little did she know, I was about to have more fun then she thought.

I could tell my sister's real intentions were to say she missed me and loved me. Those were the words she said to me before getting off the phone and giving it back to my mother.

My mother let me know they would be back the next morning and that I was supposed to go to my cousin's, Big Tank's house to stay with him for the night. She said she would call to check up on me to see if I was okay.

"Love you, son," my mother said before hanging up the phone.

When my mother hung up the phone, I just knew I was going to have some fun. To be real though, a bit of sadness came over me. I knew it was because I was missing my family.

We don't realize how much we miss our loved ones until they are not in our sight. It felt like three weeks but it had only been seven hours. I looked at the time on the TV, it was seven thirty and Angel's party was at nine.

Looking down at my t-shirt, I saw a lot of hair. I couldn't walk around anymore with that hair all over me.

I unlocked the back door before I got in the shower.

Feeling refreshed from the shower, I told myself it was on for the night.

I knew my ears weren't deceiving me. I had heard the sound of females voices and laughter. Woodz called for me to hurry up. I put on some of my stepfather's Blue De Chanel cologne. I noticed he'd left his 14k rope gold chain. He wouldn't be back until the next morning so I put the chain on. I got downstairs to see Woodz, his cousin and three of her friends.

I wanted to say something to him for bringing them into my house without letting me know but with the looks Woodz's cousin and her friends were giving me, how could I say anything? Besides, all of them looked good.

"I'm ready, Woodz. Let's go. I wanted to stop at the store to get some gum before we got to the party."

On our way to the store, I talked to Woodz's cousin. I could tell she was hittin' on me. She was asking my age and where I was from. By the time we got to the store, she already had it in her mind that I had to dance with her. What she didn't know was that I had already planned to ask her for a dance. She and her three friends commented on the cologne I had on. Saying I smelled good. I looked back to see which one of them had said it but I got smiles from all four of them.

By the time Woodz and I got to the store we already had which girl we were going to talk to for the night in mind. Little did he know, it was his cousin that I was interested in. Other than her smart mouth, out of her and her friends, she was the one I could see myself talking to.

We got to the store and it seemed like the party was there. I'd never seen that many people at a corner store before. I didn't know how the store owner could keep an eye on everyone there. I got my gum and a bottle of orange juice then went outside. It seemed like more people were out there. All I heard people talking about was going to Angel's party. I looked around for Woodz but couldn't find him.

His cousin, Misha walked up to me. "Rome, Woodz said he'll meet you at my house. He had to go do something."

I had a good feeling she wasn't lying to me. Besides, that would be a good time to talk to her alone. "Where'd your friends go," I asked.

"They went to get a bottle of Grey Goose. They'll meet us back at my place," she said. "Why, do you like one of my homegirls?"

"No, I like you," I said.

"How long have you known Woodz?" she asked.

"For about a year, why?"

"Because I saw you one time before, but then I didn't see you for a long time."

"That's because my mother moved back to Connecticut."

"That's where you from?" she asked.

"Yes," I said.

I didn't know we were at Misha's house when a dog come running full speed toward us. I looked at her to see if she was seeing what I was seeing.

"No O-girl!" Misha yelled out. "Don't run, Rome. That's my dog."

Misha had a pretty, light brown female pit bull.

Misha's mother, Ms. TP, welcomed me like she'd known me all my life. She invited me in to her house and the sound of slow jams played from the system. It made me feel right at home. Misha ran upstairs. The back door was open and the dog ran in and out. It seemed like her dog was checking things out. It would go out back for two minutes and come back in and look at me. It went up the stairs, came back down and went right back outside.

Ms. TP came in.

"Honey, you okay?" Ms. TP asked Misha.

"Yes!"

Misha's three friends walked in with a big bottle of Grey Goose and asked me if I wanted a cup.

"No," I said. I'd never drank before.

I heard Ms. TP calling Woodz's name. I went to the back door and saw him getting out of a car, knowing he didn't have a license to drive. I asked him where he got the car from. All he said was that it was his people's car and that he had it for the night.

When it came to the street life, Woodz always was ahead of the game. Woodz asked if I wanted to hit his bottle of Hennessey. Everyone was drinking around me but it would take a lot more pressure to get me to drink.

Misha and her friends came outside, amped up and ready for the party. It seemed like everyone and their mother was walking to the party.

***

Woodz had his arms around Misha's friend and I had my arm around Misha. We made it to Angel's party. It was live. Ass was everywhere. People were rollin' up. People in the kitchen rolled dice and there were bottles all over.

Misha took me to the darkest room and pushed me on

the wall. She started throwing her ass all over me. Damn, she could dance! My hands were all over Misha's fat ass. I was convinced I was leaving with her that night.

I looked beside me. Damn, for one of Misha's friends to be a white girl, she could sure dance. Woodz was having a hard time handling her but I could not talk myself, I was having a hard time with Misha. The music stopped, so someone could find their phone. When the light came on, I scanned the room; there were bad ass girls everywhere.

I instantly changed my mind on leaving with Misha. The more I looked around the more girls I saw.

I followed my homeboy into the kitchen to see if he was okay. Walking in the kitchen, I saw some boy rapping his ass off. The way the boy was rapping was like something I'd never seen. He had about six to eight females around him. He stopped flowing just to sip on his bottle of Patron and went right back at it, not missing a beat. He rapped like he'd been doing it all his life and the crazy thing was he looked like he was only about twelve years old. The boy had real true talent.

Woodz and I walked out back to get some air. It was so hot in there, the walls were sweating. Woodz's house was only up the block from the party. We walked there. I told him that would be a good idea, considering I had to let my cousin, Tank, know I was okay.

Woodz walked to his house and I walked eight or ten houses up to Tank's house. I saw him sitting on the porch, talking on his cell phone. He covered up the phone like he didn't want someone to hear him talk. He whispered to me, "Cousin, this is your mother on the phone."

He had a few more words with my mother and then hung up the phone. "Cousin, your mother just wanted to know where you were. I told her you were asleep. That's why I covered the phone, so she would not hear you talk. The problem is, I was your age before. I know how it goes. I saw you walking with some girl earlier. Was that your girl?"

"No, that's Woodz cousin, Misha."

"I hear it's a party down the block. Don't get into anything and if you're going to stay out, you can stay at Woodz's house. I'll see you in the morning."

I walked down to Woodz's house and knocked on the door.

Woodz opened it. "Hold on, I have to get something from my cousin."

I was impatient. I just wanted to get back to the party. *He's got to hurry up*, I thought to myself.

Woodz came back down. He said he had to go somewhere for his cousin.

I was mad as shit because I wanted to go back to that party but I was not going to let my homeboy walk by himself.

As we walked up to Misha's house, I thought of the good time I'd been having at Angel's party. I was so busy thinking, I'd forgotten about the car Woodz had for the night.

We hopped in and Woodz put in a CD before we rode to that corner store where I got my gum and orange juice from. Some guy walked up to the car. Woodz handed him something and the guy handed Woodz some money. We stayed there for a couple seconds so Woodz could count the cash and then pulled off. I had a good idea of what my homeboy was doing but I never asked him. We drove back in the direction of the party. When he stepped on the gas pedal, the horsepower of the car threw me back in my seat. *Slow this shit down,* I thought to myself.

Before we drove by the party, he rolled all four windows down, turned the music up to its max, and pulled up to the party. People were looking at us, bobbing their heads to the music. We stopped in the front of the party. Angel came to the car, looking like the next top model.

"Hi Woodz, can I drive your car?"

I looked at Woodz to see what he was going to say.

Being that it was Angel's B-Day, of course, he would say yes to her. Angel jumped in the driver's seat, Woodz got in the passenger seat, and I went back in the party.

By the look on Misha's face, I could tell she was upset with me for leaving her. Trying to make me jealous, she pulled some boy to her and started dancing with him. I hoped she didn't think I was getting jealous. There were too many good looking girls in there to be jealous over one.

I felt someone pull on my hand and I looked back to see who it was. There were two Hispanic girls, one got straight to the point. By the way the girl danced you could tell she knew what she was doing.

The door opened to Angel's party. I looked to see who it was. Woodz and Angel came walking in with big smiles on their faces.

I could not believe my eyes, it was Butterfly.

I didn't know if she had walked in with Angel or not,

but I knew one thing, I was not going to leave without talking to her. As soon as she walked in, the guys were all over her.

There were a lot of fly niggas in the party. But for some odd reason, she wasn't giving any of them the time of day. Then, I saw the boy that was in the kitchen rapping walk over to Butterfly and say something in her ear. He walked out and she walked behind him.

Damn, that's got to be her boyfriend. Fuck it! I'm not going to leave this party without getting the Hispanic girl's phone number, I thought to myself.

I looked over in the corner where Woodz and Angel were at. I saw a lot of commotion. I walked over to see if everything was okay with Woodz.

"Let's get out of her before they start to fight," he said.

I could feel the tension in the air. The party was about to get bad real fast. Before I knew it, a fight had broken out.

Someone got hit so hard that he fell back into the TV. The screen broke and people ran out the front out the back doors. *Damn, I've got to find that Hispanic girl,* I thought to myself.

Walking with Woodz to the car, we saw Misha and her friends. They were alright. The only one left I had to make sure was alright, was Butterfly. It seemed like every time I seen Butterfly was on my mind.

I asked Woodz if he knew her. I described her to him so he'd know for sure.

"Yes," he said, like he had known her for a while.

We got to the car. I had to find out everything I could about her. *I hope she's not a hoe.*

"Does she get around? How do you know her?" I asked Woodz. I was a little nervous for the answer, but more than ever for if he was going to say he'd fucked her.

I know Woodz was thinking to himself, "Out of all the good looking girls at the party, Rome keeps asking about this one girl."

All he said was, "Rome, you know that's Angel's cousin?"

"No, I did not know that."

Woodz called Angel to see if she would get her cousin to come back to her house, me not knowing the type of girl Butterfly was.

Woodz laughed at me. "Rome, she can't be out like that. Her mother doesn't let her do anything but go to school and back home."

"How old is she?" I asked.

"A year younger than you," Woodz said. "Do you want to go to Misha's house with me? Her homegirl just texted me and said she wants me to bring you."

"Let's go. I don't like sitting in the car like this while people keep walking by. Plus, I'm in the mood to drive"

Woodz let me take one ride around the block to see if I could bag some girls. I rode right by the two *Hispanic* girls from the party.

"Where y'all sexy girls on your way to?" I asked.

One replied, "We're on our way to the house. Can we get a ride?"

"Sweetheart, you can get a ride anywhere you want," I said.

I know my homeboy was feeling one girl and I was

feeling the other. They got in and I put on some slow jams for them. We stopped by McDonald's to get them something to eat. The girl I was talking to acted shy like she didn't want to eat. "No thank you," she said. *If she thinks I was going to take them home without getting them something to eat, she is wrong.* I ordered them something anyways.

She told me where they lived. I pulled over by their house and got out to walk her to her door. I could tell she was feeling me. I had to get her phone number, and that's what I did. She thanked me for the ride, followed by a kiss good night. I got to the car and learned my homeboy Woodz had gotten her home girls number. He stored her number in his phone. Me not having a phone, stored Sayna's number in my homeboys phone.

I knew my homeboy smoked weed and he knew I didn't. He still asked if I wanted to hit the weed. It smelled good and all, but I was scared of the effect it would have on me, I told him no but I did ask to hit the bottle of Hennessey. One sip had my chest on fire. I didn't know how he could drink that shit. I guess drinking wasn't my thing. Woodz's phone was going off like crazy. He answered it and handed me the phone. It was Misha, asking me if I was going to come to her house because she wanted to see me.

Playing mind games with her, I said, "No, I'm going home." I knew damn well I was on my way to her house.

We pulled up to her house, not knowing if her mom was in the house. Before we could get to the door, a head popped out of the second-floor window. I looked and saw Misha. By the time we got to the door, she was already opening it.

Damn, she had to jump down all the stairs! I just seen her upstairs in the window.

The first thing I looked for was O-girl, her dog. I didn't see Misha's mother but slow jams were playing softly. One of Misha's friends was asleep on one end of the couch and the other friend was on the other end.

I didn't know where her friend that was dancing with Woodz was, but I knew he was going to be mad at me because I was going upstairs with his cousin. I didn't know where he was going to stay that night.

I guess I was wrong.

"Cousin, my homegirl is upstairs," Misha said. "Come on."

We walked upstairs behind Misha.

She really does have a fat ass in those pajama pants. Misha's friend was in her pajama pants also, carrying four cups and a half bottle of Grey Goose. She filled the cups to the top. That one sip I'd taken from Woodz's Hennessey already had my head spinning. I felt like I was going to throw up. I couldn't take one more sip of anything, not even a sip or water. All I wanted to do was hold Misha and that fat ass of hers, and that's what I did.

CHAPTER 4

I woke up to an empty bed with the sun shining in my face. I heard footsteps coming up the stairs. I jumped up. I didn't know if they were Woodz's, Misha's, or Misha's mom's. I stood up and the room started to spin.

It was Misha with a plate of food and a bottle of ginger ale. I sat back down. Misha must have known I wasn't feeling good at all. She treated me like a baby, rubbing my stomach and feeding me. She showed me a lot of affection.

"Where's my homeboy, Woodz?" I asked.

I had forgotten he took Misha's friend home.

"He told me to let you know he was going to stay at her house and that he be back to come get you."

I knew I had to be at Tank's house so I asked Misha to call Woodz. Before she could call him, I heard a horn.

I got up, still feeling dizzy. I stumbled to the window to see if it was Woodz. It was.

This boy is crazy. I know he did not bring Sayna and Roseanna to Misha's house.

I walked downstairs to leave Misha's house. Her two friends were still sleeping on the couch. I gave Misha a hug and told her I'd talk to her later. I walked out and got in the car.

It smelled like a pound of weed.

"How'd you get up with Sayna and Roseanna?" I asked him.

"Roseanna called and asked me what I was doing. I told her I was about to come get you. She said her sister Sayna wanted to see you," he said.

I felt someone's hands rubbing on my face from behind me. I looked back to see that it was Sayna. She must have seen it in my face that I was not feeling good. I leaned the seat back. The feeling of Sayna's hands on my face put me right back to sleep.

I couldn't have been out for long but I know I had slept hard enough not to notice Woodz and Roseanna leaving the car and Sayna in the driver seat. The only thing that woke me up was the feeling of Sayna going in my pants. I looked down to see my zipper open.

I looked at Sayna she looked at me.

"Damn, your dick is big and you not even hard! If that's how big your dick is when you're not hard, I got to see how big it is when it gets hard."

I looked around to see where we were. I saw we were in the parking lot of a mall.

"Where my homeboy?" I asked Sayna.

"He went in the mall to go do something and Roseanna went with him," she said. "Relax."

She put her hand in my pants, pulled my dick out, and began to stroke it. She then put her hair up in a ponytail and whispered the word, "relax".

She went down and began sucking my dick. I could tell that was not her first time doing it. Sayna was sucking the life out of me. I was under the impression she was a good girl, but I was wrong. Ten minutes into Sayna giving me head, I could not hold back anymore. I tried to warn her but she kept going. I nutted in her mouth and she swallowed all of it.

This bitch is nasty, I thought to myself.

Sayna then reached in the backseat in her bag and pulled out a baby wipe. She wiped my dick off and then put it back in my pants.

"Rome I'll be back would you like something to drink?" she asked.

She got out of the car, walked to the soda machine, and got two sodas, one for her and one for me. She got in the back seat and sat there like nothing ever happened. One thing I could say about her was that I was never going to forget about her.

I finally saw Woodz and Roseanna coming but it seemed like a guy was following them. The closer the guy got to the car, the more he looked like a cop. Knowing my homeboy had been selling drugs for his cousin, I thought my homeboy had gotten set up and that the car was an undercover cop car. Not knowing the truth, I got out and told Sayna to get out too.

We walked away slowly, thinking at any moment the cops were going to surround us.

Woodz called my name. I looked back. Woodz must have known I thought the guy he was with was a cop.

"Rome," he called out. "He's cool. He works with my

mother at the store."

I was still unsure if he was a cop or not, Roseanna walked up to us and started to talk to Sayna. She said the guy's family was in the mall and that he came out to get some crack from Woodz.

I saw Woodz go in the car and. hand the guy something Then the guy walked off. Woodz walked up to me.

"You want to get the guy's car later on?" Woodz asked.

"I'm good," I said.

We got in the car. Woodz must have known I was mad. We didn't say anything the whole way to dropping Roseanna and Sayna off at their house. When we got to Roseanna and Sayna's house, they got out. Sayna gave me a hug and told me to call her later. We drove off. Woodz looked at me and said, "Rome, you alright."

I knew if I didn't say something then, he would keep doing the same shit, so I told him what was on my mind.

"No, I'm not okay. You left me in the car with drugs in it. You didn't say anything or wake me up to tell me about it. Next time, let me know before you come get me."

"I went to get Roseanna this morning but her friend Sayna wanted to see you bad. The whole way to Misha's house all Sayna kept saying was, 'I really like your homeboy, Rome. But I don't think he's feeling me.' Last night when we were at Misha's house, Sayna called my phone for you like ten times. Rome you were so fucked up, you wouldn't get up. So I went to Misha friend's house and fucked the shit out of her and then went to sleep. I got a phone call around 6:30 this morning from Roseanna so I went to her house and then came to get you. Anyways, did you fuck my cousin Misha last night?"

With Woodz being my homeboy and all, if I did I don't think I could have told him.

"No, Woodz. But she made a big plate of food."

"Rome you're my homeboy. But that's my cousin, don't play her. She really likes you."

I had to respect my homeboy, besides I wouldn't want him to play one of my cousins.

On our way to Tank's house, we rode by Angel's house first. I could not believe who I saw standing outside with Angel, Butterfly. I tapped Woodz to park the car so I could talk to Butterfly. I hopped out and she looked at me with that million dollar smile. I knew I had her.

I said, "Hi," to Angel and asked Butterfly if I could talk to her for a minute. She was hesitant on walking with me.

"Where we going?" she asked.

"Right by the car," I said.

She walked with me to the car with her arms crossed like she was cold. I started the conversation off.

"You are a very cute girl. I would like to know if it would be alright if I had your number?"

She smiled. "No, but I'll take yours," she said.

I went in the car to get a pen and wrote my house number down. She looked down at the paper I wrote my number on then looked at me.

"Your name is Rome?"

I said, "Yes!"

"Is that the name your mother named you?"

I said, "No."

I asked for the paper back and wrote my real name. I

handed it back to her.

She smiled and said, "Ok Jerome. I'll call you."

From the party the night before, to getting drunk and falling asleep at Misha's crib, to getting some head from Sayna, running into Butterfly was the icing on the cake. With Tank's house being only up the block, I said goodbye to Butterfly.

CHAPTER 5

I walked up the block to my cousin's house with a big smile on my face. It stretched from ear to ear. I got to my cousin's door and saw a woman leaving the house. My cousin smacked her on her ass. She looked back at him and told him to call her later.

"Did you have fun at the party?" Tank asked.

"The party was live," I said.

"I will take you to your house to get some clothes for a few days until your mother gets back from out of town?" Tank said.

"I thought my mother and dad would be back today?" I asked.

"They were but your grandma wanted them to stay until Monday. Also, your mother told me to let you know she misses and loves you and for you to call her when you get up."

I missed my mother and all, but I had Butterfly on my mind. I wanted to get back to my house to wait on her phone call and that also would be a good time to take a shower. Tank yelled downstairs to let me know he was going to take a shower and then take me to my house to get a shower and a change of clothes.

I kept nodding off as I waited for Tank, no doubt from being up all night. It seemed like I was asleep for hours but it really was only twenty minutes. I went in the kitchen and saw that Tank was dressed.

He looked at me. "You ready?" he asked.

"Yes," I said.

He went on top of the refrigerator, pulled a gun down, cocked it, put it on his waist, and grabbed his car keys. We walked out the door, got in his car, and drove to my house.

On our way there, he asked how was the party.

"There were a lot of bad bitches there," I said.

"You get any numbers?"

"Yes. I got one." He looked at me like that's it.

"Did you get some pussy?" he asked.

"No, but the girl who gave me her number also gave me some top.

"Cuz', I busted this bitches ass last night! She had a fat ass!" He passed his phone to me. On it, all I saw was ass and pussy. Her tits were big ass shit. He looked at me.

"Cousin, you would not know what to do with that."

All I could say was, "I know, she's got a lot of ass."

I handed him back his phone after I got one more look.

"Cousin it's not nothing to pull a woman. But the thing is to pull a good woman and keep her."

I wasn't sure if he was talking about his wife. Thinking to myself, that the girl in his phone didn't seem like a good woman, doing the things she was doing. All I could think about is the conversation we were having the day before when he dropped me off at the barbershop. When he'd said his wife is thinking about leaving him because he had some girl at the house. I didn't want to bring up the past so I just let him continued on talking. The whole time he's talking to me about women, I heard him.

"But I was under the impression that she was a good girl to now, not having any respect for her," he said. "Cousin, I know you're young, but if you ever get the chance to love a woman and know she loves you as much or more, don't break her heart. It's like a boomerang. It'll come back and that feeling, it's not good. But also, don't let them play you." And speaking getting played…

"That money I gave you yesterday, how much money you still have left over?"

I counted it. "$68," I said.

"How much cash did you give the girl from the party?"

I told him I hadn't given her any cash but I did get her something to eat from Mc D's.

"Cousin they always start off small and then next thing comes. You know, they be asking for everything from some new J's to an LV bag to a new car.

Pulling up to my house, I thanked my cousin for his advice.

"I'll call you when I'm ready for you to come pick me back up," I said.

Tank was telling me something that I already knew, but it was always good to hear things like that again to keep me up on my game.

It would be awhile before I could buy any girl anything. I don't even have money to buy myself a cell phone, let alone minutes for it. The night before was fun, but something has to change and fast. There were a lot of good looking girls at that party that I couldn't have gotten their phone number because I don't have a phone. I know one thing was I wasn't going to come in to night without a cell phone.

I took a shower, got dressed, and called my mother before I left the house. I let her know I was fine and that I'd see them on Monday.

Walking down to my boy Woodz's block, I was in deep thought about how I could make some money without selling drugs to my peoples.

The feeling of seeing everyone around, wearing new clothes and having new things made me feel like I could do it too.

My mind frame changed as soon as a cop rode by with the look in his eyes of catching someone. To me, it was always easy to figure out the ones that were selling on the block because they would be the first ones to walk off at a fast pace. Standing on the block for just a few minutes, I could tell there was a lot of cash on the block. I realized I was just standing there in the way and there was no need to be on that block standing around.

I went to knock on Woodz's door to see if he was there but before I could, his older cousin told me that he was sleep. I hardly ever saw Woodz's cousin, and when I did it would be for a brief moment. I know one thing, he was not like his brothers or anyone on that block. You could tell by the way he carried himself, that he'd seen it all and done it all. And that he loved cash.

Knowing my homeboy would not be asleep for long, I thought of what I could do until he got up. My mind was still running, thinking about how I could make some money.

I went and sat on Tank's porch to get my thoughts right. The more people I saw driving by in nice cars and having fun, the more I thought.

It didn't make it any better seeing Woodz walk up the block with a sleepy look in his eyes.

"Where are you going?" I asked.

"The alley, to meet someone, he said.

I got up to walk with him.

"I'll only be two minutes," he said. I don't need anyone to come with me."

He turned down the alley. It seemed like less than two minutes before he came walking out with a handful of money. He stopped in front of me.

"That bitch ass nigga got me for $100," Woodz said.

Looking at Woodz's face, He did not seem mad at all. I know if someone got me for $100 dollars, I would have put hands and feet all over them.

That's what I would have done, but my homeboy wasn't me.

"I'm going to the store to get a razor. You want something?" he aske

"No," I said. I knew he'd just gotten played for $100 and I really didn't need anything from the store anyways.

Knowing my homeboy, he wouldn't have cared if I asked him to put me on to the drug game. He'd said something to me before about helping him move some, "work" for his cousin but I didn't want the headache his cousin would give him when it came to getting the cash. I know how that is when others take long with your paper. If I'd gotten in the drug game, there was not going to be any playing around with my cash.

For the most part, I really didn't see the need for anything because I had my mother and stepdad. They would do anything for me, but it did not sit right with me.

All the handouts coming from my stepdad and mother, and knowing I had three little sisters that they had to look out for as well made me feel guilty.

One side of me was telling me to get in the drug game and the other side kept saying you really don't need anything.

I was feeling that it was time to become a man and stop depending on my mother and stepdad but I wasn't about to ask a nigga for shit. If I was going to get it I was going to get it on my own. I just had to come up with some cash and I knew what I had to do to get it, catch a pussy sleeping.

CHAPTER 6

The only things I was missing was a pistol and someone to rob. My uncle always told me if I ever did anything, to do it alone because I wouldn't tell on myself. My uncle was right about that. If I wanted something done right, I had to do it my way and by myself.

I kept that in the back of my mind. I was pretty sure I knew the right person to talk to about getting a pistol and that was my boy, Dee. Dee was really cool, stayed to himself, and loved to rap. I knew where I could find him – his house, writing raps with a bottle of E and J.

I walked over to his house with paper on my mind and hoped he was home. I saw his mother just pulling up to the house. She waved for me to come to the car and help her with the groceries.

"Are you looking for my son?" she asked.

"Yes," I said.

"Go upstairs. He's in his room rapping and playing instruments," she said. "Do you rap?"

"No, ma'am."

"Is there anything you're good at?" she asked.

That was something I really hadn't spent a lot of time thinking about. The only thing I knew I was good at was football but I know Dee's mother wasn't talking about sports. "No ma'am," I said.

"It's good to know what you're good at. So then you can do it and get to know yourself," she said. "You can go upstairs, I'm not going to talk your head off."

I heard the sound of instrumentals playing over and over again. I walked in the room and saw Dee and the boy from Angel's party, in the kitchen rapping. The boy looked up at me, down at his notebook, then over at Dee before asking him to play the instrumental back.

Dee moved over for me to sit down. I sat down, knowing that the boy was about to kill the beat.

He went in on the beat, he really could rap. He had true talent. They say music entices people and the things the boy was rapping about had my mind on getting cash.

Since I didn't know the boy Dee was with, I waited until he went to the bathroom before I spoke. With Dee not know what I was about to get into, I told myself I couldn't be mad at him if he said no.

I asked for the gun and Dee said yes, warning me that the gun only had six or seven shots in it. Dee, being a real nigga, never asked why I need it the gun. All he asked was if I wanted him to go with me and I told him I didn't.

When the boy that had been rapping came out the bathroom, Dee introduced me to him. "Rome that's Money. Money that's Rome."

We shook hands.

"Do you rap?" Money asked.

"No," I said.

I really wasn't up for talking. I wanted that pistol so I could do what I needed to do to get on my feet. Dee could tell by my body language that I wanted that gun so I could go take care of my business. Dee told Money to give the pistol to me. Money reached down inside of his boot and pulled out a little black pistol and handed it to me, but not before wiping it off. Money then went in his back pocket and pulled out two blue latex gloves. He handed them to me. I didn't know what they thought I was about to do, but one thing they did know – I wasn't playing. As soon as I got the pistol, I left Dee's house and walked toward Woodz's house to see if he was up. Before I could get there, I saw Woodz walking out.

"You want to use the car before I give it back?" Woodz asked. I knew it would help to get a car with what I had in mind.

"If you're going to see Sanya," Woodz said. "Bring it back before one. The owner has to be at work."

With Woodz being my homeboy, I had to put him on to what I was about to do. "I have to get some cash, Woodz," I said.

He looked me in my eyes and said, "Rome I would give you some work, but I had to give my cousin his cash so I could get some more work."

"How much cash do I need to get some work for myself?" I asked.

"One hundred for three point five," he said.

"How much can I make off that?" I asked.

"Three hundred to three-fifty if you bag it up right."

47

I didn't want to be in my homeboy's business but I did want to see how much cash he had saved up. I was shocked by the answer he'd given me. I had to make sure my ears were not deceiving me so I asked him again. He told me he only had $180 and $160 of that went to his cousin. Right then and there I realized what he was doing. He was working for his cousin for a car and a couple of dollars. That explained why he'd asked me to rent the car out. He'd run out of work.

I knew one thing. If he really was done working for his cousin for a couple of dollars, he could make the power move with me. I told him my plans but he passed on it. I guess he felt comfortable with what he had, and that wasn't a lot. At the moment, my homeboy was doing a lot better than me but that was all about to change. He walked away and I got in the car.

First, I rode around from one side of town to the other. The car was getting low on gas. I was getting upset because I had to spend cash on gas. If I didn't make a move that day, I would be doing the same shit I was before I got the car –nothing except looking at everyone get cash.

I parked to get my thoughts together and to put on the blue latex gloves. I pulled the little gun out my pocket to wipe it off and see how many shots were in it. I'm glad I looked at the clip it only had four shots in it. *Fuck it!*

Four shots were all I need to get the job done. As soon as I sat the gun on the passenger seat, I saw a Hispanic boy walk into a house. I didn't think anything of it until he came back out the house counting cash. Automatically, my mind started racing. My blood started rushing, there wasn't anything stopping me from getting that boy.

The block was quiet. I didn't see anyone else out besides the Hispanic boy. Considering it was a Saturday at about ten am in the morning, people were most likely still asleep.

I knew one thing, he was getting robbed. I put on the black bandana and hopped out the car with the pistol in my hand. I got closer to him. He must have heard my footsteps but before he could turn all the way around, I was on his ass with the pistol damn near in his mouth. He fell right to the ground.

"Give it up," I told him.

He handed over the cash that was in his hand but my instinct was telling me he had more.

"Let your pockets breathe," I said.

When he did, I was surprised by how much cash he had on him. He got up and took off running one way. I took off the other way, jumped in the car, and got the fuck from over there.

I was so nervous. It felt like every car I passed was a cop. *If I did get away with it, I'm going to get myself caught driving this fast.*

I was hot like a gun at the firing range. I had to get to the other side of town before I could get out the car. I parked the car two and a half blocks down from my house. I walked to my house and went straight to my room. I got out the cash I'd taken from the boy and threw it on the bed.

I walked in circles with the pistol in my hand. I looked out my window, feeling like someone had followed me. I looked at the one-hundred dollar bills on top of each other, it was time to see how much cash I'd gotten off him.

I'd taken four one-hundred dollar bills from his hand. The four notes was a start to get me in the drug game. I unfolded one of the knots held by rubber bands. *Damn! This Hispanic boy had some cash on him*, I thought to myself.

The roll had all twenty dollar bills, fifteen of them. The second knot held six ten dollar bills, eight five dollar bills, and twenty-five dollar bills. Altogether, it came up to $825. Besides the $68 I had put in my socks before I hit that lick, I had $893 to get me on my feet.

I knew I needed to get the car back to my homeboy before one but I wouldn't be getting back in that car and knowing what I did. I wasn't going to let my homeboy get back in it either.

My mind was running. I wanted to get out of the house. I didn't want to walk with only four shots in the gun, so I called Tank. The first two calls he didn't answer, but he picked up on the third.

"Can you come get me?" I asked. "I need to get a phone with the rest of the money you gave me."

Tank was a little hesitant. "I'll be there in a lil'. Be outside," he said, eventually.

I knew Tank would be on my top asking how I'd gotten the money if he saw it on me.

I knew I had to get a phone and minutes for it. I also needed new shoes because I knew the Hispanic boy wouldn't forget how mine looked.

It seemed like I was the only one in York at the time with the new Retro 13s. So, I took them off and put on my old Nikes. I grabbed the gun off the roof, put $400 inside my Bible, and took the rest of the money with me.

I went downstairs to wait on Tank but he must have been just around the block because he was already outside, beeping. I ran out, got in the car, and he pulled off.

"Where do you want to go to get your phone?"

I thought about how I could kill two birds with one stone, and get the phone and new pair of shoes. "The mall," I said.

"That's good. I wanted to get something from there any ways," he said.

On the way to the mall, I and my cousin didn't say anything. I kept looking at the pistol that sat in the cup holder. I couldn't tell if it was a 9mm .40 caliber or a .45 caliber. All I knew was that it was nice and I wanted one. My cousin had always been a cool, laid back down to earth guy.

"Do you mind if I see your gun?" I asked, knowing he wouldn't.

He took the clip out, ejected bullet that was in the head, and handed it to me. It felt like it could have been a .45 but I was wrong. It was a .10 mm. I'd never seen one before that day.

Tank looked at me. "Cuz, that's a lot of power there."

"I know," I said, handing it back to him.

We pulled up to the mall. I knew damn well I was not going in the mall with that gun on me. As soon as Tank got out the car, I put the gun under the passenger seat and locked the door.

My cousin looked down at my shoes then looked at me. "Cousin where are your Retro 13s?"

I didn't want to tell him I'd robbed someone in them or lie to him. "I didn't want to wear them. I didn't want them to get fucked up."

I knew he really didn't want me to be out with him looking any kind of way. "I'm not trying to be out long. I still want to get dressed for tonight," I said.

"Me too," he replied.

We got in the mall and I went right to the cell phone store while Tank went next door to the sneaker store.

A cute brown skinned girl walked up to me. "May I help you with anything?" she asked.

"Yes I'm looking to get a cellphone," I said.

She showed me the display of new phones they had but I already had my mind made up. I was in and out. I'd gotten the first phone I liked and added minutes to it before I left.

I went next door to the sneaker store and showed my cousin the phone I'd gotten.

"How much did you pay for it?" he asked.

"$80.00 for the phone and $20 for the phone card," I told him. Knowing I'd hit that lick earlier in the day, I couldn't walk around with the same shoes on. And I damn sure wasn't about to walk around with these old Nikes on, but I had that in my mind from the beginning.

I wanted to kill two birds with one stone. With one bird dead, all I had to take care of was the other one without letting my cousin find out I still had $393.00 on me.

I looked at all the shoes they had. I was feeling a pair of Retro 7s, I had to get them. They only cost $190 which only left me with only $200.00. But that was all the cash I really needed to get some work from my homeboy's cousin. The cash was gone just as fast as I had gotten it. I got to get out of this mall before all the cash I'd come with was gone. While I waited on Tank to get everything he needed, I waited outside the sneaker store.

I risked my life for $800.00 and all I have to show for it is a new phone, new Js, and $600.00, I thought to myself. But there wasn't time to be bitching. I had to man up and do what I needed to do so I'd never have to ever do again. Things from here on out weren't going to be the same for me or my family.

CHAPTER 7

I thought Tank was going to ask where I got the cash to buy my cell phone and New Retros, but he never did. He just asked me to help him out with some of his bags. He popped the trunk to his car and put our things in it. He must have been on a shopping spree, considering all the bags he already had in his trunk.

Knowing I had to get back in town to give the car back to Woodz, I said, "Time is money."

Tank looked at me and said, "You right. Time is money and I got to make back everything I spent."

I didn't know if he was saying that to let me know he was in the drug game and I never asked. I just let it go.

We went back to his house and Woodz ran up to the car. I started thinking the Hispanic boy knew it was me that had robbed him and had come on the block looking for me with his people. Not thinking, I grabbed the gun from under the seat hopped out the car, looking to see if I could see the Hispanic boy.

Woodz kept saying Dee had put someone to sleep for catching cash on the block. I wasn't sure if Dee had another gun or not, but I knew I had to find out before the boy he had put to sleep came back with a pistol.

Woodz and I walked down to Dee's house. Dee was outside with Angel, Butterfly, Money, and Woodz's mother, Mary. I could tell Dee was not in the mood to talk, his eyes were red as shit.

I didn't want to talk to him in front of everyone, so I pulled him to the side of his house. I asked him what had happened and if he needed his gun back. I was hoping he had another pistol. I didn't want to be walking around without a weapon after getting that Hispanic boy. But it was Dee's gun and the odds of me seeing the Hispanic boy again was one out of ten.

The way Dee had fucked that boy up, I knew he'd be back. I told Dee his gun only had four shots left in it, handed it back to him, and walked back to Tank's house.

I hadn't been at Tank's house for five minutes when Woodz came knocking on the door, asking me where I'd parked the car. The guy that owned it wanted it back.

Woodz's grandma, Mrs. Fish was in her car. I knew she wouldn't mind giving us a ride to my house. I asked her if she would give us a ride to get the car and she agreed. I grabbed my things I'd gotten from the mall and got in Mrs. Fish's car so she could take us to my house. She dropped us off at my house and I went in to put my things down.

Woodz and I walked up the block where I'd parked the car. I told Woodz that I'd robbed someone in it earlier so to be safe driving it around. I hoped my boy wasn't dumb enough to ride around in a car that I robbed someone in.

He got on his phone and called the owner, telling him he

could come get his car and that the keys were under the driver's seat.

Time flew. It was almost one p.m.

"I've got $200 for some work," I told Woodz.

At first, he seemed like he didn't want to give me any work.

I don't know if he didn't want to get me in the drug game or what. All he said was his cuz didn't have any.

"Let me know when he gets some work, so I can get some," I said.

"Okay," he said, but his body language was saying no.

He was being real funny toward me. I didn't know if it was because I'd said something to him about leaving me in the car with the work or he was being funny because I wanted to get in the drug game. I then asked him to come with me.

"You want to come with me to my house while I got dressed?"

Being my homeboy, I thought he would say yes. But he didn't.

"No," he said. "I have to go to my grandma house to wait for Roseanna."

If it wasn't for me he wouldn't have known her. My main thing though, was he was putting her before me and I was his homeboy.

I was still a little scared walking by myself after robbing that boy. And without a pistol, I really was scared. Even with the cash I'd gotten, I still did not feel good. I couldn't do what I really wanted to do because of what I did.

I went to my house, played around with my new phone

for a couple of minutes, and then got in the shower. I put on my favorite movie, "Shotta" and got dressed. I sat in my room counting my cash over and over. One hour turned into two hours, two turned into three and I still hadn't gotten a phone call from Woodz letting me know if his cousin had some more work or not. I couldn't take being in this house any longer. So, I walked down to Dee's house.

I could still feel the tension on the block. Dee came and opened the door, dressed in all black.

"Lock the door and come upstairs," he said. "You want to go with me to the store?" he asked.

Not having anything to do, I went with him to the store. We went in and they had all types of things, from guns to bullets to safes. Dee got some bullets and I got a little $50 safe that I really didn't need.

I just wanted shit. I only had $400 to put in the safe at the time. I asked Dee to take me to my house. I put my safe up. I knew Dee was in the drug game and he could help me get some work. Woodz's cousin was taking too long and my cash was getting lower and lower.

"I can get you some work, but will cost you $1400," Dee said.

He'd said that that was some, "fish sell". I did not know what fish sells was and I damn sure didn't have $1400 for it.

"What can I get for $150?" I asked.

"Rome, you can't get anything for $150, but you can get three point five for $175."

"How much can I make off three point five?"

"$350 if you use a scale and weigh it out," he said.

I ran in the house to put my safe up and grabbed $50 dollars from my Bible to replace the $50 I'd used to get the safe.

Damn my cash really was getting low.

I'd gone from $893 to only having $550-$350 in my Bible and $200.00 for some work.

Dee was about to get the work for me and all I had to do was get a scale to weigh out my work. I ran back down the stairs, got back in the car with Dee, and went back to his house. We pulled up to Dee's house and Money came up to the car, asking Dee if he could take him to the liquor store to get a bottle. Dee told him yes. He said he had to go there anyways to get a bottle for himself.

Money got in the car. I wanted to ask Money if Butterfly was his girl because this was my second time seeing him and her.

My pride was in the way so I never said anything to Money about Butterfly. Money asked Dee when he was getting the gun.

"He's bringing it to my house around seven when he gets back in town," Dee said.

"What kind of gun is it?" Money asked.

"A 9mm S&W," Dee said.

Money asking Dee about the gun brought up old memories for Dee.

"I'm not going to let anyone that's not from the block get paper. If anyone tries, I'm going to put something hot in them," Dee said. As far as I knew, he was not playing.

Dee gave Money some cash to get him a bottle and told Money we'd be at the store next door.

"Wait for us in the car," he said to Money.

Dee took me in the store to look at some scales. I really didn't want to spend $60 on a scale, until I saw one that looked like a CD case. I didn't know it was a scale until Dee showed it to me.

Shit, why not get one $60. That's a steal and that would be easier to hide then the safe.

Dee, I, and Money drove back to Dee's house. Woodz was standing outside, talking to Angel as we all went in Dee's house. Dee went upstairs to get the CD he and Money had made and played it.

I pulled Woodz to the side. "Did you cousin get some more work?" I asked.

"No, he won't be getting any more work until the morning."

"Dee said he was going to get me some," I said.

The only one that seemed like he really was getting paper was Money. His phone was doing numbers. I didn't know what he was selling until he came back in from making a run.

Do you smoke weed," he asked.

"I don't," I said.

"You want to hit this bottle of Patron?" he asked.

I took a cup of the Tequila, it was not as strong as the Hennessey Woodz had let me taste. I liked the taste of the Patron Money had.

I went in the kitchen. "Can you call and get me some work?" I asked Dee.

"I just called. My connection is not going to be back in town until Monday." I didn't know Woodz cousin and

Dee's connect was the same person, but I had to make some cash.

"If you want you can hold my gun for the night. I filled it up with more bullets," Dee said before I left the kitchen.

I went back in the living room with Angel, Woodz, and Money. Money was cool as shit. They say real recognizes real. Money filled my cup back up with some more Patron and told me to come outside because he wanted to talk to me about something. At first, I thought he wanted to talk to me about Butterfly and me giving her my number, but I was wrong. He wanted to talk to me about getting some paper with him. Shit, I was down with that.

He told me whatever he grabbed his connection would throw him double.

"I only have $200," I said to him.

"I can get you two o's of some Arizona and my connect will throw you two more on top of that. I have $200 I'm going to spend with my connect too. We'll both end up with four o's a piece."

I could tell Money was about his business. Still, one thing I needed to know was if Butterfly was his girl or just someone he just fucked from time to time. I still wasn't man enough to ask him But I knew I'd get around to asking him since we were about to become business partners. Dee came out to see if everything was alright between Money and I. He told us the guy was about to bring him the 9mm.

"Let him see the .25 caliber pistol I let you hold," Dee said to me. We went back inside and Money said, "Rome as soon as my connect calls I'm going to need that paper from you for the weed." I gave Money the $200 right then and there. I wanted to make sure I was in on the deal with his connect who had the Arizona.

Angel come up to me and asked to talk to me alone. She grabbed my hand and pulled me into the kitchen.

"Did you have fun at my party before those boys started fighting?" she asked.

Yes," I said.

"Do you date the Hispanic girl you were dancing with?"

"No. Why you want to know?" I asked. By this time I was getting the feeling Angel was trying to get with me, unless she was fishing for Butterfly. Or, it could be that Angel was feeling the three shots she'd knocked back before Money and I walked outside. *Maybe she's trying to make Woodz jealous?*

Whatever she was trying to do, I wanted to know right then and there. I grabbed Angel's hand. "What do you want out of me?"

"Rome, I don't want anything from you. I just wanted to know if that was your girl last night because my cousin, Butterfly wanted to know... So?"

"Angel, that is why you pulled me into the kitchen to talk? Because your cousin is feeling me?"

Before she could answer me, Money came in and told me he would be right back, his connect was outside with the Arizona.

"I thought that Butterfly was Money's girl," I said.

Angel started to laugh and said, "Rome you crazy, that's her brother."

That explained why she was talking to him at the party. Shit, now that I knew that, I was on her top. But first, I had to get some paper.

***

I was hoping Dee's boy had come back with Dee's new gun so I could hold his old one. As soon as Money got back with my green, I was hitting the block to make my paper back.

Dee's phone started ringing. He answered it with a grin and went outside. A minute later, Money walked in and told me to meet him in the kitchen.

"Rome, I got good news and bad news." The look on his face did not seem like anything was wrong but I could've been wrong. "Rome, the bad news is my connect only has 4 o's and is going be out until the morning. The good news is, you can get all 4 o's and pay me when you get the paper for the other two ounces and I'll give it to my connect."

I did not know why Money was so happy until he told me his connect sold him a pistol for $200 and pulled out a .380 caliber pistol. I liked Money's .380 until Dee come back in the house with his new gray and black 9mm S & W. The look of Dee's 9mm would make a nigga want to shoot someone. Everyone in Dee's house, beside Woodz and Angel had a pistol. Money had his .380 he'd just got. Dee had his 9mm and he'd handed me back his .25.

I knew if the guy Dee fucked up earlier came back on the block with some bullshit, it wasn't going to be good for them or us. I was not for any BS. I just wanted to get some paper.

Angel left. Woodz, Money, I, and Dee stayed at Dee's house. Dee went to get his scale for me and the bullets he'd got from the mall. Woodz was just sitting there, texting on

62

his phone and Money was counting his paper. Dee came back downstairs, gave me his scale to bag my weed up and began filling his clip up with the new bullets.

Money's phone went off. He answered it and looked at me. "You want to take the drop?" he asked. Shit, I need all the paper I could get. I had to make my $200 back and get the $200 for his connect that I still had to pay.

My first sell was $40 and that was off Money's phone. I was not going to make paper staying in Dee's house all day. As soon as I got done bagging up my green, I hit the block. The first person I ran into was Woodz's cousin. *He could be a good client to have*, I thought to myself.

I told him I had some Arizona and gave him my number. A couple people that were around overheard me and copped some from me.

I really didn't want my name out there like that but if I wanted to make some real paper, I had to get my name out there. The way things were going it wouldn't hard.

The first twenty minutes on the block, I got almost all my paper back and some of the paper I still owed Money's connect. The block was poppin' and my phone was too.

I didn't feel comfortable with all that shit on me – weed, a gun, and all that paper. I called Money's phone to see where he was at so I could give him the $200 I owed his connect.

Two rings and he answered his phone. Wherever he was there were a lot of girls. I let him know I had the cash I owed his connect and asked him where he wanted to meet.

"I'm still at Dee's house," Money said.

"I'll be there in ten minutes," I said.

No sooner than I got off the phone with Money, my phone start ringing. The female's voice on the other end sounded familiar.

"Is this Rome?" she asked.

"Yes," I said.

"This is Woodz's mother, Ms. Mary. Where are you?" she asked.

"Outside your house."

"Stay there I'm coming out."

I did not have any idea what Ms. Mary wanted to talk to me about. But the way she sounded, it had to be about something bad.

She came outside and walked up to me. "Rome walk with me to the store," she said. "Are you selling weed, Rome?"

I wanted to lie to Ms. Mary but I couldn't get myself to do it. So, I just looked at her with a dumb look on my face.

"Rome if you are, sell me two dime bags."

"Ms. Mary, your son, Woodz, is my friend and I don't want to disrespect him," I said.

"Boy! Friendship's got nothing to do with it! Just sell me two dime bags!"

I didn't want to sell my boy's mother any weed because I would want the same respect from him, but the cash was calling me. I took the $20 dollars from her and walked down to Dee's house feeling, really bad for selling my homeboy's mother that weed.

All of that went away as soon as I got in Dee's house and saw all the girls. I knew Angel was having another party, but the way things looked, the party was going to be at Dee's house. Out of all the girls in Dee's house, the only ones I knew were Angel and Butterfly. Dee, Woodz, and Money were not around.

"Where's Money, I asked Angel. "Upstairs with Dee," she said.

I went up to see what they were doing and to give Money his paper I owed his connect.

Before I could get upstairs, Butterfly came out of her mouth with, "You can't say hi?"

I didn't know if she'd said something to me because there was a room full of girls or because that was her way of letting me know she was feeling me.

I did not want to be rude and not say anything so I said hi and continued going upstairs to Dee's room. Dee was doing the same thing as he was before I left. Getting drunk and playing with his new gun. Money was doing what he liked doing and that was counting paper. For Money being so young, he had his mind made up that he was going to get paid. I gave Money the cash I owed him from the other two ounces.

Dee looked at me. "Rome, the block doing numbers like that off weed? Shit got to be flowing off the work," he said.

I knew Money sold weed and I knew Dee sold work, but I did not know he was getting it like that until Dee went in his shoe box and pulled out a ziplock bag full of work that was already bagged.

Everything started to come to me. *That's why Dee always stayed in the house.*

He always had paper and that was because he had work, and a lot of it. Dee grabbed about six or eight balls, put his pistol on his hip, his chain around his neck, and grabbed his bottle of Hennessey.

Angel and Butterfly came upstairs. "We're about to go get dressed for Angel's party. The party starts around ten."

Butterfly already looked like she was dressed for the night. I really knew Money was Butterfly's brother when he told her "You're not going to be out all night. Mom has to work overtime," Money said to Butterfly. That's when I knew he was really her brother.

At first, she tried to get smart with him but he put her in her place like a brother is supposed to do.

We all walked downstairs. Butterfly, Angel, and all her friends went on their way. Money, Dee, and I went to the block. As soon as we got to the block, my phone started to ring. It was Woodz.

"Where are you?"

The first thing I thought about was me selling his mother that weed. I told him where I was.

"Stay there, I'll be there in a little bit. I need to talk to you about something." Before he hung up the phone he said, "Rome, Sayna wanted to know if she can get your number?"

The way Sayna sucked my dick in the car, hell yeah, she can get my number. "Give it to her," I said.

He said okay and hung up.

Money walked over to me and said, "Rome you want some more of this Patron?"

In a way, I forgot I had already had two shots of his tequila.

Shit, why not? I liked it. It didn't leave a burn when it

went down and it didn't taste like that Hennessey. Woodz pulled up in a new car. "Get in," he said.

I told Dee and Money I would be right back and got in the car with Woodz.

"Are you selling weed?" he asked. I didn't know if he was asking me that because someone told him that I sold his mother some weed.

"Yes," I said.

He gave me a look I'd never seen before. "I got a sell for you," he said.

I still wasn't sure if he knew I'd sold his mother some weed. That look he gave me was fucking with me.

"How'd you know I was selling weed?" I asked.

"Someone called me for some weed, and I told them I didn't have any. They called me back and said they'd gotten some from you."

That still hadn't explained why Woodz gave me that look. He took me back to the block he was at the night before, where he got the paper from that old head.

Someone walked up to the car and asked if we had some work and weed. Woodz gave him a $60 piece of work and I gave him a $20 bag of weed. Woodz then took me to the person's house that had originally wanted some green.

Woodz told me to give him five dime bags, I did. He went in the house, came back out and handed me $40.

"Where is my $10? I gave you five dime bags and you only gave me $40."

He looked at me and said, "I need it for getting you that drop."

Woodz had never told me I had to give him ten dollars

for letting me get the drop. But it was cool. I'd let him get it.

I did not know if the Patron had my mind playing games on me, but it seemed like Woodz was acting funny to me. He wouldn't even let me drive the car he had. I asked him if he'd given Sayna my new number. He told me he'd forgotten to.

I did not know if he was being like this to me because he knew I sold weed to his mother, so I had to ask. I just kept it real with him and told him his mother got two dime bags off me. He took it a lot better than I thought.

"She gave you the paper?" he asked.

"Yes," I said.

"Okay," was all he said back.

My phone went off from a number I did not know. I answered it. There were a lot of girls in the background. It was Angel. She wanted to know where I was at and tell me that someone wanted to talk to me. She handed someone else the phone, from the voice I knew that It was Butterfly.

"Rome?" she asked. "You know who you're talking to?"

"Yes, this is Butterfly, right?"

"Yes, are you coming to my cousin's party tonight because I want to see you?"

"Yes, I'll be there."

I really wanted to see her but my mind was on getting paper. I told Woodz to go back to the block where Dee and Money were.

My phone was blowing up. I didn't know if it was someone that Money had given my number to or someone that was friends with Angel and that was at Dee's house.

She tried to disguise herself from me, but I could not put it together. The only way she was getting some weed from me was if she met me on the block where Dee and Money were at. I told her I was on my way to the block and to meet me there.

Woodz and I got to the block. There were more people there than earlier when Dee knocked the boy out. I saw all those people and all I was seeing was more paper. Everyone and their mother smoked weed. There was so many people on the block.

The girl that called me for the weed couldn't find me but we all saw them. Angel was like the leader of all of them, and there was a lot of them. She walked up to me. There were so many girls with Angel that there weren't enough guys for them. Shit, it was two girls for every one guy on the block and there were a lot of niggas there.

The only ones I was cool with were Woodz, Dee, Money, and Woodz's cousin. All the other guys, I did not know. If one of those niggas were to try anything dumb, I had seven .25 shells for them and my boy, Dee had eighteen 9mm. Followed by his boy, Money with ten .380 shots. Shit, for the most part we just wanted paper and there was a lot of it that night.

I saw Butterfly looking over at me and I wanted to go talk to her. I was just waiting for the right time. Plus, I had to see how she carried herself around guys. I can't lie, I was liking what I was seeing. Every guy tried to talk to her. She wasn't with it. Maybe she was acting like that because her brother was around, but he was there doing his own thing with some bad ass brown-skinned girl.

Money came up to me and asked did I have any more weed. He wanted to buy some before he went to Angel's party. I sold him three bags.

Everyone began walking to Angel's house for the party. The only one who stayed on the block with me was Woodz's cousin.

"Why didn't you go to the party with everyone else?" he asked me.

"Because I still have drugs to sell," I said.

He got his paper and I got mine. We stayed on the block for fifteen minutes or more, seeing people walk by going to Angel's party. It made me want to go, but every time I wanted to leave someone would come on the block looking for weed.

I know I'd made my paper back that I paid for the four ounces with. I knew I was almost done with everything that I had because my pocket was full of cash and my ziplock bag was almost done. Woodz called and told me where he was at. He asked if I wanted to get the car for the night and that he'd pay for it if I wanted it.

"Yeah," I told him.

He went over to a nice, all white Chevrolet and gave the guy something. The guy got out and went across the street into the house. Woodz's cousin came over and handed me the key.

"You got it until seven in the morning," he said.

I hopped in the Chevy. It was clean inside and out. The first thing on my agenda was to take the paper I had to the crib and then come back to the block to get some more paper. I took the cash I had on me to the crib and put it in my safe. I'd almost forgot about the cash that I already had in there.

For this to be my first day, I honestly thought I was doing a good job pulling it off. Shit seemed like if I kept it up the way it was going, I'd have a car in no time. For the moment though, I just wanted paper so I hurried back to the block.

I didn't want to miss a dollar. For Woodz, Money, and Dee $50 wasn't shit, but to me it was a lot when it came to selling weed.

One thing I knew about myself, I knew when I had to get off the block. It had been my second time seeing a cop car. The first time was when Woodz's cousin was out there with me. As soon as the cop turned the corner, I went to Angel's party. It wasn't like the night before. A couple people were drunk.

It felt like a lot of tension was in the place. I saw Money, Dee, Woodz, Butterfly, Angel, and Angel's friends on one side of the party. Everyone else on the other side. The music was playing really low. I went over to Dee to see what was going on. He said one of the guys, who was fighting the night before, brother was there wanting to know where the boy that had fought his brother was. Dee said for the most part, things were cool and that Butterfly wanted to talk to me. I looked over and saw Angel and Butterfly looking at me.

Angel called me over. "Don't act like you don't like my cousin. She's been trying to talk to you all day. She even called that number you gave her but you didn't pick up."

I stopped Angel right then and there. "I'll be back," I

said.

I grabbed Butterfly's hand and walked with her out back. I looked her right in her eyes, and asked her to tell me how she felt about me. Playing hard to get, she acted like she did not know what I was talking about. I wasn't up for the games. I gave her my cell phone number.

Angel's friend walked over to me and told me Angel wanted me. I walked over to where Angel and her friends were. Angel handed me a cup and asked me to take a shot with her for her B-Day. I was just hoping she wouldn't ask me to take another one. I already was feeling it from the shot I took with Money.

There were too many girls around for me to go back over there with Woodz, Dee, and Money. Well Money, he was doing his own thing with some girl.

Butterfly was giving me this look like I was doing something wrong being around all these girls. The brother of the boy who was fighting the night before was tripping. He was getting me mad with the damn shit he was doing. People started to leave because he was pulling out his gun. I could see in Angel's face that she was about to end her party and that's what she did.

Woodz, Dee, I, and Money were the last people to leave Angel's house but that did not stop a thing. The party continued outside.

"Rome, Butterfly is upstairs if you want, you can chill with her," Angel said.

I wanted to make sure my homeboys were good before I chilled. There were too many girls out tonight to be trying to chill with Butterfly. Money got in the car with the girl he'd been with the whole night. Myself, Woodz, and Dee went to the block where most of the people from Angel's party were.

I knew Dee wasn't going to like that there were a couple people getting paper and I was on that same shit. It wasn't my block, but they were taking paper out my pocket. I was cool with it until they started talking shit, saying how they could go anywhere and get paper and claiming the block as their own.

Dee gave me a look that said, "These niggas is on some shit."

We walked across the street and Dee asked them to leave. He blocked one guy that was with them who kept putting his hands under his shirt like he had a gun. I didn't know if Dee saw it but I did. I knew if he would have pulled out, Dee wouldn't have the chance to get his gun out in time.

"Let's go, Dee," I said.

Dee being drunk wasn't helping.

I was thinking that the only way I could get Dee to walk away was to lie and say Angel had called my phone for him. Dee walked across the street and that's when I gave Dee the heads up and let him know the guy with his hands under his shirt had a gun. By the look in Dee's eyes, I knew then that was the wrong thing to tell him. He pulled his 9mm S & W and I pulled out the .25 and looked across the street and saw the boy with his hand under his shirt pull out a long nose revolver. Before I knew it, Dee let off a shot and I followed up. Eight shots and my .25 was out of bullets. I looked over at Dee and his 9mm was still firing.

People were running in all directions. I don't think the guy across the street got a chance to let off one shot. He got the fuck out of there! Shit, for the most part, all of them got the fuck off the block, including me and Dee!

The people ran one way and Dee and I ran the other way. I was unsure if the guy fell because of the shots that he'd fired or because he got shot.

We got the fuck from over there and went to Dee's house, turned all the light off, and put the guns on the roof of his house. I did not know if Dee or I had shot someone but I was doing everything I could do to make sure I would not get caught.

Before I could take the battery out of my phone it started ringing. It was a number I don't recognize. At first, I wasn't going to pick it up, but I did. It was Butterfly, seeing if I was alright.

"I knew you were on the block. I heard the gunshots," she said.

I really didn't want to stay in Dee's house so I used Butterfly to my advantage and asked her if I could spend some time with her.

"Yes," she said. "How long will it take you to get to Angel's house?"

Butterfly must have been really concerned or just really wanted to see me. I told her to open the door, that I would be out front of Angel's in five minutes.

I was not sure if I would be at Angel's house with Butterfly for an hour or two or all night, but I wasn't going anywhere without a gun. I asked Dee to give me some more shells for the .25 caliber before I went to Angel's house with Butterfly.

It wasn't ten minutes after the shooting on the block that it became full of cops. *Damn!*

Butterfly must really cared about me because it wasn't two minutes and she was calling me again. I didn't know what it was with this girl but I was going to find out. I walked a couple houses down to Angel's house. I couldn't believe how many cops were out. I'd just gotten to the front of Angel's house when a cop was riding up the block. The door to Angel's house was open.

Butterfly was standing in the doorway looking sexy ass shit! I walked right up to her and gave her a hug and closed the door. She must have known something was up with me. She looked at me and said, "Is everything alright with you?"

"Yes, why would you ask?"

"Your heart is racing!"

I knew my heart was beating but not that hard for her to feel it. I did my best to keep her mind off her thinking about if I'd shot someone or not. But I couldn't. Butterfly did her best to make sure everything was alright with me but my communication skills were low. She asked me if I was interested in watching a movie with her. I knew that would buy me at least two hours to chill in the house with her. I could tell she knew I'd done something but she never asked. She just played it cool.

We sat on Angel's mother's bed, side by side for thirty minutes. We looked at the movie. She got up to go to the bathroom and I got up to look outside to see if I saw any more cops riding around. She came back and sat on the bed beside me and put her arm around my arm and her head on my shoulder. I could tell she was trying to buy time. I knew it. The movie was over and she was asleep holding me. I didn't want to leave, but paper was back on my mind. I had turned off my cell and missed some calls but the most missed calls came from Dee. He was the first person I called back.

Being that it was 3 a.m., and the last missed call I got from Dee was at two fifty, there had to be something up.

From the sound of the background, there didn't seem like anything was wrong with him. It sounded like he was having a good time wherever he was. I didn't say anything at first to make sure it was Dee on the other end of the phone. It was him.

"You okay?" he asked me. "Why didn't you answer the phone?"

"I was sleep," I said.

"Woodz, Money, and I are on the other side of town with Money's girl and some of her friends."

Money took the phone from Dee. I could tell he was drunk.

"You want me to come get you?" he asked.

I couldn't tell him to come get me from his cousin's house and that I was with his sister. Money and I were cool but I knew if I would have told him I was looking at a movie with his sister at 3 a.m., he wouldn't believe that's all we were doing. So, I never said anything about being at Angel's house with his sister. "I've got a car for the night. Woodz's cousin got it for me. I'll meet y'all over there," I said.

Money handed the phone to Woodz so he could give me the directions to where they were.

"Be safe, there are cops out tonight," was the first thing he said.

I guess Dee had told him what we did on the block. "Alright," I said.

He gave me the directions to where they were. He told me It was right around the corner from Sayna and Roseanna house. I really wasn't going to go on the other side of town until Dee got back on the phone, saying how some girls over there were looking to buy some green.

All I could think about was getting all my Arizona off in one day. I knew I could do it. I had an ounce and half left to move and I'd be done for the night.

I woke Butterfly up and told her I'd talk to her later.

"You can stay here if you want, but you have to be gone by seven when my aunt gets home from work," she said.

I thought about it but the cash was calling me. So, I gave her a hug and left. It was dark outside, with a full moon in the sky. With my hand on my pistol the whole time, I walked to the car. There wasn't a soul out.

Everything seemed dark except the white car I was about to get in. As soon as I got in, my phone went off. It was Dee seeing if I was on my way. I told him I'd be there in ten minutes.

"Some girl wants to talk to you, so hurry," he said.

I got off the phone with Dee and called Butterfly. I knew she would be asleep but I wanted to talk to her. She picked the phone up right away and asked me if I was coming back to the house.

"Will it be okay if I come back in half an hour," I asked.

"Okay. Just call when you get out front."

I wasn't sure if I was going to get some pussy from Butterfly, but I had to have a backup plan.

So, I shot over to Money's girl's house. Dee and Woodz were there with a couple good looking girls. The girl that wanted to talk to me looked okay, not as good looking as Butterfly or Sayna. I wasn't feeling her at all. I sold her some weed and told Money, Dee, and Woodz I'd see them later and headed back to chill with Butterfly.

Soon as I turned on the block I called to tell Butterfly to open the door, but she did not pick up. I called back again and she finally picked up. I told her to come open the door.

We went back upstairs and chilled. She seemed like she wasn't in the mood to do anything but to go to sleep. I was tired myself. My eyes were getting heavier and heavier. Before I knew it, we both were knocked out on Angel's mother's bed.

By the time we got up, Angel was just coming in the house. She must have gotten some dick, the way she was walking told me that.

She tried to spin it off on me and Butterfly, saying, "Cousin you finally let someone pop that 'V'?"

Angel must have thought I fucked her cousin. Little did she know, all we did was watch a movie and go to sleep.

But I did thank Angel for opening that mouth of hers. I wouldn't have known that Butterfly was a virgin if it wasn't for Angel saying something. From the look Butterfly gave me, I could tell it wasn't a lie.

Angel looked at me and said, "Rome, my cousin must

really like you for her to give that pussy up."

I and Butterfly knew Angel was drunk so we just let her assume that we'd had sex. I was hoping Butterfly would have said something to her cousin but she must have been too embarrassed to say anything.

Shit! I didn't know why Butterfly was so embarrassed for her cousin telling me that she was a virgin. Shit! That only made me like Butterfly even more. From the first time I saw her, I knew It was something about her that I liked. I wanted to spend more time with her.

I knew it was getting closer to Angel's mom to be getting off work and for me to take the car back to Woodz's cousin. *Damn! I did not get any pussy last night but it felt good being with Butterfly. I can chill with her any day of the week.*

The girl was full of surprises.

"It would be nice if I could see you later, after I get out of church."

Considering me and my family were church going people too, I liked finding out her family was church going people. I don't think there was anything about Butterfly that I didn't like. I could see her being my girl, but it was going to take more than one night chilling with her for me to decide. Only time would tell and I couldn't wait to chill with her again.

CHAPTER 8

I told Butterfly after church would be fine. Looking at her lips, I wanted to get a kiss but I didn't just kiss on girls the first time chilling with them. Plus, I didn't know if she wanted to be kissed and I wasn't sure if she would kiss me back. So, I just gave her a hug and left.

I got in the car and sat there for five minutes just thinking about her. She had my mind running. I'd think about paper, then go back to thinking about Butterfly, then back to thinking about paper, and back to Butterfly.

She had me open like a book and I hadn't even gotten the pussy yet! I spent another five minutes thinking about her.

I rolled down the window to see what the owner of the car wanted. It was his car that I was in. He must have thought I sold work because he asked me if I wanted to rent his car out until four. I did not know what to do so I told him hold up. I called Woodz so he could call his cousin for me.

Before I could dial Woodz's number I saw his cousin walking up the block toward us. I had no idea what the guy was doing outside the car. I don't know if he was high or not. He was looking at every spot on the car. I got out to see what he was doing.

"What are you doing?" I asked.

"Someone was shooting over here by where my car was parked. I'm looking for bullet holes.

My heart was racing, I was waiting to hear from him that someone had gotten shot. The only thing he was worried about was his car. I didn't want to ask him if anyone got shot but I had to know. I played it off like I didn't know what had gone on.

"What happened last night? Did someone get shot?" I asked him.

"No," he said.

I was at ease until he said a black car was riding around the block the night before, after the shooting.

Then again, that could have been anyone. I just knew I had to be on my P's and Q's from there on out.

By this time, Woodz cousin was asking me if I wanted to get the car until four. I really didn't need the car because all the paper I got came off the block and most of the time the car just sat there. There really wasn't any use for it. Plus, I did not want to spend any cash. I wanted to save all my paper, and the way things were going, it wasn't going to be hard to do. I didn't want to spend any paper but I wanted the car so I could go to the crib to take a shower and count my paper before Butterfly got out of church. So I got it again until four.

Woodz's cousin and the guy went up the block. I just was about to pull off when I heard Butterfly calling my name. I looked in the rear-view mirror and saw Butterfly running to the car. She shook her head in the window and said, "You left something." She handed me three .25 caliber bullets and then asked me if I was going to come see her when she got out of church.

"Yes," I said to her.

She ran back to Angel's house. I forgot I'd taken some extra bullets and put them in my pocket. They must have rolled out of my pocket when I was asleep. All I could do was shake my head. I was slipping. I had to tighten up because that was not the impression I wanted to leave on Butterfly.

I still wasn't sure why she liked me the way she did. I didn't pull any cash out in front of her. She did not know I sold drugs. The only thing I knew she knew was I was from out of town, but for the most part that was about it.

There were still a couple bags of green I wanted to get off before going to the crib. The way they were buying this green it would not take long to get the rest of it off. I just had to wait on my phone to ring. I drove around for a little and then decided to go to the crib to shower and nap before Butterfly called.

After getting out the shower and getting dressed, I tried to relax but that was not going to happen. As soon as my eyes closed, my phone started ringing. It was Butterfly asking about my whereabouts. She told me she was in church bathroom, using her mom's cell phone to call me to see if I was still interested in seeing her when she got out of church. Before she hung up the phone she let me know that she was praying for me. She was putting in a lot of effort into letting me know she cared about me. I had to give her that day.

I didn't know what she had planned for us to do, but whatever it was I was up for it. I was going to take a nap but just thinking of the sound of her voice gave me the motivation to get some more paper so I could spend time with her.

First, I had to get my paper and I wasn't going to let any girl stop me from doing that. My mind was made up. I was going to get paper. Those few bags of green were not going to do me any good If I did not get any more. The weed game was going well for me but I knew it was going to be slow for me with the kind of cash I was looking to get. I was not trying to hear that, slow paper is better than no paper. I wanted paper and wanted paper fast.

The block was dead. No one was on it. I tried to call Woodz but I got no answer. I'd been trying to call him all day but he wasn't picking up. I sat in the car on the block to wait and see if any paper was going to pop up.

It was Sunday so it was slow but I did end up seeing Woodz. I doubt he saw me in the car. I beeped the horn to get his attention and he came to the car.

"Why haven't you picked up the phone," I asked.

"I was doing something. I was going to call you when I got done," he said.

I was getting the feeling he did not want to be around me. It could have been because he heard I'd shot at someone after the party, or it could have been because I was on my feet.

They say cash changes people but cash changes people

around us too. For the most part, no one knew how much cash I had. Shit, even I didn't know how much cash I had in the safe! I just put cash in it and locked it back up. I really knew Woodz had something against me when his cousin came out and asked me if I'd seen Woodz because he was just looking for some green. I sold Woodz's cousin the last couple of bags I had. Shit, I didn't want to have the temptation to spend any cash, so I drove back to the crib to count my paper I had in the safe. I knew I hadn't spent any cash so I should have had a nice bit of change in my safe. I didn't want to count the cash. The cash that was in rubber bands, I knew it was $350.00 left over from the robbery. The loose cash was from the four ounces of green I sold was $1100. Plus, the thirty I'd just gotten from Woodz's cousin put me at $1130. Plus the $350, that put me to $1480 in cash.

That was the first time I'd seen over a thousand dollars and it was all mine. I couldn't believe that I had $1480! There was one person I had to thank and that was Butterfly's brother, Money. If it wasn't for him, I wouldn't have gotten the green and would not have this wad of paper.

I called him to thank him for getting me the weed and to see if he could get me some more. I called his phone, instead of him picking up his girl did and told me he was asleep. I knew the only way I could get his girl to get him up was to tell her I had some paper for him and to call me back ASAP.

I couldn't wait to catch up with Butterfly. I really was hoping she would call me before Money called me back.

Butterfly was bad and all but I was about my paper. I was not going to let anyone stop me from getting paper. No One.

It felt like it had been forever by the time Butterfly called me. But when she did, I was smiling from ear to ear.

"Are you ready to come chill with me? I'll be at Angel's waiting for you... and don't take long," she said. The way she said that made me think I was about to get setup.

I know from what Angel told me that she was Money's sister but for all I knew Angel could have been lying. I never asked Money if Butterfly was his sister. I still had Dees gun, so if It was setup I was prepared. I made it to Angel's house and knocked on the door. I waited for two minutes and knocked on the door again. I was beginning to think she'd played me. I began to walk back to the car until she came walking from around the back of Angel's house. She explained to me why it took her so long to get to her cousin's house.

"It's not a big deal," I said. "You came."

"Did you think I was going to stand you up?"

I said no, but that was exactly what I was thinking.

We sat on Angel's porch for about an hour talking about any and everything. She was making me laugh and I was making her laugh. She made me feel real comfortable being around her. Anything I asked, she would look me in the eyes and answer the questions. It seemed like she was too good of a girl – Banging body, gorgeous face, and lived in a neighborhood like this.

She must have had her share of me. I wasn't a sucker for love but I was falling for her. I thought I would be doing something by asking her to take a ride in the car I had. However, she was okay with just walking with me to the park. Butterfly wasn't ashamed of letting girls know she liked me. Every girl that walked in our direction and looked at me, Butterfly would put her arm around me.

At first, I thought she was only doing that because she was scared of the girls until some girl she knew walked up to us and asked Butterfly if I was her boyfriend.

Butterfly looked at her and said, "He's about to be, Why?"

The girl looked at Butterfly and said, "You two make a cute couple. Do he got any friends?"

By the way the girl was looking at me, I knew if I wasn't with Butterfly she would have tried to talk to me.

Butterfly wasn't with it. She never gave the girl an answer. She just grabbed my arm and told me to come on. I asked Butterfly why she just ignored the girl.

Butterfly told me, "Because she is always in someone else's man's face. I wasn't going to let her get you."

I don't know why she thought the girl had a chance to get with me but that was just one more thing she did to show me she really liked me.

I knew it would be any moment before Money called my phone back to see what I wanted.

I wanted to know everything about Butterfly. Her likes, dislikes, everything and this would be the proper time to do so, while she was opening up to me.

Before I could ask, she took the initiative to tell me something about herself. She started with the conversation she and her cousin had had about her being a virgin.

"Jerome, I want you to know what Angel was saying was not a lie. I tried to have sex with my ex but things didn't work. He always tried to come see me at 2 a.m. and 3 a.m. I'm not that type of girl, so he told me it was over. So, Rome if I call to spend time with you throughout the day, it's because I really like you and want to get to know you."

Everything Butterfly was saying told me she was the type of girl I wanted to be with. But still, all in all getting paper was on my mind. I had to get it without her knowing I sold drug. I knew that was going to be harder than I thought with my phone going off. I didn't know if it would bother her or not. I did a lot of bad things that weekend that made me feel a little uncomfortable being outside with Butterfly. So, I insisted we go to my house but she insisted we go to her house. Considering I didn't know where she lived, it would be a good idea if I found out where she stayed and got from outside.

***

We got to Butterfly's house. I thought she was going to take me in the house but instead we sat on a bench by her crib. It was in the cut and if anyone would try to get the drop on me I would see them fast. I looked at my phone and saw I had missed a call from Money. I immediately called him back to see where he was. He told me he was at his mom's house. If he really was Butterfly's brother, he would be at her house and I was right out front of his crib.

I told him to come to the block, that's where I'd be.

"Who are you talking to?" Butterfly asked.

"Your brother, Money," I said.

He was on his way outside to meet me.

"I'll be back," I said. "I'm not ready to let your brother know that I'm talking to you." I gave her a hug and began to walk to the block to wait on Money.

Before I could get to the block, Money was walking out of his mother's house.

He looked at me and said, "How did you know that I lived here?"

"I didn't." I looked back to see if Butterfly was still sitting on the bench but she was gone. I don't know where she went, but she was ghost.

Money knew that I'd gotten all that green off to all the people he gave my number to. That is why I hadn't picked up because I was out and I did not have any more to sell. Money told me that his connect wouldn't be back until that night and that he really didn't come out on Sundays. That was his time to spend with his family.

Money always had something to sell and those days, he was selling phones.

"If you take me to sell them, I'll give you cash for the ride," Money said.

I gave him a ride but I couldn't get myself to take the cash. Money went into some crib and called me to say he would get a ride back on the block. I would have gone back to chill with Butterfly but I didn't have a number to get back in touch with her. So, while I waited for Butterfly to call, I went to pick up Sayna.

CHAPTER 9

Sayna was down with whatever and she was a bad bitch with a fat ass! I liked being with her as much as she liked being with me. She played her part when it came to me. By the time I got to her house, she was on the porch waiting. She got in with that fat ass.

"Hi Daddy!" she said with that sexy Mexican accent of hers. She put on her lip gloss. I pulled off, not knowing where to go. I just wanted to do something. Sayna left it up to me to decide. I knew Butterfly would be calling me back in a little so I got right to it and asked Sayna for some head. She would have done it right then and there but I didn't feel comfortable getting top in the car. So, we went back to her house.

First, she introduced me to her mother and father. They barely spoke any English. Sayna said something to her mom in Spanish and took me to her bedroom. I asked what she'd said to her mother.

"I told her you were here to help me do homework," she said. "She told me that she'd be back, she was just going to the store."

As soon as her mother and father left, Sayna came in the room and took off her clothes. They said Hispanic girls had fat pussies and they were not lying. Sayna's pussy was so fat! I didn't have plans to fuck, but after seeing that fat ass pussy and her fat ass, I did.

She locked her door to the bedroom and turned on some Hispanic music. I took off my things and put on a condom that I had saved for Butterfly. Sayna climbed on top of me. Her pussy was on point.

Sayna only weighed about 150 pounds. I tossed her all over that room. Her back stroke was mind-blowing and that pussy was water as shit. I'd had some good pussy but her pussy was the best by far. The way she was moaning in my ear, I knew she was about to cum, and she did. It wasn't long before I got my nut off as well. She took me in the bathroom to take a shower.

I thought I was done until we got in the shower. I stood behind her and watched the water run off her long black hair down the middle of her back, between her ass, and off her pussy lips. My dick got back hard and I slid in from the back. The more I pulled on her hair the harder she threw that ass back. She stopped and got on her knees and threw my dick in her mouth. It didn't take long to get my second nut off. She grabbed the soap and the rag and began to wash my dick off and did the same to her pussy. By the time we got done washing up and got out the shower, her mom and dad were back in the house.

Sayna had my mind completely off of Butterfly. I looked at my phone. I had ten to twelve missed calls from a number I did not recognize. I knew it had to be Butterfly but looking at Sayna laying on her bed, ass naked, on her stomach with her ass in the air, I was mesmerized. She was looking at a Spanish soap opera trying to keep herself from falling asleep. If it wasn't for my phone going off, I would have went to sleep. I looked at my phone. It was the same number that I'd missed. I picked it up. It was Butterfly asking me where I was and if I was still going to chill with her.

I wanted to say no because I was drained from Sayna but I told Butterfly I was on my way back to her cousin's house. I woke Sayna up. She put on some booty shorts, a t-shirt, and slippers and walked me to the door.

Before I could get to the car, the sky started to get dark and a light mist of rain began to fall. By the time I made it back on the other side of town, it was pouring. By the look of things, it was going to be like that all day.

Butterfly called my phone to let me know her mother wouldn't let her back out because of the rain. At first, I thought it was a lie until I heard her mother yelling for her to get off the phone and go close all the windows. Butterfly told me she was going to call me later before hanging up. I wish I'd known that before I left Sayna's crib.

Fuck it!

I was sleepy and tired, I needed some rest. I headed to my house. On my way there, I noticed some girls on the porch. It happened to be Woodz's cousin, Misha and her friends. I rolled down the window to see if they needed a ride. They didn't hesitate at all. They hopped off the porch and hopped in the car. I dropped Misha and her friends off at her grandma's house. Misha seemed like she wasn't interested in me the way she was before. I did not care. She went in her grandma's house and I drove off.

CHAPTER 10

There wasn't anything to do. I called Tank to see if he was home.

He answered the phone, "Cousin, where are you?"

I didn't want him to know I had a car and I sure didn't want him to know I was driving. I was about to tell him I was at the house but before I could, he asked who I was in the car with.

"My homegirl is about to drop me off at the house," I said.

"Have you already ate?" he asked.

"No."

"Ok, I'll see you in a minute."

I headed to Tank's house. I knew I would be taking a gamble by driving by my cousin's house to find a parking spot. It was raining so I wouldn't think he would be outside. What a coincidence, that he was standing in the doorway of his house, looking right in my direction. I was not sure if he saw me. I parked and sat there for six minutes, waiting for him to go in the house.

As soon as he went in, I got out the car, ran to his door

and knocked. I was expecting him to open the door but I was in for a surprise, It was my stepdad! I knew if he was here, my mother was as well. *I was for sure they were supposed to be back from Connecticut tonight.* I could hear the sound of my sister in the kitchen and sound of my mother's voice. My sister being the way she was, ran in the living room calling my name. She didn't know why I was telling her to be quiet. She didn't know I did not want my mother to see me with my new Retros, new clothes, and new cell phone that my mother or father did not get for me.

I tried to turn my cell phone off, but I knew if I would have pulled it out and my sister would have said something to my mother. She already was running back in the kitchen to let my mother know I was in the living room. I could hear the sound of my mother's voice getting closer and closer to the living room. I had just enough time to turn my phone off.

As soon as my mother embraced me, she said, "Hi, son. Why did you not called me at all yesterday?"

As I tried to come up with a lie, I could tell she was eyeballing my new Retros and new clothes. I guess she was happy to see me because the only thing she said was, "Come eat."

I was instantly relieved. I went in the kitchen, washed my hands, and sat at the table. I was happy to see my family back in York, safe and having a good time.

After everyone finished their plates, the next thing was the upside-down pineapple cake that my mother made, with vanilla ice cream to top it off. I didn't have any more room in my stomach, but I made room for the upside-down pineapple cake. I was so sleepy I was ready to go to sleep. My stepfather must have read my mind. He called for my sisters and mother. "Come on so I can get to the house," he said.

I still had to find a way to get Woodz's cousin the car keys. I could not pull my phone out my pocket. I was hoping Woodz or his cousin was outside since it had stopped raining, but nope. The only ones that were out were Poo and her friends. I called Poo over and asked her where her cousin was.

"He's in the house," she said.

I handed her the keys. "Take these to him, please?"

"Okay," she said, before she ran to her house. My mother, stepfather, sisters, and I got in the car and headed to the house. I could tell everyone was tired from the long ride back from Connecticut.

Everyone in the car was sleeping, besides me and my stepfather. The gospel station was on the radio. It made me think about Butterfly. How she was a beautiful soul sister. I couldn't wait to get to the crib to turn my phone back on. By the time we got to the block we lived on I could hear cop cars and ambulances. The cops had our block yellow taped off. We had to go around the block to get to the crib. Our neighbors were out on their porches. My mother asked what was going on up the block. I overheard the neighbor tell my mother that some guy got shot and died. It wasn't a big deal to me.

The cops made their way up the block, house by house, asking people if they saw anything. They were a couple of houses down from ours. I knew I didn't have anything to do with the guy dying but I was scared staying on my porch with this gun in my pocket.

My mother and stepfather weren't up for the cop's questioning. We got our things from the car right before the cops got to our door. We went in and closed it. Being that my sister's room was next door to mine, I headed up to my room to hide my safe. I was happy that my family was back home but a lot had changed in just a week's time. I'd robbed someone, bought my first safe, sold weed, shot at someone, and saved my first $1000. Things were about to be different around the house now that my family was back in town. I would be selling weed.

As soon as I got time alone and turned my phone on, it started popping right that second. Every call I picked up had to do with paper. I was getting mad that I didn't have any more weed to sell. The couple days that my sister, mother, and stepfather had been back was spent doing family things around the house.

Woodz and Dee stopped by from time to time to see how things were going with me. They knew I wanted to chill with them but my mother would always find something for me to do around the house. Even though it made me mad that she would do my homeboys like that, I was never a disrespectful boy. I always listened to what my mother would say.

***

After two weeks of not talking to Butterfly and not getting any paper, I started to get anxious. I was running out of things to do. I didn't know how many times I had watched set it off, counted my paper, cleaned my room, and worked out. If I stayed in the house one more day, I was going to lose my mind.

I did 100 more pushups before jumping in the shower. The longer I stayed in there, the more my mind ran. There was no way I could not make any paper that day. I was going to find some type of drug to sell.

I got dressed but for some reason it felt like something was missing out my room. I did not know what until I went in my drawer and found out Dee's .25 pistol he'd let me hold was gone. I moved it nine times throughout the two weeks that my mother was back so it could have been anywhere. I looked under my bed and in my shoe boxes. I looked all over and I still couldn't find it. I walked by my sister's room and from the look on her face I knew she knew where my gun was. First, she tried to lie to me, but with a couple shots to her body, she let me know that she'd given it to my mother.

"How did you get it?" I asked.

"I went in my room to get something and saw it," she said. I was not worried about my mother calling the cops on me for having a gun in her house, but I was worried that I was not about to get it back from her. The other thing that had me confounded was that my mother didn't say anything to me when I walked past her when I got out the shower.

Things were not adding up to me. I had to find a way to get that gun back. *If my stepdad says something to my mother about giving it back to me because it's not mine, she might give it back*, I thought.

I took the chance and talked to my stepdad about getting

the gun back for me from my mother. Taking a deep breath, I told him about the gun.

"How did you let your mother find the gun?" he asked.

I told him that my sister was in my room, found it and gave it to her.

"It's going to be a really hard thing to do, knowing that your sister found it and could have shot herself with it," he said.

My mother poked her head out her room door. "Come here," she said.

I was more nervous than I'd ever been in my life. I walked behind my stepfather toward my mother's room. My mother was sitting on her bed with the TV volume really low.

"Close the door and sit down," she said in a calm voice.

My heart was beating out of my chest and my head was shaking.

She looked at me and said, "Don't lie to me! Where did you get this gun from?"

I was real big on not ratting, so I told her I was walking home and I saw it by a trash can. My mother had the look on her face as if she knew I was lying.

"You not getting it back!" she said.

I just nodded. I wouldn't have cared but it wasn't my gun to just let my mother keep.

I know I could have easy lied to Dee and made up a story and said I lost his gun and that I had $150 for him for losing it. But I needed the gun for myself, especially after the bullshit I was in three weeks ago.

My stepfather walked up to my room to talk to me about

where I'd really gotten the gun from. I don't know why he thought he was going to get a different answer from me. I told him the same thing I'd told my mother.

"The only reason she's not going to give it to you is because she likes it and wanted to keep it for herself."

After my stepdad told me that, I went right downstairs to talk to my mother about giving me the gun back so I could sell it to put some cash in my pocket.

My stepfather came in the room and talked my mother into giving it to him to help me sell it. I ran upstairs to get some cash out my safe and rode with my stepfather. I told him that I knew someone that would buy the gun off of me. My stepfather saw Dee a couple of times out the house. I told my stepfather I was going to sell it to him, but little did my stepfather know, I was just going to give it back to Dee and was going to get one later.

I walked in Dee's house "My mother found the gun and was going to keep it until my stepdad said he was going to help me sell it, so I brought it to you as if I was going to sell it to you."

Dee laughed. "Come get it later and also, Butterfly was asking about you." I left, got back in the car, showed my stepfather the cash that I already had on me as if I'd gotten it for the pistol.

We went back to the house my mother was standing in the doorway, waiting for us to come back. She asked did we get rid of the gun and how much cash we got for it. I showed her $125 that I'd taken out my safe before leaving the house. She asked me for $25. "Don't ever bring a gun in my house again," she said before going upstairs.

I went upstairs to see if anyone had called my cell phone. I had a couple missed calls from Dee. I called him back to see what he wanted.

"Soon as you left, Butterfly came walking around the corner, asking if it was you she saw getting in the car," Dee said.

"If she really wanted to talk to me or see me, she would have called. She's got my number but tell her I'll be on the block in a little, so be out if she wants to see me," I said.

I grabbed my hoodie and went to the block. In three weeks, a lot had changed and the block was one of them. Come to find out, Money wasn't around due to him going to Job Corps.

The guys that I shot at, never came back to the block. Dee was heavy on drinking. Woodz stopped moving work for his cousin and started selling his own work. Sayna and Roseanna got locked up for stealing from the store. Angel had moved off the block. So the only time anyone would see Butterfly was when she would go to the store or home.

With Money at Job Corps, I got to spend more time with Butterfly. Even though Butterfly and I never had sex, I knew one day I would get caught by her mother, sneaking in and out of her house. I remember those days like they were yesterday.

The first time Butterfly and I got caught, we thought her mother was going to work but she was off and was paying some bills.

I had ordered some pizza for us to eat while watching a movie. If it wasn't for Butterfly's dog, Butterfly's mother would have made it all the way to her room. The dog's barking gave me some time to get in the closet to hide from her mother. Knowing that her mother's room was right next to hers, it was going to be impossible for me to make it out her house. Butterfly did everything she could to get her mother to leave her room.

Her mother knew something was up and my Retros gave her more of a reason to see if anyone was there in her daughter's room. She opened the door to see me sitting in just my boxers and t-shirt. Her mother looked at me as if she was going to kill me. She was yelling at me, telling me to get out her house before she called the cops.

Butterfly knew she was in trouble but she wasn't going to let her mother talk to me any type of way. I didn't expect anyone to disrespect their parents but that showed me that she would stand up for me even against her mother.

I was catching feelings that were worth more than millions. I wasn't going to miss the chance to show her I loved her before I left her house. I hugged her and kissed her, it seemed like forever. I told her I loved her and went to the block.

All I could think about was if she was alright and when the next time I was going to see her was. Before I could get back to my house, it started to rain. My mind was thinking about Butterfly. I walked slowly.

I didn't care about a thing. It was so crazy what love would have you doing. And there was no doubt in my mind that I was deeply in love with Butterfly.

By the time I got to the crib I was drenched from head to toe. My mother was in the kitchen, preparing dinner for the night. I went upstairs to take off my wet clothes. My sister came up to let me know that my mother wanted me to come eat. I was not in the mood to do anything. I'd lost my appetite. My mind was still on Butterfly and when the next time I would see her was going to be.

My mother came upstairs to talk to me about not coming down to eat.

"I just received a phone call from a woman saying she caught you in her house with her daughter. Next time she catches you in her house she's going to call the cops."

My mother gave me some good advice and told me to look up, 1 John 4:18 that reads: "There is no fear in Love; but perfect love casteth out fear: because fear hath torment. He that feareth is not made perfect in love."

Before my mother left my room she said, "Son if you really love that girl, you would respect her mother and ask to sit down and talk to her about her daughter. Let her know how you really feel about her daughter."

I took my mother's advice and did just that. I thought about saying something that same night to Butterfly's mom, Ms. T, but I knew it was still fresh on her mind and she wouldn't hear a thing I had to say because she was still mad.

The next day, I called and asked Ms. T if it would be alright if I came to her house to apologize.

She had a little attitude at first, but she said yes and that I'd have to wait until she got back around 5 p.m. She said she'd call to let me know that I could come by the house. I sat in my room all day, waiting for 5 p.m. to get a phone call from Ms. T. The time was moving by slow as shit. I had to find something to do until I got that phone call from

Ms. T.

I called my homeboy, Woodz, to see where he was at. He was on the block about to go to the park to play basketball. I told him I would meet him there. It was nice. A lot of people were out, but I wasn't all there, I was with Butterfly.

Even my homeboy knew something wasn't the same with me. I told him I was love sick. It was 5:12 p.m. when I got a call from Ms. T, telling me she was home and that I could come by.

I did not say a thing to anyone. I just got up and left. There wasn't anything that was going to stop me from going to talk to Butterfly's mom. I was out in front of Ms. T's house and called to let her know.

"Hold up, my daughter is going to let you in," she said.

My heart was beating fast as shit. Butterfly opened the door. She looked like she'd just stepped out of heaven. She gave me a hug and kiss and asked me if I wanted something to drink. She got me some OJ and said her mother would be down in a little bit.

Butterfly sat next to me. *What was I going to say to her mother?* I couldn't give her an answer because I did not know myself. I just knew I was going to let her mother know how I felt about her. I heard her mother's footsteps coming down the stairs. My heart beat faster, with each of her steps down the stairs. I tried to keep my composure. I knew Ms. T wasn't going to let me get off easy.

Ms. T started up the conversation. "I don't appreciate you being in my house when I'm not here. And how long have you been seeing my daughter?"

Butterfly just sat there with a grin on her face. I didn't find it to be funny at all. I felt like I was getting questioned by the FBI. Her mother didn't ease up at all. She put her foot on my neck even harder by asking if I and her daughter had sex. The word, "no" couldn't come out my mouth fast enough. That's what her mother really wanted to know that from the get-go.

After that last question, she said, "Jerome I could tell you really like my daughter and she really likes you. All I ask is that you respect me and don't be in my house when I'm not home or without my permission."

She told me I was allowed to stay until 10 p.m. that night, but then I had to leave.

Ms. T went upstairs and left me and Butterfly to ourselves. I was trying hard not to disrespect Ms. T but Butterfly wasn't making it easy for me, kissing on me and rubbing her hand on my dick. Every little sound I heard, I'd jump up and move to the other end of the couch. I wanted to fuck Butterfly so bad but I was not going to disrespect Ms. T the first day she let me in her house. Besides, her mother's vent was right over us. I knew she could hear everything we were saying.

Every thirty to forty-five minutes, Ms. T would come down to check on us. I had to keep Butterfly off me before we got caught by her mother. Butterfly didn't want to stay in the house. Plus, her mother needed something from the store.

Butterfly was going to let everyone and their mom know I was her man. We got the things her mother needed and went back to the house. Butterfly waited for her mother to go upstairs to let me know she wasn't feeling that I didn't hold her hand when we got to the block around those people. I had to let her know it wasn't that I did not want to hold her hand, I just had to be on point. See, Butterfly really did not know I would let go of her hand and put it in my pocket on my pistol because I did not know those people.

There were a lot of things that Butterfly was going to have to go with the flow on and that was one of those situations. I didn't mind spending time with her but I had to get to some paper and staying in the house with her all day wasn't going to cut it. But I was going to give her the day and show her I could chill with her for hours on end. I did not mind being around her, she kept me out of trouble and I really was feeling her. She let me know how she was feeling and she spoke her mind about everything. Having Sayna's number in my phone was something she wasn't having. She said I had to call Sayna and let her know she couldn't call my phone anymore. At first, I'd said no, until I thought about something my mother had said to me. *"Don't miss the next chance to show her you love her."*

I had my mind made up. Butterfly was going to be the one. It was getting late and I knew it was almost time for me to leave. I told Butterfly to go get her mother so I could thank her for understanding me and letting me visit.

She came downstairs and I told her how I felt.

"Jerome don't hurt my daughter's heart," she said. Ms. T smiled and walked me to the door. If it wasn't for Ms. T's phone ringing, I don't think I would have gotten a good night kiss from Butterfly. I gave Butterfly a hug and kiss and headed home.

It went a lot better than I thought. Ms. T was a very nice lady and I could tell she really cared about her daughter and wanted to see her happy. Ms. T knew I was the one to make that happen. Week after week, I would go over to see Butterfly. We would talk for hours on end, while her mother would be in the kitchen, cooking or upstairs in her room.

Ms. T knew if she would have left us in the house alone, Butterfly and I would have had sex. There were plenty of times we were out and I would ask her to go to my house. She did, but she wasn't ready to give the pussy up. It would take me showing I really loved her to get that pussy and considering I really did love her, it wasn't going to be hard to do.

Butterfly's mother began to trust me being in her house that she started leaving us in the house alone but still, all in all, Butterfly wouldn't give that pussy up! The only thing she would let me do is suck her tits and play with her pussy, but she wouldn't let me fuck. I walked Butterfly to her house, not saying anything to her. She knew that I was mad and why I was mad. I started to think she had something that is why she would not let me fuck.

We had a long conversation and I told her how I was feeling about being with her for a month and still not fucking. She told me she'd made a promise to herself that she wasn't going to let the next guy she fell for fuck her before a month was over. She said if he couldn't wait for a month, he wasn't the one she needed to be with.

"My mother told me if a guy really loves you, he'll

wait."

I was still a little mad. So a lot of things she was saying went in one ear and out the other. I told her I would call her back. I didn't call or go see her for two days, and every time she would call I wouldn't pick up. She would leave a message telling me she loved me. The third day, she called me over sixteen times and left me over eight messages, telling me she really needed to talk to me about something.

I was still in my feelings so I never called her back. If it wasn't for Dee calling me and letting me know one of Butterfly family members had passed away, I would have never known. *Shit, my girl was calling and she really needed my support.*

I ran down to her house and knocked on her door. She opened it and looked like she had not slept in over a week. Her eyes were bloodshot red. A tear rolled down her face.

"What's wrong?" I asked.

"My grandma passed away last night," she said.

I'd never seen Butterfly down like this. I brushed the tears from her cheeks. Your grandma is in a better place and she loves you."

Butterfly fell in my arms. She cried and cried. I did my best to comfort her. "I miss my grandma, why'd she have to die?" were the only words that escaped her mouth.

That day being with Butterfly made me realize when the people you really love pass away, there's not anything you can do or say to bring them back. I did everything to help Butterfly get her mind off her grandma's passing.

I put on her favorite comedy movie, ordered her favorite food, and got her favorite candy. I even rubbed her feet, telling her over and over and over again how much I loved her. Still, none of those things seem to comfort her. She cried and cried and cried some more until she went to sleep.

Ms. T came in and asked how her daughter was doing.

"She's been crying all day," I told her.

"Did she eat?" Ms. T asked.

"I ordered her some pizza. But she took one bite of it and put it back in the box."

Ms. T thanked me for being there for her child and told me I could stay with her until midnight. I went back in the living room and sat by Butterfly. Looking at her while she slept, I noticed the dried up tear marks on her cheeks.

***

I lost track of the time. It was 12:20 a.m. and I was supposed to be out of Ms. T's house twenty minutes ago. Ms. T came down and realized I was still in her house and asked me to leave.

I woke Butterfly up to let her know I was about to go. Butterfly did everything she could to get me to stay. I didn't want to disrespect Ms. T for she'd just come downstairs and asked me in a polite way to leave her house. Butterfly gave me a kiss and said she was going to ask her mother if it was cool for me to stay a little while longer. Butterfly came back downstairs with her blanket and photo album. She turned off the TV, lit a candle, and began to show me photos of her grandmother who'd just passed away. With every page we turned to, Butterfly's eyes started getting glossy, like she was about to cry.

I made her laugh by commenting on her baby photos. She closed the photo albums and started smiling. She hugged me and thanked me for being there for her.

I knew it was my job as a boyfriend to be there for her.

"I Love you, Rome," she said.

I told her I loved her too. That was the first time I or Butterfly had ever said we loved one another.

I knew it was getting late and I didn't want to cause any problem for Ms. T. I gave Butterfly a big hug and kiss and went home. We talked on the phone until the sun came up. I knew I had to get some sleep.

"You can come to my house and get some rest, My mother just left for work," Butterfly said.

She didn't have to tell me twice. I stayed on the phone with her the whole way there. She opened the door, wearing something I wasn't expecting to see her in, a bra, panties and nothing else. My dick got rock hard. Butterfly's body was something out a magazine.

We went to her room. I took off my things and got in bed. I was tired until I got in bed and my dick rubbed against her fat ass. Butterfly knew what she was doing.

She rolled over. "Rome, I really love you. If you ever break my heart, you are going to pay," she said.

I knew she meant everything she was saying. I put my hand on her pussy, I couldn't believe how wet her pussy was. She wanted me as badly as I wanted her.

She got up and took off her bra, then her panties. My dick was rock hard like Medusa was staring me in the eyes. I got up, took off my things, went in my pants and grabbed a condom.

The look on Butterfly's face was like, "Damn, his dick is big." I put the condom on and began to get on top of her.

She stopped me and said, "Boy take it slow."

I did just that. Her pussy was like a whole hug and I could not get enough of it. The more she moaned the slower I made love to her. When she came, I knew. It was like a waterfall. At first, I'd thought she pissed on me until it happened again. I turned her over to hit it from the back. I could tell she really liked it from the back with all that ass. I knew she knew what to do with it. I don't think there wasn't a position I didn't put her in. By the time we got done making love, there wasn't a spot in her room our bodies hadn't touched.

She wiped the sweat from my face and got on top of me, riding the shit out of me as if we were going to die the next day. When we got done, we just laid there, my dick still inside of her. We fell asleep until her house phone rang. She told me to be quiet that it was her mom.

Butterfly sat on my lap to make me sure I didn't go anywhere and to let me hear her mother on the other end of the phone.

I could hear Ms. T telling her she was just checking up on her. Butterfly let her mother know that she was fine and about to get in the shower.

Butterfly washed me and I washed her. I don't know if I was uncomfortable or just paranoid but if Butterfly was setting me up I wasn't going without a fight. Everywhere I went I brought my .25 pistol. Everywhere, even in the shower. Butterfly and I got out the shower and went to her room and I put lotion on her body from head to toe.
Sayna's body was sexy but Butterfly's body was out of this world and she knew it. Now that Butterfly was dressed, I

had to do the same.

The way I'd dicked her down, she didn't want to leave my side at all. So, I let her walk with me to my house. She'd been there a couple of times but my mother and sisters were never there and I knew for sure they would be there that day. That didn't bother Butterfly, she wanted to meet my family. If we were going to be together, I would like for her to meet them. I could see my little sisters outside playing and my mother on the porch doing her nails. I could tell Butterfly was nervous. The closer we got to the porch the harder she squeezed my hand.

My mother greeted Butterfly and Butterfly greeted my mother. I took her up to my room, put on a movie, and got my things to get in the shower. By the time I got done, Butterfly was gone. I went downstairs to ask my mother where she'd gone but I didn't have to ask, she was on the porch, doing my mother's nails. That was a good thing to see, Butterfly and my mother interacting.

I went back upstairs to finish getting dressed. Butterfly came upstairs just as I was getting done. I asked her what her and my mother were talking about. She started by saying that my mother had told her she could come to my house anytime.

All I could do was smile. Even though it was still the week her grandma had died, I wanted to do something to keep her mind off that. I took her downtown to get her some shoes and get her hair done. I got myself a hat and a gray hoodie. We went back to her house, ate some Chinese food that I'd ordered for us and relaxed for an hour before her mother got off work.

Tank called me to see if I wanted to go with him to wash his car. He came to get me. We washed his car and headed to my Aunt Rob's house.

CHAPTER 11

Aunt Rob was the aunt that was cool with everyone. I doubted there was one person that didn't like my Aunt Rob. She had a great sense of humor. Her house stayed full of people and the guys she had over there were real bricklayers. They got paper for real. Every time they would come in town from New York to see my Aunt Rob, she would throw a block party. Cook a lot of food and everything. My aunt smoked a lot of green and only the best. I knew one of her guys would be the one to become my connect. Since Money went to Job Corps I hadn't had any more green to turn into paper. I recognized one of my aunt's friends from the last time she'd thrown a block party. I remembered, he had told me if I ever wanted to make some paper to come talk to him. Before I could say anything to Scrap, he recognized me and asked me to come talk to him.

"How are you. Do you need anything?" he asked.

"I'm looking to buy some weed."

"To buy or sell?" he asked.

"To sell," I said.

"Give me an hour and I'll be back to talk to you."

I hadn't been in my aunt's house for ten minutes and I'd found a connect. I went out back to talk to my little cousin, Lox. He was very happy to see me.

The last time his mother had a cookout and I was over here and he wasn't. He was in New York visiting his dad. So, it was good to see my cousin. Being that my cousin was younger than me, there were things I was into more than he was – one of those things was girls.

While he wanted to play the X-box game, I wanted to get paper and girls. There were a lot of my aunts home girls there, but this one, in particular, kept looking at me. I didn't recognize her. She was very popular and everyone seemed to know her.

My aunt called everyone to come get something to eat. The crazy thing was, I didn't have to go get my plate. The girl that had kept looking at me brought one to me.

I started fucking the food up. There were so many people in my aunt's house I could hardly hear myself speak.

I thought I heard someone calling my name. I knew I wasn't tripping. It was my aunt's homeboy, Scrap, from New York. He was going to look out and sell me some green. He took me to his car and reached in the backseat and grabbed a bag. He handed it to me and told me to open it.

When I did, it wasn't what I was expecting at all. There were six guns in the bag, and they weren't small guns. The first one I pulled out the bag was a black long nose .44 caliber Bull Dog. The next one was a 357 S&W, followed by a .40 caliber with a red light on the bottom, two 9mm Rogers – one P89 and the other P94 – that I really liked, and lastly a blue-steel .8 caliber.

I know I asked him for some green not guns, I thought to myself.

I didn't know what time he was on but I had to get the fuck out his car!

"What's up with the weed?" I asked.

He reached in the backseat and grabbed another bag. "How much do you wanna buy?" he asked.

"Just an ounce for now," I said.

He showed me two different weeds. One called Blue Dream and the other, called Sour. It wasn't hard for me to choose which ounce I wanted. All the people that called my phone when I was selling Arizona, I knew they would still be interested if I could get some Sour for $400. It was not going to be hard at all for me to make back the cash I'd just spent for the weed.

I still was unsure why he'd showed me six guns in the bag

Was he trying to intimidate me or did he want to sell them?

The next thing that came out his mouth let me know exactly what he wanted from me and that was to get down with him and his team. Don't get me wrong. They were getting some real paper but the bad side of that was a lot of people didn't like them.

They were from New York, drove nice cars, stayed with bad bitches, and got paper. The chance of making it with them was slim. I already had my mind made up that I wasn't going to get down with his team, but I told him I'd think about it. He also let me know that anytime I wanted to buy any one of the pistols, I could. I went back in my aunt's house.

The ounce had me smelling like I had just chopped a pound of the shit! Everyone in my aunt's house must have known I had some of that load on me.

My aunt came up to me so I could taste some of her pie she'd made. She smelled the weed on me and asked if I'd been smoking.

"No," I said.

"Well if you got some weed on you, I want some," she said.

I pulled out the ounce and gave my aunt a pinch. Before I could put it back in my pocket, I had like three to four people around me wanting to buy some. I knew I would have made out more if I free handed it but I didn't want to take the chance of giving out more than I had to.

"Do you have a scale?" I asked.

She told my little cousin to go upstairs and get the scale for me.

The people couldn't beat a gram for $20, when the people that had the same quality as mine was giving out point seven for $20. Point three extra might not seem like much but when it comes to the drug game every point makes a big difference. Even though I was making my paper back fast, it didn't make any sense to only make a $160 profit.

To some people, that was cool but to me. It didn't add up. But I did love the clientele coming from my aunt's house. For just being there a few hours, I had already made most of my paper back. I knew if I would have gotten back in the drug game that it was going to affect me and Butterfly's relationship.

I had not been away from her four hours and she was already blowing my phone up, asking me my whereabouts. I didn't want to lie to her about being at my aunt's house making some paper, especially when I knew she needed me to be there for her after her grandma had just passed away.

Butterfly didn't want anything but to let me know her mother was taking her to get her hair done for her grandma's funeral and to see if I would like something to eat while she and her mother were out.

"Yes," I said. That would give me some time to make my paper back before she asked me to come see her. The whole time I was on the phone with Butterfly, the girl that had brought me my plate earlier was all in my face. I got off the phone with Butterfly and immediately she got up off the couch and walked over to me. She asked if I had any weed to sell her. I was surprised. She wanted to buy everything that I had on me. I thought she was kidding until she pulled out every bit of $200. I was going up the price on her but her demeanor made me think she was not slow to the drug game. I sold her the rest of what I had and gave her my number. If her first time spending with me was like that, she would be the only customer I would need to have in my phone!

My cousin knew that I was making some paper while he was at my aunt's house but he was ready to leave and he was my ride. I sold out of all the weed that I had and I needed some more before I went back to my side of town.

I called my connect. He picked up the phone and I let him know I needed to talk to him. He told me he'd just pulled out front of my aunt's house and to come out. I ran out front, hoped in the car, and told him I was done with the ounce I had, that I wanted to buy another one.

"If you buy two. I'll give them to you for $300 a piece."

"That's a good deal, considering I just paid $400 for one," I said.

The only thing was, I was going to be a little short due to only making $160.

"Don't worry about it. Just pay me the next time you come up," he said. He seemed like he was in a rush to go so I got the two ounces and went on my way.

Butterfly had called me while I was getting my weed. She called me back and asked where I was. If I'd thought she was going to bring me my food I wouldn't have told her I was at my aunt's house.

It was too late to tell her that I and my cousin were on our way back to the other side of town. She told me that her mother just got her nails done around the corner from where I was. I wouldn't have minded for Ms. T and Butterfly to come get me, but I had just re-upped and smelled like a pound of weed. That wasn't the impression I wanted Ms. T to get from me. I had to do something, fast before Ms. T and Butterfly called me. I ran upstairs to the bathroom to look for anything to cover up the smell of the weed I had all over me.

I had missed a call from Butterfly but she had left me a message letting me know she and her mother were outside waiting for me. I could tell Ms. T wasn't happy at all being on my aunt's block, and more so, not happy with me being over there on it. There was a lot of traffic in and out of my aunt's house and it didn't help that some guy was trying to get my attention while I was talking to Ms. T.

I told her that he was my uncle and he wanted me to help him out with his car, knowing he did not look anything like me or my family.

Ms. T handed me the bag of Chinese food she'd gotten me. I went to the other side of the car, gave Butterfly a kiss and some money and told her I'd see her in a little bit.

Ms. T pulled off.

Something didn't sit right about the guys that were in the car behind her. They had all black on and I thought one of them was putting on a mask but I wasn't sure. My mind was stuck on this guy in my face, asking me if I had some dope for sell. I don't know why he'd come up to me out of all the people that were out on the block. But if I did have some drop, I would have sold it to him.

I saw Scrap walking up the block. The guy that asked me for the dope walked right up to Scrap and handed him some cash. Before he could give the guy the dope that same car with those guys in it rolled back up the block.

Before I knew it, Scrap had pulled out his pistol. At that same time, my little cousin was walking out the house.

I didn't know what was going on but I pulled out my .25 auto pistol and realized the guys that were in the car had a problem with Scrap and Scrap wasn't for the bullshit. He let a couple shots go at the car and I did too. Before I knew it we were side by side, shooting at the car.

We ran our separate ways. I ran to the back of my aunt's house and went inside. Everyone that was in my aunt's house was on the floor or hiding under something. My aunt was pulling on my head, for me to get down. Little did she know, that the shooting was over.

After everything settled down, a couple people went outside to see if anyone had been shot.

For some odd reason, the girl still couldn't keep her eyes off me. She had me mad that I had to see why she'd been all in my face ever since I came to my aunt's house.

I walked over to her. "Why are you in my face?" I asked.

She smiled and said, "You're bad!"

I did not understand what she meant by that but I had to get from out my aunt's house before the cops came. I told Tank to I had to get the fuck from over there.

He grabbed the plates that my aunt made us and we left.

As we were leaving, two cop cars drove through.

My heart was racing. If they pulled my cousin's car over, it was going to be over for me. I had two ounces of green on me and an empty .25 with gunpowder all over me.

God must have been with me because the two cop cars rode right past us. When we got to Tank's house, he asked me if I knew who did the shooting. He knew wasn't the one to ask because I wasn't going to tell.

I just looked at him and told him I didn't know. My phone rang and it was a number I had not seen before. I answered it and asked who it was. It happened to be the girl that was at my aunt's house who was in my face, Sad'e.

She had called to give me heads up that some lady just

came to my aunt's house and told my aunt that the guy that did the shooting was over there. Sad'e also told me it would be a good idea to change clothes.

I thanked Sad'e for giving me the heads up. I couldn't go home with this weed on me and I wasn't going to Butterfly's house, so I called Dee to see if he was home. I knew he wouldn't mind if I bagged up at his house.

When I called his number he told me that he was out of town and would not be back until that night but that his brother was at the house. I could have gone there but I really did not know Dee's brother like I knew Dee.

Me and homeboy, Woodz weren't on the same time. I hadn't talked to him in a week. I made the choice to go to my house and bag up and change clothes. The only good thing with me doing that, was that my mother was asleep so I was in and out before she woke up. I walked past the store where I first walked Misha.

CHAPTER 12

What a surprise, she was standing right there at the store. The last time I'd seen her was when I dropped her and her friends off at her grandma's house. She was happy to see me like I was happy to see her. Our conversation was all laughs and smiles. Her friends were up to the same old things, she told me. I let her know I had some weed for sale and if any of her friends wanted some weed to call my phone. While I was having a conversation with Misha there were three guys standing a couple houses up from us. They seemed like they weren't happy to see me talking to Misha or standing on their block, even their demeanor spoke.

I was feeling the tension that they were giving off and I could tell from the bulge on their sides that they had pistols on them. I wasn't looking for any trouble, so I told Misha I'd talk to her later and I left to go to Butterfly's house.

I got to Butterfly's house, just catching her mother leaving the house. I tried to stop to give her some paper for gas but she was in a rush to go somewhere. I called to tell Butterfly to come open the door. I know I heard some guy's voice in the background. I couldn't wait until she came to open the door so I could see the nigga she had in the house. First, she tried to play me and say there wasn't anyone in the house. She was smiling but I didn't find anything funny. Knowing I'd heard someone in the background, I was surprised now to hearing sound coming from upstairs. It was her brother, Money. He had left Job Corps to go to attend his grandma's funeral that was taking place the next day. I was happy to see him but I did not know how he felt about me talking to his sister. Come to find out he already knew. His sister had said something to him the night he called me to come to his girl's house when he, Dee, and Woodz were over there. I guess him telling me there was some girl that wanted to talk to me was just a test to see if I would have talked to the girl. If she would've been alright, I would have. I'm glad I didn't because I wouldn't have been with Butterfly.

Not a lot had changed, but still I had to put Money on to what I was into.

"Let's go somewhere to talk," I said to money. Butterfly was getting upset, thinking I was acting different since her brother was back. She was going off on me. That was the first time I'd seen Butterfly go off like that over something small. Money told me he was going to his room so I could talk to his sister. I did not know why she was going off. She told me because she'd called for me to come chill with her and that she thought I would be acting funny after I got her pussy. To her, it might have seemed like I was acing different but I was not the type of guy to let his girl know everything that was going on, especially when it came to street shit.

If it wasn't for her grandma passing, I wouldn't have felt sorry for her. I wasn't in the wrong for not letting her know my business.

She said she was done with what I had to say. She went in her room and closed the door.

There wasn't anything that I could say to get her out her room, so I went upstairs with Money to catch him up on things that had been going on. He didn't need me to put him on a thing. Job Corps didn't have him miss a beat. He went from selling weed to selling work. I knew he sold work before. But by the amount he had, I could tell he was all in and had put the weed game down.

"You done selling weed?" I asked.

"I'll never put the weed game down but the work is where it's at right now," he said.

Compared to crack, the weed game was slow. I could not understand why Money was moving the way he was. I didn't know if he wasn't allowed in his other house, or because he did not want to get caught bagging up all his work, or because he was on some type of drug.

"Why are you moving the way you move?' I asked.

"Look at my phone," he said.

I didn't know how looking at his phone was going to explain to me why he was moving the way he was moving, but I looked at his phone. Things started to make sense about why Money was moving the way. He had over three hundred missed calls! I didn't even know phones held three hundred missed calls, but apparently they did. He asked what the last number that had called his phone was. I read off the number he immediately finished bagging up his work and began to put it in the bag he had sitting on his bed.

Butterfly was yelling up to us to give us heads up that her mother had just pulled in the driveway. I could tell the from sound of Butterfly's voice that she was still upset but she didn't want me to get caught being in her mother's house. I knew I wasn't allowed to be in Ms. T house without her permission and the only thing that would save me was that Money was in the house with me and his sister, but I didn't want to take that chance.

Money grabbed the bag off his bed with the work in it and ran downstairs. We made it to the front door in the nick of time as Ms. T was walking in the back door, Money and I was walking out the front. The number that had called Money's phone looked like a number I remembered. It was Dee's number. He was calling Money to come over and drop his bars for the CD that they were about to put out.

One thing I knew was when it came to Money and his music, he always put that first over everything. Money asked me if I wanted to go with him to Dee's house while he dropped his bars for the CD. I told him that I had something to take care of and that I'd get up with him later.

I had to make some paper. The block was dead so I headed up to the block where I just had seen Misha.

There were a lot of people up there. I knew I could easily get some of my weed off. Misha was in the same place she'd was when I left from up there, and so were the three boys. I already wasn't in the mood for any bullshit, thanks to Butterfly getting mad at me for some dumb shit.

It didn't help when one of the boys walked up to me

while I was talking to Misha and had the nerve to tell me I had to get off their block. I already had a chip on my shoulder and when the niggas came with the dumb shit, I had to show them I meant business. I knew I was out numbered and I knew all three of them had a pistol on them and were looking for trouble. I was the one to give it to them. I left their block and went right to Dee's house.

Dee and Money were laying their last bars. As soon as Dee got done I told him how some boys tried to play me and told me I had to get off their block. I lied to Dee and told him they'd also pulled their pistols on me. Dee and Money wanted to go with me to take care of it but I told them no and that all I really needed was to hold Dee's .9mm S&W. "Where's the .25 I let you hold?" he asked.

"I have it on me, but I want something bigger."

Dee was not at ease to give up his .9mm like he was his .25 pistol but he did. I headed right back up to the three guys' block.

Misha and her two friends were leaving and asked me where I was headed. I told her back to the block. Misha tried to stop me from going back up there but I already had my mind made. That's where I was headed.

Misha told me be safe. "Those boys are drunk and have been acting crazy all day."

I did not say anything to her. I just went on my way thinking to myself, *I don't have to be drunk to let my pistol off.*

I kept repeating it in my head how the boy had said I had to get off his block. The only thing that stopped me from replaying it over and over again was that Butterfly had text me and said if I didn't want to be with her then to let her know and if I wanted to talk I could come to her house. Her mother had left to go find an outfit for the funeral. Butterfly said it was okay for me to come over. I never responded to Butterfly's text message. I turned my phone off, thinking of the best way to get them boys. I could see them standing in the middle of their block, so I walked on the opposite side of the street.

They had to be drunk. I was damn near across the street before one of them noticed me. Before they could get on point, I had my pistol out and pointed at them across the street. As soon as one tried to take off, I began firing. Crazy thing is the one that told me I had to get off his block was the first one to take the fuck off.

I wasn't moving swiftly. No mask, no gloves, and it was broad daylight. I know I could've killed one of those pussy ass niggas. The only thing that saved them was that they had run in a house.

There was no way I didn't hit one of them. I was so pumped that I put the pistol back on my hip and branded the shit out of myself. I walked away like I wasn't the one that was just involved in shooting.

There was a white tinted out car following me and I was out of bullets. I was about to take off until I looked and realized I'd seen that car before. I just did not know from where.

The window rolled down. It was Ms. Santiago, the woman I'd met at the barbershop. She told me to get in.

Her face was balled up as if she was mad at something. "I just got back from York. You were the first person I recognized, but you were just shooting some people. Why would you do that?"

I never answered her, I just sat there, quietly.

"Whatever it's about, it's not worth losing your life or taking someone else's. Where do you need to go?"

"You can drop me off around the corner at my girl's house."

She advised me to take some time to get my thoughts together and not to come outside for at least a month and that if I did hit someone, I needed to get out of town.

Things didn't set in until Ms. Santiago dropped me off. Butterfly came and opened the door. She still had a little attitude. I wasn't up to arguing with Butterfly.

My mind was racing. It had been only one month and I already had gotten myself into three shootings. And, I had just found out that I had shot one of the guys.

I was becoming my own worst enemy. Everything began to be different. Butterfly knew something was wrong with me but she thought it had something to do with the little argument we'd had an hour ago.

She did not know I wasn't the same me because I had just shot someone and I did not know if he was going to live or die. I never did turn my phone on, so Money and Dee could not get a hold of me. They came to see if I was at Money's house with his sister. I knew from the look on Dee's and Money's face that something was wrong. I just could not understand why Dee and Money kept smiling.

As soon as Butterfly went upstairs to use the bathroom, they told me what the word on the streets was.

They said four guys had just been shooting and two of

them had gotten hit. Dee and Money knew I had just come to get the gun but I also knew they were fishing for information. Dee said one of the guys got shot in the arm and the other guy got grazed in the head. Dee and Money were not dumb at all. They knew I had something to do with it. They came prepared and handed me a glove full of .9mm shells and Money handed me a bottle of Grey Goose.

They told me to be safe and if I needed anything to call their phones, then they left. I did not want Ms. T to come home and tell me that I had to leave her house and I didn't have bullets in my gun. I hurried up and filled the .9mm S&W back up. I got done just before Butterfly came back downstairs. She asked me why her brother had left the bottle of Grey Goose there.

Butterfly knew I said sold some weed and carried a gun from time to time but she did not know I had been in three shootings or that I had shot someone and grazed the other. She didn't know why her brother had left the bottle for me, to ease my mind.

Butterfly's mother, Ms. T had just called the house to let her daughter know that after she had gotten her outfit that she was going to work from there and that she would see her daughter in the a.m.

Ms. T thought that just because her Money came home from Job Corps that she wouldn't have to worry about me being in her house with her daughter. But what Ms. T did not know was that Money and I had become real cool and he did not mind me being at the house with his sister while his mother was gone. I didn't have to worry about Money saying anything to his mother.

I had just gotten some of the high-grade weed and my phone was going off crazy but I had to be safe. All I could think about was what Ms. Santiago was saying and she was right. I had to get out of town for a little bit. I was getting into a lot of shit in York and it wasn't like I had the paper to just up and leave town.

Butterfly had finally told me why she was upset and that was because I hadn't commented on her new hairstyle. After letting me know what was wrong with her, it wasn't hard to make it up to her. I could tell Butterfly really was looking for pure love. I was too, but the street was getting a hold of me fast. Money and Dee weren't helping the situation. Every time they called me they would call to let me know a black SUV kept riding around the block. I thought if they really were my homeboys that they would have put some holes in that car for me.

The word must have gotten back to Woodz. He called my phone, not to see if I was alright but to tell me I couldn't come to his mother's house because I was hot. He never asked if was I okay. He just called to say not to come to his house. Out of Dee, Money, and Woodz I would have thought Woodz would have had my back and be there for me the most. But like they say, you see who your real friends are when you're going through something real. Woodz didn't even help me get my weed off he knew I was hiding out at Butterfly's house. Instead of helping and calling me to get weed he would call someone else.

If it wasn't for Money, I wouldn't have made my paper.

***

Money got off everything I had. I had to look out and

give him a $100 and he still really didn't want to take it. By this time, Butterfly was hip to me giving her brother my weed to get off for me, but that was the least of my problems.

I had so many things on my mind that I couldn't stay still. Every little sound I heard, I told Butterfly to turn down the TV.

After a while, I began to be at ease, counting the paper that Money had brought me for my weed. I felt like it was time to open the bottle of Grey Goose that Money had left me. Butterfly was doing her thing in the kitchen, cooking me some food while I was counting my paper. Things were going good for the most part. I was relaxed with Butterfly. She seemed like her old self until my phone rang and she answered it. I had forgotten that I had given Misha my phone number to call me if any of her friends wanted some weed. I was not in the wrong and neither was Misha or Butterfly.

Misha did not know I had gotten into a relationship and Butterfly thought I was playing her. Instead of Misha just asking for me she started to argue with Butterfly. Butterfly had never answered my phone until that. I let her know Misha was just looking for me to sell her some weed. Butterfly didn't want any females to call my phone. And that was going to become a problem for us. Most the people that called my phone for weed were girls. After telling her that, she kind of understood. Plus, if I was cheating on her, I wouldn't have let her pick up my phone. Butterfly was crazy over me and I liked it. That night, things got more interesting between Butterfly and I. She prepared us a meal.

I didn't know, but she had gotten herself some lingerie. She even bought me a pair of silk boxers.

Things started to make sense, why she was so mad. She had planned this day all for me. She broke down to me about everything she wanted out of life and she wasn't going to let anyone bring her down, not even me.

She had asked what I wanted out of life. I had not really thought about it. But I knew one thing, I didn't want to be anything like my dad. That brought up the conversation of Butterfly's dad. Butterfly's dad was never in her life. She didn't have a father figure. It was just her mother and her. Ms. T was one hell of a mother. Besides Money selling work, he was still going back to Job Corps to make something out of his life. Butterfly was still in school, getting good grades. On the other hand, I had my mother and stepdad there for me and I still was turning out to be worse than Money and Butterfly. I wasn't doing well in school, I stayed in fights, and my grades weren't that good. I was selling drugs and getting into shoot-outs.

My life was on the way to destruction. If I didn't get a hold of my life, I wouldn't make it to see my 17th birthday.

Everything I thought about doing, good and bad, I did it because I wanted to. That goes back to Woodz's sister, Poo. How is it that a little kid like Poo could be positive in a seventy-five percent negative environment? It's because she chose to be. We all have the choice to do good or bad, and I was choosing to do bad. I knew when I got in the drug game there were going to be things and people that wanted to bring me down. But I never thought I would become my own problem. I was beginning to think I could not help it. After me and Butterfly got off the topic of talking about our dads, she asked me to help her wash the dishes before we got in the shower.

I knew I was in for a surprise. I was going to bust her ass. I ran some bath water and put some candles around the tub to set the mood. I didn't know how I was going to explain to Butterfly why I wasn't going to see her for a while. It would have been best to tell her the next day.

That night was all about us. I went in the room to tell her that the bath water was ready. She had just taken off her panties and was messing with something on the bottom of her foot that she had just stepped on. She told me to come see if I saw anything on the bottom of her foot when I got closer. She pulled me on top of her. Before I knew it one thing led to another. The first time we'd fucked was good but this next time was great. I don't know if it was because I had liquor in me but her pussy felt tighter than the last time we'd fucked.

After we got done, I didn't know why she was so quiet. I knew for sure she'd got her nut off. I went to the bathroom to run some more hot water in the tub. She came in handed me a towel and silk skin boxers she got for me. She sat on the toilet and was just looking at me. I lit the candles and took her hand to help her get in the tub. I got in behind her and slowly started to wash her back. She seemed like she was melting in my arms.

I'm guessing she was enjoying the moment. I was very confident in myself with making sure she got her nut off. Still, I had to ask because she wasn't being herself. She was real quiet. She told me she definitely got her nut off.

"Why are you so quiet?" I asked.

"We haven't used a condom and I'm trying to figure out, if I got pregnant would you take care of the baby, or leave me on my own."

"No, I wouldn't just leave you," I said, but in the back of my mind, I wasn't even thinking about kids.

Just to say, if I did end up getting Butterfly pregnant, I wouldn't have any problem taking care of her. That was always something that made me like Butterfly the way I did. She didn't have any problem with letting me know what was on her mind. And with me knowing that, I knew it would be the right time to let her know I had to leave town for at least two weeks.

"Okay," was all she said.

It wasn't the answer I was expecting from her. She didn't even ask why. Her response had me a little upset and I wanted to know why she'd just said, "okay" as if didn't care if I stayed in town or not.

It was bothering me like it was bothering her. She looked over her shoulder and gave me a kiss. She said, "Bae, when my brother and Dee came in the house, I went upstairs to use the bathroom and I stopped in my mother's room to turn off her AC. I overheard the conversation you, Dee, and my brother were having. I heard everything. I didn't say anything because I was waiting for you to say something to me."

Me being me, I still lied and told Butterfly that her brother and Dee weren't talking about me being in a shootout.

And her being her, she said, "Bae, I love you. I don't

want to see you get killed. So if you got to leave town for a lil' then go and leave. When you get back I'll be waiting for you."

I couldn't say anything. I was the one that was now quiet. We sat there in the tub until the candles burned out and our skin became wrinkled. We got out the tub and went to her room to get dressed. She put on her lingerie and I put on my silk boxers.

***

It had not been later than 11 p.m. and I still had a half bottle of Grey Goose.

Love and Basketball had just come on which happened to be her favorite movie. Butterfly ran downstairs to get a glass of apple juice and a glass of ice for my Grey Goose.

Her mother had just called again to check on her and to remind her to feed the dog before she went to bed because she wasn't going to be home until 9 a.m. Ms. T had asked Butterfly if I had been over to the house. With me sitting right in Ms. T's house, Butterfly did not hesitate in lying to her mother. Butterfly said, "goodnight," and hung up the phone.

Love and Basketball had been on for 5 minutes and it was just starting to rain. Butterfly hugged me and asked me if I was going to stay the night with her. Little did she know, I already had that in mind.

"Yes sweetheart," was what I said, while rubbing on her sexy ass body. I kept looking at her gorgeous teeth every time she smiled. From the look she kept giving while watching Love and Basketball I knew we would not make it through the whole move.

For me and Butterfly to only be in our teens, we were doing things only grownups did. If this was the way Butterfly really was, I wouldn't mind at all making her my wife. But first, before I even thought about being a family man or husband, I had to get my life right. While she watched the movie I was thinking about the best way to handle the situation I had with the two guys I'd shot. Butterfly had fallen asleep and I could not get any sleep. Love and Basketball had gone off and come on again and I still was wide awake. I finished up the last sip of vodka while Butterfly slept like an angel. Being cooped up in this house wasn't anything I was going to get used to.

I didn't know if the liquor was talking for me, but I woke Butterfly up. I told her I needed to talk to her so I could express the love I had for her. She knew if I would have stayed in York that I would have died or killed someone. She knew like I knew that this was going to be the last time I saw her for a long time. I finally fell asleep. Those five hours of sleep felt like the ten minutes. I really didn't want to leave Butterfly's house but I had to before her mother made it home. We had sex one more time that morning but it only made it more difficult for me to leave her but I couldn't let my dick think for me.

My chances were already slim and they were getting slimmer by the hour.

I was leaving Butterfly's house. I ran into Money. He had just pulled up to the back of his mother's house.

"Where are you on your way to?" Money asked.

"Going to my house," I said. He informed me that he had been at his mother's house two hours ago to see if I was still there and saw me and his sister asleep so he didn't bother us. I was thinking to myself I was out cold. Money had dropped me off at my house, smelling like a bottle of booze. I didn't care if my mother smelled the liquor on me or not. I was just happy to be home. I put the pistols under my pillow and hopped right in the bed. I slept all day my mother thought I was sick.

I had forgotten that Butterfly's grandma funeral was that day and I had not talked to Butterfly since that morning. They always say God works in mysterious ways. Well, I had gotten myself in a lot of shit in York, PA. Just the other day I'd shot two people that my mother and my father did not know anything about.

My mother asked me if I was going to go with my dad to Connecticut to help him put up a wall on the side of my aunt's house. Like I said, God is always there when we need him the most. That was my way to get out of York, PA for a while. My mother had told me that my dad was leaving in two hours and to be ready if I was going with him. I still had Dee's two guns that I knew he would be looking to get back before I left to go to Connecticut. I had asked my mother how long we were going to be up there. She had told me for 3 to 4 weeks. Getting my things packed to leave was the best thing that could happen for me. I called Dee to come get his guns. He told me that Money was going to come get them.

Money came sooner than I thought. My sister yelled upstairs to tell me someone was out back, beeping the horn, and that she thought it was for me and then the phone rang. It was Money, letting me know he was out back. I wiped both guns and put them in a shoe box and gave the box to him. He asked me wherever I was going, to be myself. I knew the only one that knew I was leaving was his sister Butterfly and I was right. Money handed me an envelope with a letter inside of it and said it was from his sister. I got back to my room and opened the letter. It was a letter, and a photo, from Butterfly pouring out her heart to me. The way she worded it was as if she was never going to see me again. I knew with me being in Connecticut that it would humble me and help me get my life right. It was almost time for me and my father to leave. My mother was standing in the living room looking at us like we were leaving for good. I knew as soon as we left, that she was going to break down and start crying but I was wrong. She started to cry before we left. She prayed for my stepfather and me. We got on the road. It was only four to five hours from York, PA to Connecticut. We stopped one time to get something to eat and gas up the car. The rest of the way I went to sleep and when I did wake up, we were just arriving at my aunt's house.

CHAPTER 13

I could tell my father was tired from all the driving. His eyes were bloodshot red. My mother had just called my father's phone to see if we'd made it there safely. Being out of York, PA, I felt a lot of weight was off my shoulders. I could go anywhere and I didn't have to worry about anyone shooting at me. Most of all I didn't have to be nervous every time a cop rode by. It was nice outside. My cousins had just come home from their friend's house and my dad was too tired to start on the wall we came down here to do. My male cousins were not around at the time but my girl cousins had just come back from their friend's house. I had not seen my cousins in a while. We all had growing up to do. I knew I was only going to be in Connecticut for a month. I didn't want to waste any time having fun but first I called Butterfly to let her know I was okay and that I loved her. Before I could dial her number, some girls were walking up the block, looking good as shit.

I didn't have to say a thing. Two of them were on me. I didn't know which one of them I was going to talk to so I let them decide.

One started up the conversation by asking if I was from New York.

"No. I was born in Connecticut."

She told me that she now lived in York, PA. She didn't know where York, PA was at but she was interested and was looking forward to getting up with me.

We exchanged numbers. I had not been back in Connecticut ten minutes and I already had gotten a shorty's number. I thought Connecticut was going to be laid back but I was wrong. I know it was crazy but damn, you would think over the years things would have calmed down a bit. But no it seemed worse. A block up from my aunt's house shots rang out.

My cousin received a phone call from one of her home girls, asking her to walk up the block and told her that someone was just shooting. My cousin asked me to walk with her to her friend's house.

The closer we got to her friend's house the more people began to come outside. We got closer and realized someone was lying on the ground and he had been shot in the head. That was the most blood I had seen in my life. I was guessing that it was the dead guy's homeboys or brothers that were standing around him, lost for words.

Shit, I would be too if that was my friend or brother with a hole in his head the size of a golf ball. Some girl was yelling at the top of her lungs. I knew that she was related. The crazy thing was, the girl that was yelling was my cousin's friend that asked her to come up the block to her house and the guy that got shot in the head was the girl's brother. I know my cousin wanted to support her friend but it was too much going on for me to let my cousin go over there where her friend was standing.

I grabbed my cousin and went back to my aunt's house. I was in a daze, thinking that could've been me or one of my homeboys if I would have stayed in York, PA.

All that day, my aunt's block was on fire. The detectives went from house to house, asking people if they'd seen anything. I was going to be in Bridgeport, CT for a month. *I think I was better off by bringing one of the guns with me,* I thought.

It hadn't been twenty minutes when all the cops had left the crime scene and more shots rang out a few houses up from the guy's that just had died. Someone else got torn out the frame. There were two bodies in one day on the same block. Shit, that was all I needed to see.

I wasn't going out to end up getting shot because of mistaken identity. There were a lot going on that made me think one day could be my last. Butterfly had called my phone to let me know how her grandmother's funeral went. She said she was trying to be strong for her mother until her mother broke down and started to cry. This made her cry as well.

"How are things going in Connecticut," she asked.

Butterfly only knew how Connecticut was from movies and TV shows. So when I told her that two had people died up the block from my aunt's house, she didn't believe me.

This made her think I was lying about being in Connecticut. Our conversation wasn't going well so I told Butterfly I'd talk to her later.

The rest of that night I watched TV until I went to sleep.

***

The next morning, my stepfather got me up to go with him to get some things to start the job that we'd come down to do. I didn't know anything about carpentry but being with my stepfather, I was going to learn a lot.

I remembered something my stepfather told me. He said, "You rather learn a lil about a lot than learn a lot about one thing."

My stepfather was like MacGyver. There was nothing that he didn't know a little about.

We went to the warehouse store. I didn't know any of the names of the tool we were going to use to do the job except for the sledgehammer. It was every bit of eighty-five degrees outside and it was supposed to reach ninety. I could have easily told my stepfather I didn't want to help put up my aunt's wall. And I really hadn't come to work my ass off. But I also wasn't on a vacation and I had to make some cash. Then only thing I couldn't understand was why we had to put up a wall on just one side of the house.

My stepfather explained to me that due to the water not draining under the grass, the house had started to slide. Because of that, it pushed the wall out and that's where we came in at. All we had to do was build a wall a foot away from the wall that was about to fall and fill in the gaps with concrete. There was more to it than that. It was hard work and time-consuming. It took one day just to put the things outside so no one would get hurt or try and sue us. The other two days we went out to get all the things we needed to make sure it would get done right. After a couple of days, I started to see it come together. I was beginning to be proud of our work, then I found out it was going to rain for two days. It was nice, not too hot, with a nice breeze blowing. I had almost forgotten about the girl I'd first met when I first got to Bridgeport, CT. She surprised me when she showed up at the job sight. I was drained from working and I smelled.

It was Friday but for me it was my Monday. I and my stepfather had a deadline to get the job done before our family reunion took place the next month. I wasn't going to let some girl get in the way of my paper. Besides, I wasn't all that interested in her. My mind was on Butterfly and what she was doing. I couldn't wait to talk to Butterfly that night.

It had been days working with my stepfather and I wanted to give up and just go inside to call Butterfly. But just when I wanted to quit, something inside of me would tell me to work. Not just for myself, but for Butterfly. If it wasn't for her, I wouldn't be doing the positive things I was doing. She was motivation, sometimes for good, and sometimes for bad. I had to get back to her.

I never did call that girl. I was too busy working with my stepfather and too tired to go anywhere or do anything. We had one more week to get the job done. I thought it would take the whole month to finish the job but we made out and got it done a few days early. That gave me a week to have fun. Even though it had been almost a whole month since I'd left York, PA, where I'd shot those two people, it was still fresh on my mind.

Reality began to set in. I knew I was going to have to go back to York in due time. I just needed some time for my name to die down. I hadn't been in touch with Dee, Money, or Woodz so I didn't know what was going. Due to Butterfly not being an, "In the streets girl," the only things she told me were those on TV and with her mother. No one knew when I was going to be back, not even Butterfly and I wanted to keep it that way.

That weekend, my stepfather had to wait to get paid for the job we did. I knew my stepfather was going to look out and give me some cash but I didn't think it would be anything much.

That night I chilled and talked to Butterfly until we fell asleep.

***

That next morning, my aunt got me up and told me to go downstairs to eat before me and my stepfather got back on the road to go back to York. I ate and one hour went to two hours and two went to three hours and my stepfather still had not made it back.

I went to get dressed when my aunt knocked on the bathroom door to tell me my stepfather was in the room waiting for me and wanted to talk to me about something. I wasn't sure on what he wanted with me. I finished getting dressed and went in my aunt's room where my stepfather and aunt's husband, whom I hadn't seen the whole time I was in Connecticut, were.

There were stories about my aunt's husband and one of them was that he was a real brick layer. So it was a surprise to see him for the first time, but I still didn't understand why he and my stepfather wanted with me. I sure was about to find out what my stepfather and aunt's husband wanted, though.

My aunt's husband was sitting on the bed, counting a bag full of cash. He handed my stepfather some cash. I'm guessing for putting the wall up on the side of the house.

That's a lot of cash but where is my cut for helping? I thought.

My stepfather peeled back a couple of $100 bills and asked me if I wanted $700 for helping him put up the wall or an $800 watch. I thought about it. I still had almost $1000 saved up at my mother's house back in York. I didn't need the $700 but it would help me out a lot. I thought about it for a few seconds until my aunt's husband pulled out a brown, leather snake skinned rose gold Old World Mastered watch with diamonds in the bezel. It only had one tiny scratch on the face of it and it was 100% authentic.

After that, there was not anything to think about. I took the watch and that was that. Before I left the room my, aunt's husband told me the only thing he asked me was to never ever wear that watch in Bridgeport, CT. From him telling me that, I knew two things. One, was he'd gotten someone killed or robbed someone for it and two, it was real and cost someone a lot of cash.

I went to put my things in the car to get back on the road. It seemed like a longer ride back to York than coming. I could not get any sleep.

My mind was racing, thinking about everything from the work we did on my aunt's house, to seeing the guy with the hole in his head and not wanting to end up like him. I realized I could do anything if I put my mind to it.

I tried hard not to call Butterfly but I could not help myself. Plus, I was supposed to call two days ago but could not get out to get minutes for my phone.

I'd been talking to Butterfly for some time, so I knew when something was wrong with her. It wasn't minutes into our phone call when she told me Money had gotten locked up for some drugs.

"Does he have bail?" I asked.

"Yes," she said. "My mother is on her way to get him out of jail."

We talked until her mother got back to the house with Money. I told her to put him on the phone so I could talk to him. I could still hear Ms. T using every curse word in the book. Money went to his room so we could talk.

Come to find out, he sold some work to an undercover cop. I fucked with Money but I didn't want to be around him knowing that he had just got out of jail for selling some drugs to an undercover cop. I didn't want to but I had to keep Money at a distance. I knew that would be a little hard being that I talked to his sister.

Me and my stepfather finally made it back to York, PA.

CHAPTER 14

It felt good to be back in town and to see my mother and sisters, smiling. But reality was, I still had to be on point for the two guys I'd shot. I called Dee to let him know I was back in York and that I needed to hold his gun. Dee told me he had gotten rid of the .9mm. The only thing he still had was the .25 pistol, but I'd have to go get it from his brother.

I took the chance on walking down to the block, thinking if I ran into the guys I shot, they would down me. The crazy thing is, I had to walk past their block. I was feeling like a still-born baby that was not going to make it alive.

All I could think about was something I'd seen in the Bible from Psalms 118:6.

"The Lord is on my side. I will not fear what man can do to me."

I made it to the block. A couple of people were happy to see me, especially Woodz's mother, Mrs. Mary. She asked me how things with me were and how my family was doing. I told her, but I had to keep the conversation short with her because I didn't want to stand on the block without a pistol.

I called Dee to let him know I hadn't seen his brother and that when he got back in town I wanted him to call me. I told him I'd be at Butterfly's house.

I knew Butterfly was going to be surprised to see me but I didn't think she would be that happy to see me.

Ms. T answered the door. She was also surprised to see me. She smiled and said Butterfly was going to be happy to see me.

I could hear Butterfly in the kitchen. Ms. T called her to come in the living room because someone was there to see her. Butterfly walked in the living room and as soon as she saw me, the look on her face was as if she'd seen a ghost. She dropped and broke the glass of apple juice she had in her hand and ran and jumped on me. She almost knocked me down. She didn't have a care in the world that her mother was standing there, by the way she was kissing all over me. Her mother understood that she was excited to see me. Her brother had come downstairs from hearing the glass breaking and all the commotion. Butterfly still hadn't gotten down off me, not that I wanted her to. It was just that she was getting heavy and my arms were getting tired. I was very surprised Ms. T didn't say anything about her daughter being all over me.

Ms. T was looking like she might be about ready to go on a date. This was my first time seeing Ms. T dressed up like that. I could've said, "Damn, she looked good!" I could see where Butterfly got her figure from.

I saw Money waving for me to come and talk to him.

Ms. T had told Butterfly to clean up the broken glass. While Butterfly did that and Ms. T finished putting on her accessories, I went and talked to Money. I would have thought he would have slowed down a little being that he'd just gotten setup by an undercover cop. But no, not Money, he still was up to his same old ways, bagging up some cocaine.

Money seemed like he did not care about a thing, not even about himself. He showed me the cash that he'd just had made that day.

"Hope you put that up before your mother walks up here and sees you with all this cash and asks for some cash for bailing you out of jail."

All he did was smile. I wasn't up for going anywhere with Money knowing he had just got booked by the cops. So before he could ask, I told him I was going downstairs to spend some time with his sister, whom I had not seen in a month.

She was still smiling when I got downstairs and Ms. T was putting on her lipstick. Ms. T knew I had not seen her daughter in a month so she didn't mind letting me stay over at the house until she got back from her date. Ms. T grabbed her handbag and went out the door.

Money came downstairs, got his bottle of Hennessey, put it in his back pocket, and went out the door. As soon as the house was clear, Butterfly and I did not waste any time. We got right to love-making for hours.

We went at it, and when I did finally cum, I took a breather for a few minutes and got right back to beating that pussy up. I couldn't get enough of Butterfly's sweet thing. Putting in overtime was what she called it. We made love until we couldn't fuck anymore. She took me to her bedroom and as soon as I went in, the first thing I saw was a teddy bear with me and Butterfly's names all over it. At first, I thought it was cute until we lay down on her bed and I looked up and saw mine and Butterfly's name was all on the ceiling. Then I started to notice mine and her names were on everything in her room. From the side of the TV to the back of her door, on her walls, notebooks, she even had a necklace with my initials on it. I was starting to think she was obsessed with me.

We lay there until I got a phone call from an unknown number. It was Dee's brother letting me know I had to meet him at the back of his house if I wanted the gun. I could tell it was bothering Butterfly that I just got back in town and just to her house and I already was about to go. Butterfly pleaded with me to stay with her at the house.

"I'll be back, I'm just going to Dee's house to get something," I said.

"If you're going to Dee's house, I'm going with you," she said.

I didn't want her to be in my business, but there was not anything I could do to keep her from not going with me. I did not want to argue with her, so I let her walk with me.

We went to the back of Dee's house so I could meet his brother. Dee's brother handed me the pistol, gave me some cash, and told me to be safe. Butterfly did not see Dee's brother hand me the pistol but she did see him hand me some cash. She did not say anything until we got back to her house.

I don't know if she just wanted to start an argument or just really cared about me. She had made a big deal about Dee's brother giving me cash and asked if I was selling drugs again. She gave me a whole argument saying how her brother had just gotten picked up for selling drugs and she didn't want that to happen to me. Little did she know, I was not selling anything. Dee's brother had just given me some cash because I'd just made it back in town and he wanted to look out for me. She went on and on, saying if I really cared about her, I would stop selling drugs and get a job because she didn't want to be with me if that's all I was going to do with my life.

All I could do was respect her. Besides, she was right. I didn't want to sell drugs all my life, and I wanted to be with her. I still had to be on point for my enemies.

It was never a problem staying in the house with Butterfly, but it was starting to get old real fast. I was cooped up in the house for a month when I went to Bridgeport and I wasn't going to do the same in York. I took Butterfly to Dee's house. A couple of people up the block that I knew came to Dee's house to see me.

I guessed Money had told Woodz I was back in town and Woodz told them, so Dee's house got packed full of people. That was all the reason to get a couple of bottles and throw a cookout.

Things were cool until the liquor got to the niggas. Dee wanted to fight everyone. He always had a problem holding his liquor and even though he didn't have a problem with me I had his gun and he wanted it now. Dee knew that I didn't have my own gun and I still had a problem with the two guys I'd shot but he didn't care because he'd then gotten himself into some B.S.

I gave the gun and told Butterfly to come on. We were going to her house.

I was mad because I had to walk home and there was a chance I would run into one of the guys I'd shot.

I chilled with Butterfly while thinking how I was going to get home safely. The good thing with that was I still had Scrap's number and he had those guns. The last time I'd called him was before I'd left to go to Bridgeport. I hoped he still had the same number. I had to call to find out. Someone picked up but I wasn't sure if it was him or not. He seemed to know it was me but he didn't sound the same at all.

I had to make sure it was really him before I ran off at the mouth and asked him about two guns. I guess he was thinking the same way I was. Before I could ask him to meet me, he was already asking me where I was at because he was going to come see me.

I got a phone call like an hour later, telling me to come out and that he was sitting in a black BMW. It was without a doubt, that it was Scrap. He had a light grin on his face.

He had asked me if I had anything to do that day.

"No." I replied.

"Cool," he said. "You're going to chill with me.

He pulled off. I didn't have a clue where we were going. I started to get a little nervous when he started to head in the direction where I'd shot the two guys.

I really started to get a knot in my stomach when he pulled out his 357 S&W and sat it on his lap. My mind started racing, thinking the guys I shot were one of his family members. I was five seconds from hopping out his car. Things went from bad to worse, we were about to ride right by one of the guys I shot.

I never forgot his face and I was sure it was him because he still had his cast on his arm.

I didn't know if Scrap was fishing to see if I was the one that had shot the two guys. He had let me know that the time we had that shootout by my aunt's house was with some of the guys that chilled on the block that we had just ridden past.

To me that was a coincidence we had beef with the same guys, but I still didn't say anything about me shooting those two guys because he could have just wanted to see if I was the one that shot them.

On the road we were on, there was not a car or house in sight. I was thinking that it was over for me. He was about to kill me and leave me on the side of the road. At any moment he was going to point that nickel plated 357 in my face and pull the trigger.

Everything started to flash before my eyes until he gave me his pistol and told me to put it in the glove box. I was filled with relief for the time. By this time, we had already been on the road for 45 minutes. We pulled up to a nice big house where an all-white Mercedes Benz was parked in the garage. We pulled in the garage. Scrap closed the garage door. Something about the Mercedes Benz had my attention. If it was Scrap's house this shit was nice as fuck. All I could think to myself was that I wanted a big house like that.

There was no one in the house as far as I knew, besides six pit bulls. He never got around to asking me what I wanted when I called until we got to his house. He took me to his kitchen and offered a drink. He had every type of liquor imaginable in his kitchen. It made it hard for me to decide what I wanted to drink. I went with what I knew and that was Grey Goose. Finally, he got around to asking me what I wanted when I called.

I didn't bullshit around with him. I told him I was looking to buy one of the guns that he had shown me a month ago by my aunt's house.

"What happened to the gun you were shooting with?" he asked.

"I borrowed it from one of my homeboys. But now he's in a situation and needs it," I said.

Scrap said, "I never got to thank you for the time you shot at the guys with me by your aunt's house. That was some thorough shit you did. By the way, how old are you?"

"Sixteen," I said.

"I was sixteen years old doing the same things you are doing now. Before you can lead, you must learn to follow. What gun are you looking to buy?"

"I liked the .38 but I really liked that P89 Ruger with the red light on the bottom of it."

"As soon as my girl comes back, I'll show you the guns again."

He put in a rap CD called, "Once Upon a Time in Brooklyn" by Uncle Murda, which I'd never heard before then. Whoever Uncle Murda was, he was ruthless and the shit he was saying in his raps was real.

If I didn't have a favorite rapper at that time, I think I'd just found him. Uncle Murda's music put you in a different mood. You did not need drugs. His music got you higher.

Scrap was in the kitchen, making a cake with all the wrong ingredients. His dogs were in the next room, barking like crazy.

"Go get the door," Scrap said. "It's my girl."

I was surprised to see the face that came through that door. I could not believe she was Scrap's girl. I said her name to be sure that it was her that was standing in front of my face. "Ms. Santiago!" I was without a doubt, it was her. I knew I recognized the Mercedes Benz that was in the garage. She handed me a book bag and told me to give it to her man, Scrap. I knew the guns were inside the bag. Scrap was puzzled that I knew his girl.

Ms. Santiago went to do something in the garage and Scrap started to ask me all types of questions about his girl and how I knew her. I didn't have anything to say but the truth which was that I'd met her at the barbershop when I was getting my haircut.

He pulled out all the guns that were in the bag and just like the first time seeing them, I liked that P89 Ruger.

Ms. Santiago came in and started running off at the mouth, telling her man that I was the one that shot those two guys. I don't know why she thought it was cool to just tell Scrap that, it's not like it was anything new. That shit happened a whole month ago.

Scrap looked at me. "Those guys only respect violence. I'm going to sell you that P89 Ruger you want and I also got something you're going to like that goes with it," he said.

He left the room for a moment and came back in with an extended clip that held thirty-two shots. I was fine with the seventeen shot clip, but that thirty-two shot extender clip was something I'd only seen in movies. The only thing I wasn't sure about was the price he was going to charge me for the gun and that clip.

Before I could ask him the price he had let me know that the guys I had shot were the same guys that were in that car by my aunt's house that day that I was shooting with him. Everything started to fit like a jigsaw puzzle. That's why those guys told me to get off their block earlier that day before I came back and shot them. It wasn't because they were just looking for trouble or because I was talking to Misha, it was because they recognized me from being on the block by my aunt's house and they did not know if I was down with Scrap and his team.

All that drama came from being with the wrong people. There wasn't anything I could do but not get caught sleeping and end up like the guy that got shot in his head in Connecticut. I wasn't going to become the one they lit the candles for.

Ms. Santiago could tell I was interested in the CD that her boyfriend was playing for me so she copied all the CD's he had of Uncle Murda's and gave them to me. I didn't know Ms. Santiago was going to be the one to take me home, but before we were about to go I needed to know how much Scrap was going to charge me for the gun and clip. I don't know what he was doing but I was ready to go.

I got what I called him for and Butterfly was blowing up

my phone. I couldn't answer because I knew if Butterfly would have heard Ms. Santiago's voice, she would have thought I was cheating on her.

Ms. Santiago went in her bedroom to get her car keys, came out and told me that her boyfriend Scrap wanted me. I was a little hesitant to walk into their bedroom. I knew that's where the six dogs were, I knocked on the door before entering. Scrap told me to come in. I didn't want to go any further in the room with the six dogs, not in their cages. Scrap knew I was scared. He said something in Spanish and two of the dogs sat at the foot of his bed and the other four went to each corner of the room.

I'd never seen someone have control over their dogs like he did but seeing that I still didn't feel right being in there. I wanted to see what he wanted and get the fuck from out of there. He handed me a crown royal bag and said bring him back $500 and keep $300. I looked inside and saw it was a half ounce of work. I told him I didn't want to sell work, I only sold weed.

He laughed and said, "You can be out there in them streets shooting people but you don't know how to get to some paper?"

Everything hit me. He was right. When I did my first robbery, I did it to get some cash and when I got some cash I was going to get some drugs so I could get the things I saw other people with that I couldn't afford.

"Okay," I said.

He handed me a box of bullets for the gun I'd just bought. Ms. Santiago was standing in the doorway with her car keys in her hand, waiting for me so she could take me home. It didn't take long for her to get me to my house. I ran in my house, grabbed the $500 for the pistol and ran back to the car. I got in. I didn't know why Ms. Santiago was smiling until I handed her the $500 and she said that I looked just like my mother.

"How do you know what my mother looks like?" I asked. "She was being a mother and came outside to see who I was, dropping her son off at the house," Ms. Santiago said.

All I could do is shake my head and smile. "That's my mother," I said. "She does things like that all the time."

I asked Ms. Santiago to drop me off at Butterfly's. As soon as I got out front of Butterfly's house my phone started going off. I told Ms. Santiago thank you for the ride and closed the door to the car.

By the tone in Butterfly's voice I knew something was wrong. She asked me where was I at. I told her open the door I was right out front.

I had just bought this new pistol. It wasn't easy to conceal like the little .25 pistol Dee let me hold. So, before Butterfly came and opened the door, I tried to fix it. Butterfly opened the door and before I could give her a hug, she smacked the shit out of me.

She hit me so hard that I lost hearing in my ear for about a minute or two. I was a couple of minutes from putting my hands on her until she started going off. She was talking about me just coming back in town from not seeing her for a month, coming her house, fucking her, then just up and leaving without saying anything to her, and not answering the phone. She felt like she was some type of whore. And on top of it all, there was a shooting by Woodz's house.

Her telling me these things it still didn't explain why she smacked me like that.

"I smacked you because you had a grin on your face," Butterfly said.

The look in butterfly's eyes said it all, that she really did love me. But I had to let her know to never put her hands on me like that again. All she could do was hug me and say sorry.

"I just was scared that something happened to you and I really got scared when you did not answer the phone," she said.

Now that she said what she had to say, she wanted to know what my excuse was for not picking up her phone calls. I could have just lied and said anything but I thought about what would Scrap say to Ms. Santiago if he was in this situation that I was in? I thought he would have told her the truth but not too much.

"I took a ride with Scrap to get something to make some paper off of and something to keep me a little safe, being back in York. I couldn't answer my phone because I couldn't hear it due to the new CD Scrap was playing for me," I said.

She looked at me as if like everything I was saying was a lie or it might be the truth. "I'm just glad you're safe and back in my arms," Butterfly said.

Many attempts to communicate are nullified by saying too much.

Now that Butterfly was okay and back to herself, I called my homeboy, Woodz, to see who was shooting by his house. He asked where I was because he had something to show me.

I told him that I was at Butterfly's house and that I had something to show him as well.

It wasn't long before Woodz was calling my phone to tell me to come out to the back of Butterfly's house. He sounded like he was out of breath, like he had ran over here.

"Why are you out of breath?" I asked.

"I ran over here to show you the new pistol I just got while I was out of town."

It looked just like Money's 380. There were not a lot of guns I hadn't seen, but that pistol Woodz had looked identical to the 380 Money had before I left to Connecticut. Woodz had told me that earlier he let off a couple of shots on the block just to see how it sounded. That explained the gunshots Butterfly said she heard. Woodz also told me that the two guys I'd shot came up to him when he was with Misha like a week after I left to go to Connecticut and said that there wasn't any beef between them and me.

Woodz told me they didn't want any smoke and they weren't bitching because they got shot.

I told Woodz there was never any beef between me and those guys. I shot them and that was that. I changed the subject so I could get right to what I had to say to Woodz. I knew he wouldn't believe that I had some work for sale so I showed him to sum up everything. It wasn't what I thought he would say or do.

"Why are you showing me that, I got my own work?"

I asked him if he'd help me make $300 to pay my

connect his paper, I'd give him $150 but the only thing he said was he had his own work to get off.

From that conversation, I didn't need to say anything else. I felt like he was hating that I had some work for sale so there was no point to show him the P89 Ruger I'd bought. He was becoming more of an enemy than my friend. If Money had not gotten set up by the cops I would have asked him to help me get my work off but I wasn't going to take the chance of him getting setup by the cops again.

Dee would have helped me but he'd been out of town and would not be back until the next week.

The rest of that night me and Butterfly just watched a movie 'til her mother got back from her date. We could clearly see she had a good time and was drunk. It was nice to see Ms. T with a smile on her face. The times I did see her, she was always working or getting some sleep for the next day of work. On her days off, she just slept. She went upstairs I'm guessing to take a shower.

Butterfly was nodding off every five minutes. I was getting tired myself. I knew I could have stayed over at Butterfly's house but I wanted to sleep in my own bed so I went home.

Being that I had my new pistol on me the walk home was not a problem. I got home safely. My mother and stepdad were on the porch, drinking their little wine coolers. I gave my mother a good night hug, realizing at the last minute she might feel the gun that's on my hip. I pulled away from her. She gave me a look like she knew I had something on me but she didn't say anything but good night and that she would see me in the morning.

I was so tired. The last thing I remembered was getting a phone call from Butterfly. She asked me if I'd made it home and told me she loved me. The other thing I thought about was how big and nice Scrap's house was and how Scrap had everything and that I was going to be just like him one day.

CHAPTER 15

The next morning before the sun rose, my phone was going off. I did not know why Scrap was calling me that early in the morning. I never answered and he never stopped calling. I figured something must have been wrong for Scrap to be calling me the way he was, so I finally answered the phone.

He had the nerve to ask me why I was asleep. He told me I had forty-five minutes to get dressed before he got to my house to pick me up. I told Scrap I hadn't gotten any of the work off.

He said that should be more of a reason for me to not be asleep.

I laid there for five minutes then got up. It was still dark outside. I went and got in the shower to help wake me up. I got upstairs and saw I had for more missed calls. I called Scrap back to see what he wanted.

"Just calling to make sure you were up and ready to go. I'll be in front of your house in ten minutes!" he said.

I hurried and got dressed, grabbed my pistol, the work, $20 and waited on my front porch for Scrap to pull up.

It didn't take long for him to pull up in front of my house. I got in the car the and the first thing he said to me was, "Never go in the house with drugs. Get everything off if you want nice things. You've got to be poor hungry."

Scrap was right. If I wanted the things, I had to chase that cash. I had to be poor hungry to make some real cash.

It was still dark outside. He drove straight to the block where I'd shot those two guys.

Everyone out there looked like zombies. All of them were drug users and they were looking to get some drugs. Scrap and I had what they were looking for.

They were all waiting for Scrap to show up. It was like we were under attack. So many crack heads came up to the car, and they were spending a lot of paper. Scrap was right. We were around the corner from my house. There was no way I should have still had work. Scrap had got off seventy-five percent of what I had to get off and his phone was still blowing up. I found myself strapped, two-stepping with the devil. Scrap had to go make some move on the other side of town. He couldn't be at two places at once, so he asked me to stay there on the block. It wasn't going to be a problem being that I had my pistol on me.

The sun was just about to rise and I knew the two guys I'd shot were going to come out to get some of this paper on their block. All it was going to take was for one client to get some of my work, and it was on.

They couldn't get enough of my work and the paper was rolling in by the hundreds. I made more by free handing it than I would if I'd bagged it up. I had Scrap's $300 plus more. And, I still had some work leftover. I wasn't going anywhere until I got the rest of the drugs off.

I don't know how my mother got my cell phone number but she did. She was blowing my phone up. I knew the only thing my mother might believe was that I'd gone to Butterfly's house, but she was not believing anything I had to say. She just wanted to make sure I was safe. There was not a doubt in my mind that my mother didn't know I was in the drug game.

Scrap was calling my phone to see if I had gone back home to get some sleep or was still on the block getting some paper. Shit, the only thing I had to say was, "Bring me some more work!"

It didn't take Scrap long to bring me some more work. He dropped me off at the crib. I really did not want to go there.

If I wouldn't have needed to drop the cash off, I would have never left. I had to get back to the block fast. None of the clientele had my number to call me and let me know they needed more work.

It was a good idea to stop at my crib. It gave me some time to see what my mother wanted and to grab my extended clip because there was a very good chance I was going to see one of the guys I'd shot and being on their block, shit could go down at any time. If they sent a shot at me, I was going to send like thirty-two back. I'd rather been a have than a have not. Scrap called and told me to be safe. One of the guys I'd shot was right on the block. I knew I shouldn't have gone back on their block, but listening to that new artist, Uncle Murda, put me on some bullshit and that paper was calling for me. It was like I was looking for trouble.

As soon as I got to the block, I saw one of the fuck boys I'd shot. He looked like he'd seen a ghost. He was talking to some guys and they walked off. My heart was racing. *If those niggas come back, it's on.*

I was playing with fire but the cash I was seeing kept me on their block. The only thing that was on my mind was Pablo de Money, and that's what I wanted. I wasn't going to let anyone or anything stop me from getting to it. Not the two guys that I'd shot, not Butterfly, not even my mother or stepfather.

I couldn't have counted how many times I had to go to my house to drop off some cash. There was one other guy on the block with me.

Misha and some of her friends had come to the block. There wasn't any time for me to give Misha any attention. I could tell Misha wanted to say something but was scared to. As soon as I was going to say something to her, I saw both the guys I'd shot get out a car with two other guys.

It seemed like everything got quiet and started moving really slow. I just knew it was on. I wanted to see what they were about to do. Instead of them walking in my direction, they walked to where Misha and her friends were standing.

The guy I'd shot in the arm said something to Misha and looked up the block to where I was. Misha walked up the to me and told me that the guys I'd shot told her to tell me that there wasn't any beef between them and me. I looked at Misha like, "Yeah, okay." Right before Misha left she looked at me and said, "Rome, you are crazy!" She walked back down the block where her friend and the guys were.

Death is certain life isn't. I wasn't ready to die anytime soon. I threw the extension clip in my pistol and got right back to the paper. I was stacking up cash like a fundraiser.

***

I began spending less time with Butterfly and more time in the streets. My heart turned cold to the point that I wasn't giving anyone any respect, not even my mother or father. Even Butterfly's mother, Ms. T saw that I was acting different. The love I had for Butterfly began to fade away and with Ms. T having two jobs and Money turning himself in to do his time for selling to the undercover cop, Butterfly and I had a lot of time to spend together. I used that time to fuck Butterfly, bag up my drugs, and get some sleep.

All the things I had enjoyed doing with Butterfly, I started doing with Sad'e. Sad'e was older than me and already had a little son. I knew from the first time meeting Sad'e, at my aunt's house, I was going to end up hooking up with her. I liked the way she moved. She would do anything for me, even get off some of my drugs. So when I would be on the other side of town and needed to get some sleep or relax, Sad'e's would be the place I'd go. I started being over Sad'e's house more than a little.

Butterfly knew there was another girl in my life. The only thing was, she couldn't prove it. The way I made love to Butterfly was as if she was the only girl I was fucking.

***

My homeboy and I weren't on the same time. He just wanted to get rental cars and buy clothes and the next day, he'd be broke. We were living in two different time zones.

167

He called to see what I was going to do for my B-day. I was so stoked on getting paper that I had forgotten about my 17th B-day.

To me it was just another year. But I was going to turn it up. I knew the best person to do that with was Scrap. But he had gone out of town for the week. Sad'e had planned something for me but she told me that I was going to have to wait 'til she got off work to get it.

I figured why not celebrate my B-day with the girl I loved most, Butterfly. She always had my back and loved me for me. When I didn't have anything, she wanted to see me. She never asked for a thing. So instead of me spending time in the streets, I took a day off to spend with Butterfly. My mother had called to say Happy Birthday and to tell me when to come to the house to see her when I had some time. I took Butterfly to the mall to get some things. I oddly noticed that her stomach had gotten a little big. I thought it may be because we had just got done eating so I did not pay it any mind.

After leaving the mall, I took Butterfly with me to my mother's house. In front of my house, I could see my cousin, Tank's car, my Aunt Robin's truck, and my grandma's car. My mother had invited a couple of my family members over.
She had even invited Dee and Woodz, that was something.

I gave it to my mother, she did her best to make me happy. I understood that she hadn't realized a lot of things had changed and in the last couple of months the people that she thought were my friends had become associates. Just because she had let them into my house didn't mean I was going to act like everything was cool.

I said hi to my family and went to my room. My mother came up to see if everything was alright with me. I felt like if I didn't explain to her what was going on, that she would have kept doing the same old things. I told my mother to sit down so I could talk to her. I explained to her that some people who saw me getting paper might have seemed like they had my best interest but deep down inside, they wanted to see me fail.

My mother just smiled and said, "Boy you think everyone is always after you. I love you, son. Happy birthday." '

Butterfly said, "If you stopped doing the things you're doing, you wouldn't be thinking like that!" She then asked to see my bible and opened it to Psalms 37:27, that read: "Deport from evil and do good and dwell for evermore."

Everything that Butterfly was saying and showing me was the truth. I just wasn't trying to hear that at the time. I told Butterfly that no one was going to look out for me the way I looked out for myself.

I took a nice long shower to get my mind right. I thought about everything my mother and Butterfly had said.

Butterfly knocked on the bathroom door. "Some girl, by the name of Sad'e, called to tell you she was getting off work early tonight and wanted to know if you had some weed to sell her," she said.

My heart was racing, thinking of if Butterfly knew that was the girl I was cheating on her with. The good thing was that Sad'e didn't care if I had a girl or not. She just asked when I had time, to spend it with her.

I hadn't spent a lot of time with Butterfly lately. I had all the shit on from head to toe, I'd even put on my new watch, but Butterfly on the other hand, wasn't looking her best. I gave her $500 to go get a makeover, that would give me some time to take care of all the people I'd missed when I was with her earlier that day. I let Butterfly off downtown to get her some outfits and shoes while I went to see what Sad'e wanted.

My phone was going crazy. People wanted weed and crack and I had it for them. Scrap even had called to say Happy Birthday and to let me know Ms. Santiago was about to bring me a present. I went to the block and in ten minutes, I had made my cash back and some that I'd given to Butterfly. If it wasn't for the cops riding by, I would have stayed on the block. But I didn't care to spend the night in jail on my birthday or any day. Plus, Butterfly was blowing my phone up to come pick her up.

The look Butterfly did with her hair wasn't something I liked at first. It wasn't until she got dressed and I saw how her outfit accented that sexy ass body. Still, there was something missing and I knew exactly what it was, jewelry. I killed two birds with one stone. Ms. Santiago was at the mall and had my birthday present. I didn't know what it was and that would be a good spot to get Butterfly some jewelry. You would have thought it was Butterfly's birthday the way I was wining and dining her. Things were going well on the way to the mall until Butterfly said she thought there was an undercover cop riding right beside us. I asked Butterfly what made her think that.

"Because he just said something on his walkie talkie,"

she said.

I'll be damned! It was an undercover. He had been following someone and just turned on his lights to pull them over. I wouldn't have been so scared if I wouldn't have had my gun in the car with a three round clip in it. I couldn't wait to get to the mall to put the gun in the trunk.

Before we got there, I called Ms. Santiago to make sure she was still at the mall. Good thing I had called because she was just about to leave. Butterfly was a little on edge riding in the car with a gun. I could see it all in her face. She couldn't wait to get out the car. There was a spot open right by where Ms. Santiago was parked. Butterfly had no idea who I'd come to the mall to see.

Damn! Ms. Santiago hardly had anything on. The bodice she wore was so tight that her tits were about to pop out. She came to my side of the car and handed me a card and a bag and said, "Happy birthday." The only thing that had my attention on was her big ass tits.

I introduced Butterfly to Ms. Santiago. Butterfly was short on words. I could tell she wasn't feeling Ms. Santiago, who was in her mid-thirties but had a body like a twenty-year-old.

Ms. Santiago told me to enjoy my B-day and to be safe. She headed back to her car, got in, and rode off. I knew Butterfly couldn't wait to ask me about Ms. Santiago. So, before she could ask, I gave her a quick rundown on how I knew Ms. Santiago.

I put the pistol in the bag Ms. Santiago gave me and put it in the trunk. Butterfly hadn't known the only reason we came to the mall was so I could buy her some jewelry.

You never know who you run into at the mall.

They say people look alike but this girl I saw looked too familiar and she kept looking at me. I never paid her any more attention. I bought Butterfly two bracelets and a pair of earrings. Butterfly wasn't feeling too good so she had gone to use the restroom while I ordered us something to eat. While I was waiting for our food, I noticed a girl was standing beside me, trying to get my attention.

"Rome don't act like you don't know me!" she said.

Then it hit me, it was Sayna. I hadn't seen her in a long time. She'd gotten crazy thick. I'd forgotten that her sister had told me she got locked up for stealing. There wasn't a doubt in my mind that I was going get back up with her, but I had to get rid of her before Butterfly came out the restroom.

It was too late. Butterfly caught me red handed getting Sayna's new number. Thinking fast, I told Sayna that I'd call her later. If Butterfly's look could've killed, I would have been dead. I don't know what had gotten into Butterfly, but she did not say anything to me about me talking to another girl.

We got the food to go and left the mall. I didn't know if Butterfly was catching the flu but she was not feeling well. She didn't want to eat. All she wanted to do was sleep. She slept the whole way back to her house.

As soon as we got in her house she ran straight to the trash can and threw up. These were all signs that Butterfly might've been pregnant. I made sure she was okay before I went outside to get the bag that Ms. Santiago gave me for my birthday. When I got back in the house, Butterfly had a gift of her own for me. She gave it to me and said, "Happy Birthday!" I was not expecting anything from Butterfly for my birthday. It was nice that she'd thought about me. The only thing I could think of that could've fit in that little box was jewelry. I opened it and got the surprise of my life. I almost passed out.

A pregnancy test strip that read positive laid in the box. That was the first time Butterfly ever saw tears in my eyes. She did not know if they were tears of sadness or tears of joy. I hugged and kissed her on her stomach.

10/9/2004 I got the best gift I could get for my B-day. I was so happy that I had forgot to see what was in the bag that Ms. Santiago gave me. If it wasn't for me getting my gun out the bag, I wouldn't have seen the Spicebomb Viktor & Rolf cologne and the $200, but I wasn't impressed.

There wasn't any gift that could compare to the gift that God was about to bless me and Butterfly with. At first, all I wanted was to drop with the head cracked like C-Low. I thought my eyes had been open before, but they really were now that me and Butterfly were about to start our own family.

There were only two things on my mind, and those were to be the best father I could be and to celebrate my birthday with Butterfly. I would catch my paper and come right back in the house with Butterfly. She made me a birthday cake while I sat in the living room, counting my cash.

I'm about to be a dad at seventeen. Two kids about to try to raise a kid. One thing I did know, we were going to do our best to be good parents. I didn't know how Butterfly was going to break the news to her mother. I told Butterfly to take some time before she said anything to her. Later that day, Woodz and Dee had called me to go to Misha's house party.

They were very surprised when I said no but they still found a way to get me to stop by Misha's party. They knew I wouldn't let any paper go. I still had like an ounce of weed left and Misha had a house full of people that smoked. I was not going to let any of that paper go.

Misha's house was poppin'. But I'd come there for the cash not anything else. Misha tried her hardest not to say anything to me but she couldn't help herself. She walked over to me and handed me $40 for my B-day and offered me a dance. I didn't want to be ignorant so I got the dance from her. I knew Misha liked me a lot and I knew there was more than one way to skin a cat. I'd have Misha get my weed off for me so I could go back to Butterfly. I knew she would not have a problem doing for me. I had told Butterfly that I'd be back in ten minutes. When my ten minutes was up and I wasn't at the house, she would be calling my phone like crazy. I got back to Butterfly's mother's house and noticed Ms. T was home.

I was hoping Butterfly hadn't said anything to her mother about her being pregnant.

Ms. T had asked me why I would buy her daughter jewelry on my birthday. I told her the truth, that I didn't want to be walking around with jewelry when the love of my life didn't have any on. All Ms. T could do was smile and walk off. My phone had been going off the whole time I was talking to Ms. T but I couldn't just run in and out her house while she was home. I could have easily used that as an excuse to leave but I really did want to chill with Butterfly on my birthday. I also had to get my paper. Butterfly and I started seeing eye to eye a lot more. Before I could say anything she read my mind and said, "Bae I know you want to go get your paper, Go ahead and be safe. I'm going to take a nap and I'll call you when I get up. But if you want to come back before that, take my house key. But don't be running in and out because my mother doesn't have to go back to work and she's going to be in the house."

Most of my paper was coming from trap house and they were spending a lot of paper with me. The only thing I didn't understand was why they just were calling me when there were a lot of people outside that sold drugs. I'm guessing it had something to do with the fish scale that I was selling.

There was this one guy in particular that kept looking at me. Something in my gut was telling me to leave that trap house, plus Misha was calling me to let me know she had my paper from the weed I asked her to get off for me. Misha's party was popping more than it was before I left. I would have thought it would have died down due to how late it was getting or because someone had started a fight. But everything was cool and when things did get a little out of hand, Misha and her cousins would calm that shit right down. A lot of the girls respected Misha and her cousins.

My day was going good until I started getting the vibe that Woodz was feeling some way that I was getting a couple dollars now but I was not going to let anything or anyone put me down. I'd just got the best news I could have heard.

The light from the kitchen was the only light in the house on besides the light coming off people's phones. I walked to the kitchen to get something to drink. I watched Misha watch me and knew her pride was in the way to say anything to me. I know she wished I would have.

Sayna and her sister Roseanna had just walked into the party. Niggas were on their top. Sayna and Roseanna were known for being one of the two baddest girls in York. A lot of bitches did not like them because their men always would try to fuck them. I had not seen Sayna in a while due to her getting locked up but I could not hold a conversation with her because I was with Butterfly. So, when she saw me at Misha's party she didn't hold back a thing. First she made sure Butterfly wasn't at the party by asking me, and then Sayna pulled me to the back of the party to talk to me.

We had a lot of catching up to do. I couldn't lie, it felt good to see Sayna. She told me how she had got locked up and all she could think about was me. How she wanted to be with me, that she was jealous the first time, seeing me with my girl at the mall. If she was mad when she had seen me and Butterfly at the mall imagine how she was going to feel when I told her that my girl was pregnant and I was about to be a father. The conversation had to be put on hold.

My phone was ringing and it was some more paper. I took Sayna with me to catch my paper. All I could think about was the time she sucked my dick. She looked at me and asked did I remember the first time she'd sucked my dick. Just thinking about it, my dick got hard.

"How could I forget," I said.

I caught my paper and went back to Misha's party. Sayna and I sat in the car going down memory lane. I could tell she really missed me and I missed her. But I was no fool that gives away which I can't keep in order to gain that which I can never lose. As soon as I was thinking about asking Sayna to suck my dick, my phone rang. It was Butterfly calling to see where I was at and if I could bring her something to eat. If it was not for that phone call from Butterfly, I would have gotten some head from Sayna. I told Sayna that I was going to call her later. That I had to go get my girl something to eat. If I kept running into Sayna, I was going to end up fucking up my relationship with Butterfly.

My mother called to see if I was coming in or staying out for the night. I had stopped by my mother's house to put up some of my cash. I had plenty of cash to get Butterfly something to eat but I remembered her saying earlier that she wanted a plate from my mother's when she got done cooking. I made up two plates of food and wrapped them. Before I left, I went upstairs to give my mother a kiss and let her know I was staying at Butterfly's. I closed my mother's room door and realized my sister, Quesh, was standing at the top of the stairs half asleep.

"What are you doing up?" I asked her.

"I was waiting for you to come home so I could tell you that mother was trying to get into your safe but couldn't figure out the code," she said.

I gave my sister my cell phone number to call me if our

mother tried to get in my safe or go in my room. I also gave her $75, $25 for her and $25 for my other 2 sisters, so they could go to the store in the morning.

Scrap always said when you start making real cash, even your family would try to get over on you. I got in the car and drove to Butterfly's house, wondering if I could trust my mother. If not, there was no one I could trust. I parked out back of Butterfly's house. I had the key to her house but the dogs were going to bark, so I waited until Butterfly called me so I could tell her to put the dog up so It wouldn't wake Ms. T. Butterfly opened the door with Ms. T standing right behind her, telling Butterfly to tell me to go home.

The first thing that came to mind was Ms. T found out that I had got her daughter pregnant. I handed Butterfly the plate of food and went back to the car, knowing Butterfly was going to find a way to call me to let me know what was going on, and that's exactly what she did.

Butterfly said when she got up to open the door she stepped on the dog and it woke and her mother thought it was me trying to sneak out the house so she followed her downstairs to watch her get the food from me. I told Butterfly I loved her and I'd talk to her the next day.

I always could go to Sad'e's house at any time, but I wanted paper so I turned my hustle up.

I was on every side of town on every block. Just me and my 32 shot Ruger that I called my best friend. It was about 4 O'clock in the morning. Sad'e had sent me a message to come to her house to fuck but I wasn't in the mood to fuck. All I wanted was some paper. If it didn't have anything to do with paper I did not want to be bothered. That night, there was this one particular woman that called me all night for 50s and 100s. When she didn't have any cash, she would have something to sell me, from DVD players to gift cards, to TVs. But the best thing she said she had was a pistol. That was the only thing that she had that I wanted to wait to steal it. I didn't want to stop at Sad'e's house but I had to get some of the things out the car. I took the TV/DVD player to Sad'e's house.

Sad'e was always someone I felt like I could trust. I gave her the cash I'd made just five minutes ago. I even asked her to put my Ruger up until I got back. This was either a smart move or just cautious because the lady I was about to go see who was going to sell me the gun could be setting me up to get robbed or could be good people.

I was about three minutes away from finding out where she wanted to meet.

***

I could see everything, and if there was someone that she had to rob me they were not with her. She was by herself and moving a lot. She got in the car and kept looking in the rear view window. She asked for two grams of crack for the pistol. From where I was sitting, I couldn't see any pistol on her. I asked where was the pistol was and she asked to see the work. I showed her the two grams. She reached in her blouse and pulled out a small pistol. I gave her the two grams and she gave me the pistol and just like that, I had my 2nd pistol. I felt more comfortable riding around with the smaller pistol, especially not having a driver's license. It was about 6 O'clock in the morning and I had to get some rest.

My phone was still going off like crazy, so I could not get any sleep because I would be missing a lot of cash. I knew Dee and Woodz were asleep, plus they didn't have the hustle like I had. So, instead I had Sad'e ride me around while I got some sleep. This was not anything new to her. The last boyfriend Sad'e was with had her on the same thing. She had an idea on how to move in the streets. It came a point where I gave her the work while I slept in the passenger seat and she'd get it off. I woke up to see her handing the work to one of my clients and getting the paper. I went back to sleep and woke up again back of Sad'e's house to drop off the cash.

Sad'e was my rider for real. By the time it was 8 O'clock in the morning I was getting sleep but it was nothing like getting rest and that's what Sad'e and I needed.

We stopped at McDonalds to get some breakfast and went to her crib. We ate and tried to get some rest but could not because the friend that rented out his car was calling to get it back. I knew if I didn't pick up the phone he would have called the cops and reported it stolen. I got up and drove the car all the way to his house. He didn't want to get the car back, all he wanted was to rent the car back out to me for a week. I gave him an 8 ball and left. I was not about to ride all the way back to Sad'e's house. I knew it was about the time in the morning that Ms. T was on her way to work, so I went to get some rest at Butterfly's house.

CHAPTER 16

I still had the key to the house so I let myself in. Butterfly was still asleep. I got right in the bed and passed straight out. That was the best rest I'd gotten in a long time. I didn't even feel Butterfly get out the bed. If I hadn't needed to go to the bathroom, I wouldn't have ever gotten up. Butterfly was cooking dinner. I couldn't believe that I'd slept until 7 O'clock that evening. It did not matter how sleepy or tired I was. I always heard my phone ringing and I never turned it off. So for me not to hear my phone ring all those hours, had to be something up. Come to find out, Butterfly had answered my phone while I was sleeping and gotten mad that Sad'e and Misha had called to see if I was okay and could bring them some weed. Butterfly told them to stop calling me. That I was ok and was asleep. Butterfly said that they wouldn't stop calling so she turned my phone off.

I would not have been as mad if I had not turned my phone back on to see I had over 30 missed calls from everyone; Sad'e, Misha, Scrap, Ms. Santiago, Woodz, Dee, Quesh, and the guy that rented out his car. Even the girl that sold me the pistol.

I called everyone back, starting with the guy whose car I had. I didn't want him to think that something happened to me and call and report the car stolen. I did not need any run in with the cops. He was good. He just wanted to see if I was alright. The next person I called was Scrap. The good thing with Scrap was I'd just missed his call 20 minutes ago and all he wanted was to see if I needed any more work, which I did after I'd got off the last fourteen grams. The next person I called was Sad'e. She was the one that had called me the most. She was seeing if I was good and to let me know she had gone to her mother's house to pick up her son. With Sad'e being six years older than me, she was more mature than I was.

I did not have to call Quesh back. She had called me and told me my mother took the $75 from her because she thought she'd stolen it from out my room. All it took to fix that was for me to get on the phone and tell my mother that I gave that $75 to my sister and that she needed to give it back. I also knew it had to do with more than my mother thinking my sister would steal any cash from me. Maybe she took the cash from my sister because I never gave her any cash before.

It was nothing to give my mother or father any cash and I was not going to have any problems doing so. As soon as I got all the cash and things from Sad'e's house, Butterfly did not want me to go anywhere. All she kept saying was that she did not feel good. I just thought it had to do with her being pregnant. Something was telling me to stay. It was looking gray out like it was about to rain but the street life had taken a hold of me. I didn't want to miss a single piece of paper. I also knew that Money had gotten setup by an undercover so I could easily be next if I didn't slow down. Usually, I had good instinct when it came to recognizing good clientele. I didn't need to go anywhere or do anything except go get the things from Sad'e's house. If it was not for my cash and my pistol, I would not have left Butterfly's house.

With that decision I made, I ran into one of the guys I seen at the trap house. I never really did like the way he was moving but I just thought it was because of all the work he was smoking. He waved the car I was in down. I stopped to see what he wanted. He fed me some bullshit about some house he was at where there were a lot of people inside, looking for some good work. The house he took me to was not that far from Butterfly's house. I was thinking that would be a good trap house when I didn't have a car to get around in. The house we went in was very nice. There weren't that many people inside and the owners of the house were two couples that I used to see around. I would never imagine them to smoke crack, but they did and I had what they were looking for. The guy that brought me to the house kept asking for a hit, which I gave him. The owners of the house spent $150 from the jump. I could tell they really liked my work. They could not speak. The only thing they could do is give the thumbs up sign, letting me know that my work was good.

The guy that brought me to the house was a big guy. He tried to run the house. He even tried to act like he was going make a move on me and rob me for my work. Little did he know, I was packing my new .22 pistol in my back pocket. The owners of the house left to go get some cash out the ATM. I sat there for a little while.

Something in my gut was telling me something was wrong. The guy that brought me to the house started moving real funny to me. When I tried to leave, he tried to keep me there saying, "Youngin' they'll be back in a lil' bit. You can look out and give me some more work until they come with the cash."

I would have looked out but I was doing that from the time he had brought me to that house and he hadn't spent a dime with me. He left the room and returned with a kitchen knife and stared in my direction. Before I knew it my 22 pistol was in my hand and I had let off every shot, except two but he didn't fall. I knew I'd shot him by the way he was screaming. Instead of running out the front or back door, I ran up the stairs. That was the wrong thing to do. He was standing at the bottom of the stairs with the knife in his hand but he didn't take a step upstairs. I pointed the pistol down the stairs at him and he took off out the front door. I could not leave the house. I was hearing the sirens howling and knew if the cops came in this house, it was over for me. The only thing I could think about doing was calling Butterfly and telling her to come to the back of the house where I was.

***

I was stuck on the third floor on the roof. I had my pregnant girl outside. She was there in no time. She had told me that the cops were all out front of the house and there was a guy in the ambulance that had got shot. There was a grocery bag that had blown to the roof. I grabbed it and put the 22 pistol and drugs into the bag and dropped it down to Butterfly to get rid of it for me. With no questions she grabbed it and left. Now that the pistol was off me, I had to find a way off the roof. I was for sure that the cops were about to be all over this house. The only way I was getting off the roof was from the same way I got on it. The other way was to jump across to the next building roof. If I did decide to jump and did not make it, it was going to be a long way down.

I did not have any more time to think. I had to make the jump, unless I wanted to go to jail for shooting someone. I took two deep breaths and jumped to the other house, ran down the fire escape, and did not stop running until I got to Butterfly's house. She didn't know what was going on. I had to make sure that I got the gun and drugs out the house. I told Butterfly to take the pistol to her friend's house and put the pistol and drugs in the grill that was in her friend's back yard, then to come right back to the house. She did just as I had asked her. She was nervous from all the cops she'd seen riding around but she never asked me anything about what had happened. She was more concerned that I was going to get locked up and not be there for her and the kid. She was right. If I made it out this one, I had to do a lot of things differently. The chance was slim that the guy I shot had my cell number or knew what car I was driving or what my face looked like.

What is going to be the outcome of me selling drugs. I couldn't complain because rose bushes have thorns and rejoice that thorn bushes have roses. I had to take the good with the bad and the bad with the good.

Butterfly was still shaken up and wouldn't eat a thing. It was making me mad that Butterfly wouldn't eat. She didn't realize that she was not just eating for herself but she had the baby to think about also. She was not thinking too clearly, neither was I. I put the love of my life in danger. If the cops would have decided to stop her when she had that gun and drugs on her, there was not any explaining she could've done to stop her from not going to jail.

I thanked God that she and myself made it out of that situation safe. I did not just have one situation to worry about. I had several but, the main was to be alive to see my unborn child. There was no way I was going to get myself out of this situation. I had already put Butterfly through a lot, just that day. Though, there was one more thing I needed for her to do. I wanted her to go see if the cops had left from in front of the house because I had to move that car.

I could tell Butterfly was really nervous but she did it for me. I didn't want to get back into that car but I also didn't want to mess things up with my car connect, so I took the chance, got into the car, and headed straight to Sad'e's house. If I made it to her house, I'd be good for a couple of days. Sad'e was my little thot that would do anything for me. So, when I told her that I needed to stay at her house for a couple of days, she was fine with it. She knew about me getting into that shootout by my aunt's house and being that she had a little son, she didn't want anything to happen to him. She said that I could stay there, but she was going to stay at her mother's house with her son. Sad'e did things a lot of women would never do but like I'd said, Sad'e would do anything for me.

I called Butterfly to let her know that I was safe. If I was on the run for attempted murder I had to move like it, and something I had to do was get rid of my phone. As soon as Sad'e got back from taking her son to her mother's house, I put things in motion.

His first thing was getting rid of the phones, the second was to have Sad'e take the car to the owner's house, the third was getting a new phone, and the fourth was to move that gun from where Butterfly put it at.

Now that I'd taken care of everything, I had to watch the 6 O'clock news to see if they had any leads on the shooting. I was very surprised to hear the guy did not want to cooperate with the cops, that was a weight off my shoulders to see he had made it and did not want to help the cops.

One thing after another was happening. I called to see how Butterfly was holding up, I could hear Ms. T in the background going off. Butterfly could not talk for long but she did manage to let me know what was going on. Come to find out, Ms. T had her neighbors keep an eye on her house to see when I was over there. Her neighbor called Ms. T and let her know that I had been in Ms. T's house while she was at work. If Ms. T thought me being in her house was going to stop me from seeing Butterfly, she's crazy. The good thing was that Butterfly's aunt lived around the corner from Sad'e's house, so Butterfly would go to her aunt's house and then come around the corner to see me. Even though Sad'e liked me, she didn't mind me bringing Butterfly over to her house, especially when I told Sad'e I had gotten Butterfly pregnant. I just was hoping Butterfly didn't find out that Sad'e was really not my cousin and was some girl I used to fuck.

CHAPTER 17

As weeks went by Butterfly's stomach got bigger. It was only a matter of time before Ms. T would find out that her daughter was pregnant.

I hadn't run into that dumb ass guy that tried to rob me. I didn't know if he got out the hospital but I had to be on point for him. Woodz had been coming around more just because he knew I had some work and all his people wanted it. He wasn't coming around as a friend but that was cool with me as long as he had some cash when he called my phone. Dee had introduced me to one of his friends, JD, who had moved to the block. I really wasn't looking to make any friends but JD was into slinging weed and I was the one he could get it from. Besides, he did not seem like the type of guy that I had to worry about. He just liked paper and girls.

Every week JD had like three to five girls over at his house. He hadn't met Butterfly but when he saw her, he tried to get her to go over to his grandmother's house where he was staying at. Butterfly being the type of girl she was, let me know that Dee's friend had tried to talk to her.

Things were back to normal between me and Ms. T, so I was around a lot more. Ms. T knew that she could not keep Butterfly and I away from one another and I damn sure could not get enough of Butterfly. By this time, everyone on the block and on the other side of town knew that Butterfly was my girl. So, if a nigga tried to talk to her they didn't give two fucks about or respect me. But every guy that did try to talk to her, she would let me know about.

Her stomach was so big that there was no hiding that she was pregnant. JD had called me to get some weed for him and the girls that was at his house. When I walked in JD's house and went in his room, the two girls were ass naked eating each other's pussy.

Anything JD told them to do, they did. I had only gone there to sell JD some weed but I couldn't stop looking at the things those girls were doing to one another. It was just me and JD and those two girls. JD handed me a condom and told me I could take one of them to the next room. I took the hottest one in the next room. Something was telling me to not fuck with this girl when I had a girl/baby momma at the house that I could fuck and do anything with. But the way the girl was pulling on my dick, I had to see if she was lying. She wasn't. She sucked my dick so good that it was hard for me to walk after she got done. When I finally did get the energy to leave a couple of JD's friends walked in the house. I was so tired after getting some head that I went to the house to get a shower and some sleep. Later that night, Dee had called me and told me that JD was having a party. I knew who was going to be in there.

If it was a party anything like Misha's party, I was going to move some cash once again. It was only about 10 O'clock and JD's party had already started. The two girls that he had at his house were still there dressed and in everyone's face. The guys just didn't know that three hours before the party started, those same girls that they were kissing on were the same girls that were eating one another's pussy and sucking dick. Butterfly had called to tell me to get the fuck out the party. She said her and her mother had just rode by and saw me walk in.

"Where are y'all going after ten at night?" I asked.

"My mother told me to get up and come to the store with her," Butterfly said.

I did not think anything of it I just hoped they weren't out all night. My work was getting low and I needed to re up. I did not feel like going to my house to get cash and I knew I had some cash at Butterfly's house.

I called Scrap to let him know that I'd be seeing him to get some more work but he never answered. I even tried to call Ms. Santiago but she didn't answer either. I gave them some time to call me back. A half an hour turned into an hour and neither Scrap nor Ms. Santiago had called me back. I was hoping everything was alright, but everything was not alright.

As soon as I was about to leave JD's house I caught a glance of the 11 O'clock news on the TV and saw Scraps face all over the news. The cops had ran into their house and found 800 grams of crack, 3 guns, and $187 thousand in cash. The police had also shot and killed 3 of his dogs. Being that the crib was in Ms. Santiago's name, the police tried to lock her up. They let her go seeing that the drugs and guns were in Scrap's car. I was hoping he had bail. I know the little bit of cash I had saved up wouldn't do much for his bail. I was about to see if Butterfly and her mother made it home so I could get my cash out of the house but there was no need to. Scrap didn't have a bail. Seeing Scrap's face all over the news fucked my whole night up. I was down to my last 7 grams of work and my last ounce of weed. I knew before the night was over the 7 grams and the ounce of weed would be gone. Butterfly calling to say that her mother might know she was pregnant because on the way to the store she made a comment on her tits getting bigger, didn't help any.

With Scrap just getting arrested, it made me realized how I could get locked up at any time and wouldn't be there for my child and Butterfly. I knew Ms. T wouldn't allow Butterfly to come out but I had to see her.

JD was selling shots of liquor. I bought the bottle that he had and went to Butterfly's house. I knew she was tired but she also knew I wanted to see her. There was a full moon out, it wasn't too hot or too cold. I explained to Butterfly what had happened to my connect and his girl and that things were going to slow down for me a lot. I told her I was going to spend more time with her. We sat outside for hours, coming up with names for our baby, talking about the things we were going to do for the baby and who he or she would look like more. I was a little tipsy and feeling good as shit to be enjoying the night with my Butterfly.

Butterfly knew everything about my likes and dislikes. There were even times where I didn't have to say anything to her. She just knew what I was thinking.

It was 2 O'clock in the morning and Butterfly and I were still outside, talking and enjoying the night when I saw two guys walk our way. I could not see their faces because of how drunk I was. They walked by me and Butterfly and commented on my watch. They got a couple houses down and stood there. I didn't have to say a thing to Butterfly.

She looked at me and said, "Bae, do you want me to go get that for you?" Our connection was so good that she went in her house and came back out with my P89 Ruger and extended clip wrapped up in her blanket. I was not going to let some niggas fuck our night up, but they never came back. The way Butterfly read my mind to go get my pistol reminded me of Scrap and Ms. Santiago. I hoped she would hold him down for whatever time he had to do. The more Butterfly and I sat out, the more I drank and the more I drank, the sexier Butterfly looked. We kissed and I played with her pussy, but that was not doing me any good. Butterfly knew if she didn't get me in her house we was going end up fucking outside. She wanted my dick just as bad as I wanted her pussy. So, she got me in her mother's house without making a sound, but that changed when we got into her bedroom. The way Butterfly was moaning, I was sure Ms. T was going to wake up. We fucked until we did not have any energy to move. Butterfly went straight out cold.

I was wide awake, I couldn't get any sleep knowing Ms. T could get up at any time and find me in her daughter room. I did not want to get back on Ms. T's bad side. I wanted to get Ms. T to let me stay over her house with her daughter, but I'd work on that another time. I had to get out the house before Ms. T woke up.

***

I didn't have a car of my own so I could not get to the people that were calling my phone and I was missing out on a lot of paper. If it wasn't for a trap house on the block it would have taken me longer to get the work off. But I did and was glad because I was tired and needed some rest. Before I went home, I ran into an old associate. I asked him why he was out so early in the morning. He said that he was looking for people to rob. "My homeboy and I saw you out with some girl. He wanted to rob you, but I stopped him."

As soon as he said that I gripped my pistol. He and I seemed like the only ones out at this time and I had a pocket full of cash. He was looking for someone to rob. He seemed cool but I also knew not having cash could change a person. He gave me his number to call him if I had anyone I wanted him to rob. He walked off and I didn't see him anymore.

Usually around the time of night it was, the street would be full of people. *Maybe it has something to do with it being the middle of the month.*

I could not wait to get home to get some rest. When I did finally get to rest, my mother kept coming in my room checking up on me as if something was wrong.

That Sunday morning, my mother asked me to go with her to church. I thought about it and was going until Woodz called me asking me if I wanted to buy his pistol.

Romans 7:19 "For the good that I would do I do not: but

the evil which I would not, that I do."

So instead of me going with my family to church, I went to meet Woodz at his grandma, Mrs. Fish's house to buy his pistol. Ever since Scrap had got locked up, the streets had been dry. I was out of work and so was everyone else. The people that did have a little bit of work were really getting paid. Scrap was supplying ninety percent of the town. When he got locked up that fucked the town up.

Niggas were selling a lot of fake work and robbing people. The people that did have cash saved up were spending it on jewelry, cars, and other things. Even I, myself fell in line by spending cash. Every week I was buying the newest J's, bottles of liquor, and things for Butterfly and the baby, not knowing if we were going to have a boy or girl. My cash got lower and lower and before I knew it I was thinking about robbing niggas myself. *But why do that when I have someone to do it for me.*

There was this one guy that was iced out like crazy. He had some work but wouldn't sell to anyone. I called O'Boy to see if he was down to rob the guy with the jewelry and work for me. He came to where I was at in a heartbeat. I showed O'Boy the guy I wanted him to rob and I left fifteen minutes later. O'Boy called me and told me to meet him at the park. I grabbed my gun and met O'Boy at the park. From the smile on his face I knew he'd pulled the robbery off. He handed me an eight ball of work, seven grams of weed, and $1300. He said that he split everything down the middle with me but I just knew he had more than what he was giving me. I took it, knowing that I hadn't had to do anything.

From that day, O'Boy would call me like every day to see if I had someone for him to rob. This one particular day, O'Boy called me and asked me to do a B & E with him. I didn't need any cash I had some. But when the sound of $50,000 came out is mouth, I was interested in what O'Boy had to say! I was not big on doing crimes with just anyone but I wanted in on that amount of cash. First I had to make sure that what he was saying wasn't some bullshit. I did my own research.

Everything seemed like it was legit. I just had to setup a date and time when myself and O'Boy were going to do the B & E. O'Boy had called me one night to go with him to check out the house we were going to rob but when he came to get me, he'd brought some white guy with him. I could tell by the white boy's demeanor that he was looking to make some real cash. O'Boy never told me how he'd found out about this $50,000. Come to find out, the plan was all the white boy's.

That explained how he knew so much about the house and the people that lived there. He was related to them. He explained why he wanted to rob his own family. I didn't care about the family problems he and his family were having. I just wanted to know if there was really $50,000 in the house and if he knew where the cash was. I was in no rush to do the B & E. If I was going do this breaking and entering, it had be done right. Besides it's not like I would get a slap on the wrist if I got bagged. O'Boy asked the white boy to take us to one of his girl's house. I didn't know what O'Boy had in mind, but I rode with them to come up with the best plan, not to be out riding around drinking and seeing some girls that did not have anything going for themselves. By just being around them, I was starting to get a migraine. O'Boy came over to me and asked why I wasn't talking to any of his girl's friends?

"I don't talk around a lot of people I don't know," I said. By the look on the white boy's, face I could tell he was not out to have a good time. He was trying to get shit in order. We told O'Boy that we were about to go to the store. We lied. Like I said the white boy and I were on the $50,000. He took me to see the house, gave me the ins and outs of where the cash was and when the best time to hit the house. By the time we got back to the house where O'Boy was at, he was in the next room drunk and falling all over the place. I knew that was my que to leave. The white boy stayed at the house with O'Boy. I already knew that when I left O'Boy and his friends that I was going to Sad'e's house. Shit it was too late to go to Butterfly's house.

When I got to Sad'e's house she was just about to get out the shower. I was going to fall back and try to be faithful to Butterfly but that was not going to happen that night. Not the way Sad'e was looking when she took off her robe. She put me right to sleep.

The next morning, O'Boy called me to see if I wanted to go over some things about the robbery. I hardly could get any sleep from thinking about what I was going to do with the cash if we pulled the robbery off. First, I was going to get Butterfly and I our own place, then a car for her and one for myself. Then I was going put some cash in a bank account for our kid and put some in a bank account for all three of my sisters. O'Boy came to pick me up at Sad'e's house. We went to get the white boy that was staying at his girl's house. I knew that O'Boy and the white boy were stick up kids so I brought my little 25 pistol with me just in case they tried something stupid. Everything the white boy had said that the people at the crib were going to do, they did. He was on point. I could tell he did his homework. He told us the best time to do the robbery, the next day, when everyone went to work.

They dropped me back off at Sad'e's house. I knew if I pulled this job off that I'd be good for a very long time. Me and the family I was about to have.

It was a Friday but the only thing that was on my mind was making sure I planned things right because if things didn't go right when we went to rob that house, I was going to have to get out of town. When you fail to plan, you plan to fail. I was not trying to fail but just in case things did not go as I envisioned, I wanted to be sure Butterfly at least had some cash to help out with the baby. While Woodz and Dee, were on the block, I came up with a plan to take all the cash. I had went from my mother's house to Butterfly's mother's house. Butterfly thought I was bringing all the cash over because I had an argument with my mother.

That Friday came and went, before I knew it. The next morning had arrived. I then fucked up and got caught by Ms. T. She had forgotten something and had to go back to the house and find me coming out the front door. I couldn't lie and say I'd just gotten there being that I had the same clothes on from the night before and it was six something in the a.m.

Ms. T cursed me out and I didn't say anything to Ms. T.

I left and sat on the block. It was about 7 O'clock when O'Boy had come to get me for the robbery. There wasn't supposed to be anyone at the house. O'Boy brought his gun and when we went to pick up the white boy, he had his gun also. O'Boy and the white boy had given me a little .38 pistol, not knowing that I had my little .25 pistol. To make things even better, we just had seen the owner of the house leaving. We gave it five minutes and we kicked in the door, going right to the bedroom, looking for the safe with the $50,000.

The safe was right where the white boy said it would be, but it was a lot bigger than I thought and getting it out the closet was a lot harder with the bed being there. Seeing a box cutter on a nightstand beside the bed, I thought fast. Being that the safe was on the rug, I cut around the safe and O'Boy and the white boy helped me pull the rug with the safe to the top of the stairs. We already had been in the house for about four minutes. We pushed the safe down the stairs. It slammed into the front door and sounded like a 12 gauge had gone off. We knew we had to move fast. We ran down the stairs to move the safe. it hit the front door so hard that it jammed the door from opening. O'Boy went around to kick the front door in from the outside. At the same time, the white boy was pulling his car around to the front of the house. It took the white boy, O'Boy, and myself to get the safe into the truck. If it was $50,000 in that safe, my life was about to change. We took the safe to the white boy's girl's house and used every type of tool in his girl's garage to try to get the safe open. It seemed like it was going to be impossible to get the safe open.

I figured if we used a sledgehammer and kept hitting the middle of the safe it would bend the corners of the safe out enough for us to use a crow bar to get it open. And it worked. The first thing I saw was a lot of fifty cent pieces and dollar coins. If there was $50,000 in that house, it wasn't in this safe. We removed a second cover that was in the safe and saw two blue deposit bags. I opened the first one, nothing but fresh $100 bills. I opened the second one and the same, nothing but $100. There was nothing close to $50,000 but something was better than nothing. We split a little over $12,000, between three people. That wasn't bad, $4,000 and some change. The white boy was happy with the $4,000 and so was O'Boy. But to me, that wasn't shit for all the work we had to do to get it. But they were happy as shit. It was as if they'd gotten the $50,000. I could understand how someone that had never seen some real cash would think $4,000 was a lot. I knew right then and here that would be the reason we would get caught. O'Boy and the white boy were so happy that they had made $4,000 that when they dropped me off at Sad'e's house and told me that I could keep the .38 revolver. The first thing I thought was that the .38 that they gave me never worked in the first place and that's why they'd given it to me. Sad'e's house was quiet. I guessed she hadn't made it home from work.

Everything didn't go as planned but I could not complain. I had a little over $4,000 dollars. All the plans I had in mind to do for my sisters and my family changed. Some I was still going to look out for my sister but not how I would have liked. I still had to make sure Butterfly got everything before the baby was born. I did not have any plans to go out for the rest of the night but Sad'e had just walked in the house with a couple bottles, telling me that she was going to have some of her home girls over for the night. Plus, Dee had called me to go out with him and a few guys on the block.

Sad'e had got a rental car for the weekend and wanted me to drive her to the mall to get an outfit for the night. Sad'e didn't know anything about the robbery I did so she didn't have any idea that I had $4000 in between her mattress. We went to the mall. Before Sad'e got herself anything, she took me to get some shoes and an outfit. Sad'e was not my girl but she didn't mind doing anything for me. After getting my things she wanted me to go with her so she could try on some outfits for herself. Shit, it didn't matter what Sad'e put on, she looked good in it. Every outfit she put on I liked it. She got about six to seven outfits and went to the women's shoe department. I went to the jewelry store with some of the cash from the robbery. I spent about $420 on two rose gold, Jesus faced earrings that would go well with my rose gold watch,

I knew Sad'e had said she was coming just to get an outfit but damn not all this shit.

We went back to her house. I wasn't going to get dressed without getting my haircut. Sad'e knew me like the back of her hand. She gave me the keys to the rental car and said be back in an hour so she could go take her mother some cash for watching her son for the weekend.

I was a little hesitant to leave that $4,000 in Sad'e's house, but I trusted her enough to leave the cash there. I could have easily taken it to Butterfly's house but I didn't want to have anymore problems with her mother. She had just nabbed me coming out her house at like 6 o'clock in the morning. Butterfly hadn't called me all day and when I called her, she didn't answer the phone. After I got my haircut, I stopped by Butterfly's house to see if everything was okay but Butterfly and her mother weren't home. I stopped by my mom's house to see how they were doing but they weren't home either. I would have been a little worried if my stepfather wouldn't have called me and told me they were at the park, having a cookout and that was where they would be all day.

I rushed my stepfather off the phone so I could answer Sad'e's phone call.

Sad'e was just calling to let me know that I needed to find a better hiding spot for my things. She could been talking about anything. I told her that I'd be there in five minutes.

When I got to her house she had a house full of friends. They were all dressed. The only one they were waiting for was Sad'e. The ones that did not know me were looking like, "Who is this boy that just walked in Sad'e's house?"

The ones that did know of me said hi. I went upstairs to see what Sad'e was doing. She had the bedroom door locked. She ask who was it. I told her it was me. She unlocked the bedroom door and explained why she had locked it. She really did not have to explain herself to me . I could see why she had locked the door. She was ass naked with a night stand full of cash.

I locked the door behind me and didn't waste anytime cussing her out and asking why she had been counting my cash. She was looking at me as if like I was the one that was crazy.

She just kept saying, "I'm not counting your cash. This is my cash!"

The cash she had on the night stand looked like every bit of my $4,000 and some. I walked over to grab my cash and she grabbed me like I was in the wrong. I thought Sad'e really believed the cash I'd left at her house was for her until she said something that made me think I might've been the one going crazy. She said that the $5,000 came from her income tax. That made me flip up the mattress to see my pistol and the $4,000. I couldn't do anything but apologize to her. The cash she had was hers and the $4,000 that I hid under her bed was all there. She did not even know that I had that kind of cash in her house. She did not say anything about the cash I had. She was more shocked that I would think she would try to get over on me for some cash. When she just had bought me all those things and was going to give me some cash to help me get a lot of drugs but ever since Scrap got locked, up the streets had been fucked up.

Everyone was being robbed or being got over on by people selling them fake work. So if I was going to buy some drugs to sell, it wasn't going to be a lot. There were a lot of wolves out that were looking for a quick come up.

Sad'e finally got out of the shower, still mad at me. She wouldn't say anything to me the whole time she was getting dressed. I wasn't going to sit in that room while she had her attitude. There were already a lot of things on my mind. I just wanted to have a good time. I took a shower and I didn't enjoy that either. Sad'e's room door would not stop from opening and closing. If I hadn't moved the cash, I would have thought one of her friends was trying to rob me.

Sad'e had knocked on the bathroom door. "I'm going with my friends," she said. "Do you need to hold the car?"

I don't know if that was her way of letting me know she wasn't mad anymore.

"Yes," I told her.

She put the car keys on the sink and pulled the shower curtain back to give me a kiss. Sad'e didn't consider us being in a relationship. So for her to say she loved me was odd. I paused for a few seconds before saying I loved her back. The sound of her voice faded and quieted as she and her friend left out the house. I stayed in the shower for about three more minutes then got out just in time to catch Butterfly's phone call.

I was so happy to see Butterfly had called me that I hit the wrong button and cancelled her phone call. I immediately called her back, hoping she was going to be happy to talk to me like I was to speak to her, but she seemed down. I had asked her was everything alright with her.

"Is everything alright?" I asked.

"Yes," she said. The sound of her voice let me know otherwise.

She asked to see me. I told her as soon as I got dressed, that I would be over there. It didn't take long at all for me to get dressed. I had put on my new Jesus faced, rose gold earrings and my rose gold watch and took the $4,000.

I didn't want to ride around with a pistol on me, but I'd be damned if I get caught sleeping that night or any other night.

I pondered on what was up with Butterfly. When I did get to the block, Butterfly, Dee, and Butterfly's cousin Angel were standing around having a conversation. They didn't see me driving the rental car. I got out the car to surprise Butterfly. I snuck up behind her but Angel gave me away. I was feeling good but something was seriously wrong with Butterfly. She looked like she had been crying.

She grabbed me by the hand and took me to the park. I thought I would be prepared for what she was about to say but I wasn't. Come to find out, while I was doing the robbery, Ms. T had taken her to the doctor's office and had Butterfly abort the baby, right then and there. It felt like a dark cloud had come over me. I could not understand why Butterfly would allow her mother to talk her into getting rid of the baby. All Butterfly kept saying was that she was sorry.

She could not understand how I was feeling. My first kid, and she'd gotten rid of it. Everything I begun to do was for her and the kid. The $4,000 was going to be a new start to our lives but since that Ms. T had killed our child, I'd lost all hope inside and Butterfly knew it. I walked her back to her cousin and went and got in the car to gather my thoughts.

I watched Butterfly talk to her cousin as if her mother had not just made her get an abortion. I don't know if that was her way of dealing with it. It sure took a lot out of me. The more I thought about it, the more I thought how he or she would have turned out. Dee must have just found out that Ms. T had made Butterfly get an abortion. He knew there wasn't anything he could say to stop the pain I was feeling. Dee wanted to stop by the liquor store to get a bottle.

Why not, it might ease the pain, I thought. Soon as I got the bottle of Grey Goose I didn't waste any time opening it. Before we made it back to the block, a fifth of liquor was about gone. I dropped Dee off. I turned right around and went to buy another bottle. My mind wasn't in the right place. I had over $4000, a pistol, and was drunk riding around in a car that wasn't mine… and with no license.

The day was all headed for destruction. I got a call from Butterfly. It must have finally hit her. She was crying so much that I could not hardly hear what she was saying. Angel took the phone from Butterfly and told me I needed to get over there and get Butterfly before she went crazy. My soul and heart were dark. As I pulled up to the block to see Angel and Butterfly, I prayed Butterfly could convince me that she didn't have anything to do with her mother making her get the abortion.

The love I had for Butterfly was mind blowing and I don't think she realized how much I loved her. But for her to not let me know that she was thinking about getting an abortion…

Butterfly got in the car and was talking about everything besides the loss of our child. I couldn't take it anymore. "Get out. I'm done with you," I said to her.

***

I was so drunk that I made it to Sad'e's house and hadn't realized how I got there. If it wasn't for my bladder about to burst, I wouldn't have known that I had made it to Sad'e house. I passed out in her bed. The only things I had on were my socks and boxers. The only one that was in the house was Sad'e. She was very upset with me because of how drunk I was. She had taken off all my clothes and put my cash and pistol up. She ran me some bath water because I had thrown up all over myself. That had been the first time I'd ever gotten that fucked up.

After my hangover went away some I realized I had slept until the next night. Sad'e even answered my phone. She said my mother had called to see why I had not come to the park for the cookout. Sad'e covered for me and let my mother know that I had fallen asleep and that I would call her back when I got up.

It might have been a good thing that my black ass did take it in the night before. Six people had gotten shot and then were robbed, and two had died. My mother had been very worried about me. She knew I was in the streets and with what had been going on she just wanted me home. She even invited Sad'e to stay over.

If I hadn't been looking out Sad'e's window, I wouldn't have known that an undercover cop had been sitting in the parking lot. He could have just gotten there but my gut was telling me that they were looking for me for one of the shootings, drugs I was selling, or for the robbery I had pulled.

Sad'e didn't know anything about the robbery I had done.

"Some guy walked up to me and asked me if I knew a guy that goes by the name Rome," she said. "I told him no. I didn't say anything to you because he looked like a crackhead. From the things Sad'e was saying, I knew I couldn't stay at her house. I told Sad'e to pack some things and that she was going with me to stay at my mother's house.

My mother had never met Sad'e but they got to know one another fast. Sad'e's son had gone out of town with her mother so she didn't have a lot to worry about. She left for work from my house, took a shower at my house, and cooked at my house. My room became our room.

It would be just a matter of time before I got Sad'e pregnant. It was the weekend. Sad'e wanted me to go with her to her crib to get some more clothes.

Everything seemed like it would be okay to stay at the house. We hadn't stayed at Sad'e house in over two weeks. We cleaned the house and decided to get a bottle and a movie and chill there for the night. At my mother's house, I couldn't fuck Sad'e the way I would have liked to, out of respect for my mother and sisters being in the house. But there was not going to be any hold back from that pussy that night, and she knew it. Everyone that called her phone to ask her if she was going out, she told them that she was chilling with her babe for the night. Sad'e asked me to walk with her to the store. With everything that had happened the night before, the streets were quiet. Something didn't feel right at all on the streets. A dark cloud hung over the city. Every car that rode by looked like an undercover. Sad'e and I got what we needed from the store and went right back in the house.

I hadn't realized that I was becoming an alcoholic. I had lost my way of life. I didn't have a care in the world and when I did down the bottle all I could think about was the child that I lost. I thanked God that he had put Sad'e in my life to help me get through that night. The next morning, my dick was rock hard. Sad'e woke up and got right on top of me. I needed that. Afterwards, I went for a walk but something was telling me to go back to Sad'e's house.

Before I knew it, three unmarked cop cars had surrounded me, telling me to put my hands up and not to move. There was nothing I could do so I did exactly what the officers told me to do. If the officer hadn't called me by my full name, I would have thought they had the wrong person. The officer read me my rights and put me in the undercover cop car. I still didn't know why they had picked me up. Every time I asked them why I was being arrested they wouldn't say anything. They pulled into a building. I had no idea where I was or what they were about to do to me. It was sad to say, I was happy to see other people that had been arrested. They walked me by a holding tank and I saw the white boy that I did the robbery with and in the tank beside the white boy, I saw O'Boy. They had picked them up too.

I hoped they hadn't said anything. But if they hadn't, how did the cops know about me? The undercover cops put me in the holding tank beside O'Boy, took the handcuffs off me, and walked out the door, closing it behind him. One of the officers came back in the room with two photos, one photo of O'Boy and one photo of the white boy. He slid the two photos in front of me and asked me if I knew them. I clearly knew both of them but I told the officer I'd never seen them before. He tried to scare me and say that I could be looking at ten-fifteen years for the robbery. I told him I didn't know anything about a robbery. I was more at ease that was all they had on me.

I thought the next time the officers came back in the room he was going to say something about the shooting but the next time he came in to talk, he let me make one phone call.

The only number I knew by heart was Butterfly's and my mother's. My mother wasn't picking up so I called Butterfly. She picked up, heard my voice and hung up. I called back and explained to her that I'd got picked up by the cops and I needed her to keep calling my house until my mother answered and let her know what was going on. The cop did not give me any time to say goodbye. He just hung the phone up. I thought he was about to put me back in the holding tank that I was in but they put me in the holding tank with the white boy and O'Boy. I might have been young but I wasn't dumb enough to fall for the trick that they were trying to pull. I knew they'd put me, O'Boy, and the white boy all in one holding tank to see if we were going to talk about the robbery. I knew what they were trying to do and so did the white boy, but O'Boy was either stupid or he was the one working with the cops.

Sitting in that holding tank, my mind was running at a one hundred miles an hour. I had bail but it was too high for my mother and father to pay. Even the cash I had at

Sad'e's house wouldn't have been enough to bail me out that morning.

They took me to Y.D.C until my court date. York Detention Center held some street young niggas that knew of me for the work I'd put in on the two boys. A couple Young Boys tried to see if I was really about that life. It was nothing to fight and let niggas know I wasn't with the bullshit. After those first couple weeks, I became cool with some of the guys there. My homeboy, Money, had just left a week before I got there to go to boot camp. On the streets, Money was a laid back guy but in Y.D.C he was someone who fought. I wasn't missing a lot besides some pussy. Looking out my window and seeing the C.O. pass out mail, I knew that I was not going to get any mail from anyone. Just as I suspected, the C.O. walked right past my door.

Once again, I hadn't gotten any mail, not even a letter from my mother. Sometimes I needed to cry to ease my hurt. I cried and cried until I could not cry anymore.

The thought of no one sending me any mail just made me realize that the people I loved didn't love me the way I thought. The best thing I had was the Bible. When I felt sad or felt like no one cared, I opened the Bible. The Bible was my way out.

The next morning, things took a turn for the better. I was the first person to get called for mail. I was surprised to see Butterfly's name on the front of the envelope. I didn't want to go to breakfast or to the gym. All I wanted was to see what Butterfly had to say in her letter. Everything Butterfly said in her letter let me know how she truly felt. There wasn't any doubt in my mind she loved me. I would see how much she really loved me once they told me how much time I was going to have to do. It was my sentencing day. I would find out everything before my court date.

I had one phone call to make. I called my mother to see if they were going to be there.

My mother and stepfather had talked to my P.D. and she let them know that seeing that I was a juvenile, I wouldn't get that much time. My mother had also told me someone stopped by the house to drop something off that was mine. After reading Butterfly's letter I would have thought it was her, but she said it was Sad'e. She was there at my house hoping I'd call.

Sad'e cared for me but when I hadn't gotten any letters from her. I thought she took my cash and guns and said fuck me. I guess I did not know Sad'e like I thought. She'd given my mother my jewelry along with my cash and said she was going to write me that night to tell me something. With all the lies people were saying to me, it made it hard to believe

My phone call was up and the C.O. was calling for me to change my clothes for my court hearing. Mostly, all the kids that were at Y.D.C had court hearings that day. They either were going to go home or get sent to boot camp.

I knew that this was my first time getting caught for something I did. I had no idea to the outcome in court. Time was moving fast until I got in the courtroom. The only people that were there was one cop and my court-appointed lawyer. I sat there while my lawyer let me know the outcome that I could be looking at. To me, she seemed unsure herself. I looked around the courtroom and wondered what was taking them so long to start. I was expecting my mother, stepfather, and sisters to show. I was very surprised to see Sad'e. She took one look at me and a tear rolled down her face. The officer there made it very clear that no one was allowed to touch me, not even my mother, which hurt even more. She tried and the officer said no.

The judge finally came out looking like a cold nut in the face. I could tell he did not want to be there, while he tapped his pen on his bench.

It was the first court date. My lawyer told me that it was just a preliminary hearing and I wouldn't know how much time I was looking at, if I did get any time. I was just there to see if the DA had enough evidence to charge me for the crime they said I'd committed. The DA called out the first witness.

I was shocked to see O'Boy walk up to the stand and raise his right hand to tell about the robbery. O'Boy didn't leave out a thing about the robbery. He even told them things didn't have anything to do with the robbery. He finally got to how he got caught in the first place. He told the judge that when he'd first got the $4,000 that we all agreed to not buy anything but on his way home, he saw a car that he'd always wanted going for $3,000. The owner of the car came out and offered to sell it to him for $2,500. O'Boy explained that he pulled the $2,500 right then and there. The guy gave O'Boy the keys to the car and told O Boy to stop by in the morning to get the registration to the car. O'Boy told the judge that the next morning he went and got the registration to the car, put it in his name, paid for the insurance, and got some tint for his windows. By the time he got done doing everything to the car, O'Boy only had $300 to his name. So he bought some work to sell but the work he got from the guy was fake. O' Boy lost out on $300 so he did what he knew best and that was to go rob someone. Not thinking, he used his new car to do it in and someone got his license plate and called the cops. The cops tried to pull him over and O'Boy took them on a high speed chase. They ended up catching him. They found drugs, along with a pair of gloves, and masks. O'Boy gave the white boys and my name to the cops to get some time off his sentence.

The judge asked the DA where the other guy O'Boy was talking about was. The DA told the officer to bring in the other guy. I turned around to see the white boy walk in the courtroom. I was thinking he was for sure the rat but he didn't say anything. He even tried to help me out by saying he'd never seen me before. I realized the only evidence the DA had, came from O'Boy. If it wasn't for O'Boy, I wouldn't have been sitting in the courtroom. They set another court date for us to get sentenced. The officer took O'Boy out first and then came back to get me and the white boy. I said my goodbyes to Sad'e and my family. They put the white boy and me in the same van. He was going to Y.D.C. I and the white boy didn't say anything the whole way to Y.D.C.

I thought it was just another way for them to try and see if we were going to say something about the robbery. The only time we said anything to one another was when we got back to Y.D.C about how bad one of the counselors looked. They took me and white boy to our cells. They put him right next door to my cell I was so tired that I made my phone call for the night and went to sleep.

My mind was so fucked up from that court hearing that I forgot to write Butterfly before I went to sleep. The next day was visits for us. It seemed like everyone at Y.D.C got a visit, everyone besides me. But my whole day wasn't that bad. I'd gotten another letter from Butterfly and one from Sad'e while people were on their visit. I was in my room, reading the letters that I'd gotten from two girls who said they loved me. Maybe they did truly love me. It seemed like they were the only ones that made sure I was alright.

Before my next court hearing, I did end up getting a visit from my mother and stepfather. They tried to prepare me for the time that I was going to get. I couldn't understand that everything they were saying was right. If I hadn't been doing the things I were doing, I would not have been in this situation. Everything my mother and stepfather were saying was right but they never said anything when I was looking out for them with cash.

***

The next week, I went to court and the judge give me and the white boy a year and six months. O'Boy got six months. They sent me to a Juvenile facility.

Getting to the new place meant from the start I had to put some work in on some boy from Philly who had a chip on his shoulder with everyone that was new there. The other guys were afraid of him but I was not. I knocked that chip off his shoulder. He said he could fight but I couldn't tell. I got mail from Butterfly, Sad'e, and even from Misha.

The only people that seemed to care were my mother, father and the girls I was talking to before I got locked up.

My so called friends, Woodz and Dee not once wrote me. It's like they'd forgotten all about me. Money gave Butterfly a letter when she went to see him to send to me. Besides him, all my mail came from my family.

This was my first time being away from my family for a long time and I missed them a lot. I missed all the little things, like messing with my sister about how her hair was longer than my other sister's hair.

I felt every bit of that time but I also learned a lot from being in there still to this day. I remember something one of the staff said to one of the other kids there. The difference about us and him is we got caught and he didn't. Every one of us weren't in there for all the same charges so that meant that the staff could have done something every one of us did.

As the time came closer and closer for me to go home, I began to think a lot about my life. Being in the juvenile facility, I found out the people on the outside who showed me their true colors. The ones that had love for me showed it. I'd be crazy if I went home and didn't show them appreciation for being there for me.

I realized that God's grace is not getting what we do not deserve and his mercy is not getting what we do not deserve.

My last week at my placement, I found out a lot. Money had just came home from his placement and found a job. Woodz was doing the same old things, renting cars out. Dee had been going through it with some guys up the block and got shot. Butterfly was talking to someone and might've be pregnant. Misha had gotten into like four fights. Sad'e had gotten her a new place. My aunt had moved off her block after two more people got shot. My little cousin wouldn't stop taking cash from his mother so she sent him back to New York to stay with his dad.

On the last day at my placement, it was hard for me to get any sleep knowing I'd changed but the streets hadn't. I wanted to do good I went home for like they say, the axe forgets but the tree remembers. I knew the only way I could make it in life was to get a job and keep my mind on God.

The placement and staff where I was at turned us into chattel and we didn't get paid for any of the work we did. So, if I could work like that for not a thing, I knew I could work at a job and get paid for it. Everything I dreamed to become, I could be if I just put my mind to it.

It was about five in the morning and I still hadn't gone to sleep. In two more hours, I was walking out the door and getting in the car with my family. Just to get in the car and ride down the long road felt good. I hadn't noticed but apparently I had matured a lot. I thought maybe it was because my mother and stepfather had not seen me in over a year. I hadn't said or done anything for them to say I had matured. No one knew the date I was coming home, not even Butterfly or Sad'e. On the ride home, I did not want to miss a thing but not getting any sleep the night before and staying up until five in the morning had my body ready to shut   down.

CHAPTER 18

When I did wake up, I was in front of my house. I couldn't wait to get to my safe. Everything I had before I left was still there, my jewelry and cash. I knew Sad'e still had two of my pistols and Butterfly had two more of them as well. While I was at my placement, my mother asked me to get some of the cash I had saved before I got locked up. I had over $4000, but seeing only $2000. I was a little upset. However, being that it was my mother that took my paper, I let it go. I was just happy to be home, spending some hours with my family. But I needed some pussy badly. Sad'e was the last pussy I'd had before I got locked up so she was all I could think about. Besides, she did hold me down the whole time I was locked up.

I threw my jewelry on and walked to the block. It was my first day home so I wanted to surprise Dee, Money, and Woodz. They didn't have any idea that I was home. Things had changed and so had people. There were a lot of new faces that I hadn't seen before. Dee was the first person that saw me coming on the block and then Woodz. They were surprised to see me. I was happy to see them and Dee had a cast on his arm from when he had gotten shot. I could tell from the tension in the air something had just happened. Every car that rode by Dee would grab on his pistol. Money had run from around his house with one of my pistols in his hand. I could tell he did not notice me at first but when he did he gave me the run down on what was going on that had Dee, Woodz, and him so nervous.

Supposedly. the guy that shot Dee had just came back in town and called Dee's phone. I was cool with Dee but I wasn't about to get into something that didn't have anything to do with me. I didn't know how the guy got down that had shot Dee, so I went to Butterfly's house to get my pistol.

I was very nervous to see Butterfly especially after she had gotten rid of our baby. I mean, she did write me and send me some photos but it was nothing like seeing her.

She'd gotten thick. She hugged and kissed me like I'd never left. I could not get her off me, not even if I tried. I did missed her a lot but I also knew I had been gone for over a year and that she might be pregnant. The thought of her keeping someone else baby made me mad. I asked her to get my pistol that she had been holding for me. While Butterfly was getting my pistol, Money had walked in the house. I knew if I would have asked Butterfly if she was pregnant she just would have lied to me so I asked Money. I could tell he really did not want to tell me, knowing that his mother made his sister get an abortion. Money told me that his sister might be pregnant. That's all I needed to hear. When she came back downstairs with my pistol, I made sure it had some bullets in it and left.

It was my first day home and I just wanted to enjoy life. Dee had gone through too much for me to chill around him.

Woodz had been riding around in cars, not saving any cash not doing anything but getting cars. Money was always at his girl's house or at work. I had no one but myself and my pistol. The only thing I wanted to do was walk and enjoy the beautiful day.

Before I knew it, I had walked all the way to Sad'e new house. I knew she was going to be surprised to see my face but I was in for a surprise. I knocked on her door to her new house. She wasn't expecting to see me and I wasn't expecting to see some guy standing in the doorway in his boxers. He looked at me like I was in the wrong for asking for Sad'e. He asked who I was to Sad'e. I could have said that I was her ex-boyfriend but I knew that would not have been a good idea, considering I could tell he was a jealous guy and he might have found my pistols in Sad'e's house. So, I just told him that I was her cousin, he called for her.

Sad'e walked down the stairs and saw me in the living room. She was lost for words. She waited till the guy walked upstairs to come give me a hug. Even though I and Sad'e weren't in a relationship, it hurt me to see another guy in her house with his boxers on. She tried to explain herself to me which I wasn't trying to hear. I asked her to go grab my things. She told me she had moved them to her mother's house because she didn't want the guy she was seeing to take them. She went upstairs to get her shoes and to let him know she was going to her mother's house.

We talked about all the things she'd said in the letters. How she said she wanted to be with me. I thanked her for holding me down the best she could while I was locked up but told her I would never trust her again. She hit me with some fake tears like that was going to make me change my mind on how I felt. Her mother was gone and there was no one in the house. Sad'e went and got my pistols, still trying to explain herself to me. Being away from pussy over a year had my hormones through the roof. I knew Sad'e had just been fucking that guy but that did not stop me from getting some top from her. It did not take me long to get my nut off. Sad'e cleaned me up and I left, my heart racing more than ever.

It was my first day home and I was walking with three pistols on me. I could not wait to get to my house. When I did, I sat in my room, trying to get my thoughts together. I came to the realization that all the people I loved and cared for were the ones that hurt me the most. Butterfly was about to have another guys child. Sad'e had been seeing someone the whole time I was locked up. My mother had taken over $2000 from me. I did not want to get back in the drug game. I just wanted to do good for myself and live life. I spent a lot of time with my family and when I wasn't with them, I was with my stepfather, looking for a job. But that was not easy coming out of placement for a robbery. The cash I did have was lasting, but not for long. My sisters needed things for school and my father needed to get the car fixed. Trying to keep my cash up I did everything positive I could to make some cash. From painting, to washing cars for a little bit of cash. Being around Dee, Money, and Woodz and seeing they just made paper and spent it just as fast, living day by day.

My mother had called me and said that some lady had stopped by the house and gave her a number for me to call. I didn't have any idea who it was that wanted me to call. Like they say when you're on the path to do right, people always find their way back in to your life. The number was Ms. Santiago's. She had found out I was home and stopped by my mother's house to see me. Ms. Santiago wanted to pick me up to give me a coming home present. Scrap hadn't been locked up for two years and Ms. Santiago had some other guy in her life.

That's what I had thought anyway, but it wasn't another guy, it was Scrap's uncle, Squalla. Ms. Santiago took me out to get something to eat and to introduce me to Squalla. When I first got in Ms. Santiago's car, I hadn't realized that from the knees down Squalla didn't have any legs. He hadn't said a thing at the restaurant or while we were in the car and when he did decide to say something he said, "You're only as good as the team you got."

He reached in the backseat and handed me his cell phone and told me to put my number in it. At first I didn't know why he wanted my number. They dropped me off at my house. Before I got out the car I asked about Scrap. Ms. Santiago said that he got life for killing two guys in jail that he had beef with. Just talking about Scrap, Ms. Santiago became emotional. I dropped the conversation and walked in the house and heard a familiar voice.

I'd be damn if it wasn't Sad'e and my mother having a conversation. Sad'e was sitting with my mother ,having a talk like she didn't have some other guy at her house. I walked right by her and went straight to my room. It wasn't even three minutes before Sad'e walked up to my room and said something to me about disrespecting her. What Sad'e failed to realize was that no one was going to respect her because she didn't respect herself. She told me all those things when I was locked up, but I come home to find another guy in her house. I told Sad'e I was not settling for less and I needed time to get my life right. It took everything in me not to fuck Sad'e, but I couldn't help myself. I fucked Sad'e and then told her she had to go. If I could not trust my mother, how could I trust any other women?

I still had not found a job and my family didn't have anything for me to do to make some cash for myself. I got a phone call from Squalla, asking me to take a ride with his girl. I was kind of nervous. I did not know him or his girl but I trusted Ms. Santiago enough to take a ride with Squalla's girl.

Before I could ask Squalla when she was coming, I heard a car horn.

"That should be her outside in a black BMW," he said. That was the car that was beeping the horn. I hung up the phone and grabbed my little .25 pistol. I had no idea where I was going or what I was about to do. Squalla's girl rolled down her window and asked if I was Rome. I nodded and she unlocked her car door and told me to get in. My first thought when I saw Squalla's girl was that she looked like a sweet woman. I was no fool to not ask where we were going? She said, "First we're going to the gas station, then I'm taking you to see Squalla."

Squalla's house was in the cut, like bandage creams was

all around his house. He asked me to sit down and told me that he'd heard good things about me. "Scrap always talked good about you. I was excited to meet you, but then you got locked up," he said. "Are you still in the drug game?"

"No," I said.

"If you ever want to get back in the game, give me a call," Squalla said.

While Squalla was saying that, the first thing that came to mind was Psalms 63:9, "But those that seek my soul to destroy it shall go into the lower part of Earth."

Getting dropped off by Squalla's girl, my phone was going off. Someone had told Misha that I was home. It was only about 10 O'clock but with going to bed at 9 o'clock for over a year, I was super tired. Misha was not going to let me go home without seeing her, though. My mother was also calling my phone and wanted me to come home. So I decided to tell Misha to meet me at my house.

By the time I got home Misha was on my porch, waiting for me. She had the most pretty smile on her face when she saw me. Misha and I walked in the house. My mother was in the kitchen and she looked at Misha, probably thinking that she was the second girl I'd brought in that day.

I smiled and introduced Misha to my mother. I knew my mother wanted to say something to me about bringing all types of girls in her house. Good thing my stepfather came downstairs in just the nick of time to take my mother's attention off of me and Misha. Misha was awfully quiet when my mother was around but as soon as my mother and stepfather left the kitchen, Misha opened right up. She was happy to see me but also mad that she was the last person to find out that I was home. Misha's conversation was a lot different from Sad'e's or Butterfly's. She really was concerned on what I was going to do with my life now that I was home. I lied and told Misha that I was getting back in the drug game, just to see what she was going to say. I was expecting for Misha to say something on the lines of, "You not going to give it some time before you get back in the drug game?"

But no, Misha looked me in the eyes and said it hurt her to find out that I had gotten locked up.

"There's a way things seem right to man," Misha said. "But at the end, it leads to death."

The way Misha said that, I could truly tell she cared for me in a way that Butterfly and Sad'e didn't. I would say Misha was in love with me but then again she hardly knew me. Misha's mother, Ms. TP had called her phone to make sure that Misha got in before 1 O'clock. It was about 10:40 p.m. and Misha's mother knew that her daughter was at my house. Ms. TP must have had a lot of trust in Misha to let her come to my house knowing I probably would try to get some of her sweet thing. Which I had tried to, but I liked Misha even more knowing that she was not going to let me get any pussy.

We sat there, looking at TV and talking. Misha let me know that the year and half that I was gone a lot had changed. People were reckless, didn't give two shits for anyone's life or theirs. She said one of the guys I'd shot got killed from trying to rob someone and the other guy got life for shooting one guy and killing another. She told me things had been real crazy and that she was scared to even go outside.

I'll be damned! While Misha was telling me how the streets had changed, we heard shots ring out. It couldn't have been more than a block from my house.

My mother and stepfather ran downstairs, thinking that I had left out the house and someone was shooting at me. While I had been gone, my mother had heard about some of the shootings. But me being her son, she could not see me doing that. Nevertheless, It was still in the back of her mind that it might be true.

Ms. TP must have heard the gun shots also because she called Misha to tell her to make it home. My mother and stepfather knew I was not going to let Misha walk home by herself and they also didn't want me to be out so they decided to drive Misha home.

My mother couldn't wait until we got back to the house so she could tell me about myself about bringing all types of girls in the house.

I cut my mother off by saying, "Mom I could be out all night and you would have no idea where I was!"

My mother knew everything I was saying was no lie, so she just asked me to have respect for my sisters and her. A year ago, it would have went in one ear and out the other, but over the year I'd matured a lot and took heed to what my mother was saying.

I was so use to getting up before six that I got up without anyone getting me up. And just in the nick of time to go with my stepfather to look for a job.

By the look of things, if I didn't find a job fast ,my mother and stepfather would be taking care of me for a while. My stepfather and I went to about twelve different places to fill out applications. I was ready to go home to get some sleep. My stepfather dropped me off at the house so I could get some sleep. All that stuff my mother was saying about me bringing all those girls in the house was some bullshit. She had the nerve to have Butterfly in the house when I got home. But I couldn't blame my mother being that she had no idea about Butterfly being pregnant and getting rid of the baby. Plus, I was happy to see Butterfly.

My mother left us to ourselves so we could talk. From the last conversation me and Butterfly had, she was under the impression that I was still mad at her. But how could I be mad at the one girl I truly loved. I still wanted to know why she hadn't called me when her mother was talking about making her get an abortion.

Butterfly stopped me in the middle of my sentence and said her mother hadn't made her get an abortion. When Butterfly said that, my heart sank like the Titanic. If I would have showed any signs of me being upset she might not had told me the truth about what had happen to our child. Every time my sister would come downstairs, Butterfly would stop talking. I knew she didn't feel comfortable talking around my sister. So I took her to my room where she opened up about everything. She said her mother didn't make her get the abortion but she did take her to the hospital because she was bleeding all over her mother's house. Butterfly got to the hospital and the doctor ran some test and said that she had lost the baby.

All I could do was hold Butterfly. *Maybe I had something to do with her losing the baby from all the stress*

I had put her through, I thought.

I told Butterfly that I could've never wanted to be the one to hurt her and by me not being there when she needed me the most I might have did just that. I brought to mind all the good moments we shared together hoping that would put a smile on her face. Considering that my mother knew of Butterfly, it wasn't hard for them to get along while me and my stepfather went to get some things for the cookout we were going to have later that day. When me and my father got back to the house Butterfly was in my room getting some sleep. Things couldn't have been any better or could they?

One of the jobs that I and my stepfather applied for called and wanted us to come in for an interview for the job. Things were taking a turn for the better. Even I and Butterfly were thinking about getting back together. I wanted to know something but she looked so beautiful while she was asleep. I didn't want to wake her. She must have felt me looking at her. Butterfly woke up and asked if everything was alright. I needed to ask her she sat up and asked me what it was.

"Are your pregnant?" I asked straight up.

"No. People are just saying that because I've gained weight from this birth control shot my mom made me get on," she said. "Is there anything else you want to know?"

"No," I said.

My mother called for us to come get our food. Before we walked out my room, Butterfly grabbed me and asked could she get a kiss. I still had crazy feelings for her and I knew if I would have kissed Butterfly my love would have reconciled. Just as I thought, her kiss was better than the first time we kissed. If Butterfly would take me back, I was going to do her right this time around.

1 Corinthians 13:11 "When I was a child, I spoke as a child, I understood as a child, I thought as a child: but when I became a man ,I put away childish things."

My way of thinking was to do right for God, myself, and my family. My mother had told Butterfly that I had been looking for a job. It seemed to impress Butterfly. All she knew for me to do was sell drugs and shoot people. So for her to hear that I had been looking for a job made her very impressed. Butterfly had finished the plate of food and wanted me to walk her home, which I didn't mind. Plus, they would have been popping up at my mother's house and I wanted to spend all the time I could with Butterfly before I started working.

Butterfly invited me in her mother's house. The young minded me would have went in but I had to think Ms. T didn't like me and didn't want Butterfly to be with me. I didn't want any contact with the police. It took damn near everything in me not to go in Ms. T's house. If I didn't have my pistol on me and had to worry about Ms. T catching me in her house, I would have taken the chance. But I had to use my mind instead of my dick. So, I gave Butterfly a kiss and went home. If I didn't have time to do things right when would I have time to do it over?

I got a good night's sleep and couldn't wait to go to my first job interview.

***

It went well. I had gotten my first job and what a

coincidence, it was something I was good at – selling. It wasn't drugs but $1,500 dollar Kirby vacuums. I had no problem selling but my paycheck wasn't adding up. One day I would sell one or two $1,500 vacuums and at the end of the week my paycheck only $300. I saw more than that in less than an hour when I was hustling. I grew up hopeless so I had to stay focused, if I wanted to become someone in life.

The way things were looking, I was doing a lot better than some of the people I knew. Woodz didn't have a job but they were hustling backwards fourteen grams to eight ball. You would think, when you're doing something good with your life people would appreciate that but you also come to realize who your true friends.

Butterfly wasn't one of those people. She hadn't loved me. She just was with me for my name. When I would go see her she would be drunk or about to get drunk. She was not an alcoholic but she drank like a toilet. Butterfly was trying so hard to fit in when she was born to stand out. She said she loved me but I couldn't tell. I almost got into something three times because people kept disrespecting her. I broke it off with Butterfly until she changed some of her ways.

Sad'e would call me from time to time but she would never get another chance with me. The guy she had been letting stay with her had her playing with her nose and to me that was borderline on becoming a crack head.

Misha seemed to be the only girl to care that I wanted to do something with my life. I found myself being around her and talking to Misha more than Butterfly.

Just when things had started to go in my favor they took a turn for the worse. The drugs I used to sell, come to find out my mother was doing them. If it wasn't for me noticing a car pulled up in the back of my house and my mother going to it, or finding open bags in the bathroom toilets that hadn't flushed all the way. I would of never knew that my mother had been on drugs. My cash began to come up short. Little things around the house began to come up missing. She couldn't buy my sisters their school clothes, so that had to come out of my. The paycheck I was getting every week was helping around the house. But then it came a time when I didn't want to go to work because of the thought of some guys in my mother's house while my little sisters were there.

It was a Friday, I'd just gotten paid and I had plans on taking Misha to see a movie but when I got home from cashing my check something seemed odd at my mother's house. My sister had told me that some guy came by the house and asked to talk to our mother and said he was calling her all types of names. Right then and there, I felt my soul turn dark and my heart race. I didn't need to hear anything else from my sisters. I rushed into my mother's room and did not hold anything back. I let my mother know that I knew she was on drugs and that she had been taking cash from me. I told her I also knew that some guy came to the house and cursed her out. She tried to deny everything just like someone that was using drugs would.

My mother had heard some of the stories of me shooting people so when I told her I would blow that niggas head off if he came back to the house she knew that I was not playing. I left my mother's room and went upstairs to change clothes. An angel was on one side telling me he had my family and wasn't going to let anything happen to them and the devil on the other side told me if I didn't take care of the guy who'd come by my mother's house he was never going to stop coming by.

The devil got the best of me. I went to the roof of my house got my P89 Ruger and my extended clip and got ready for the guy to show up at my mother's house. I totally forgot about taking Misha to the movie so when she called to see if we were still going, I told her no. I was expecting her to be mad but she just wanted to make sure that I was okay.

That whole day, I could not wait for that nigga to come back to my mother's house. It wasn't going to be good.

***

That next week, I was supposed to be at work but I still was hoping to catch that guy. Missing those days from work cost me my job.

Squalla called to see how I'd been doing. He wanted to see me in person. There was something he had to tell me. Squalla's girl came to get me. When we got to Squalla's house, Squalla wasn't in a good mood and Ms. Santiago was sitting in the corner crying. Squalla told me that someone had killed Scrap the night before.

Scrap was like a father to me so when Squalla told me that I dropped a few tears. There was not anything any of us could do. Scrap didn't go out without trying to take someone with him but the guy had lived. The hardest things in life can be saying hello for the first time and goodbye for the last. No one was feeling it like Ms. Santiago was. Squalla had a lot of Scrap's drugs. If anything ever happened to him, Squalla had people that would move the drugs. But he knew Scrap talked good about me being on time when it came to that cash with the drugs. Squalla was going to throw work my way. *How could I say no?*

And like a dog that goes back to its own vomit, I was back in the drug game. In just a couple of days, I went from lukewarm to hot with a couple Young Boys that were working for me. Young and in control, those boys would sit you down like an injured would. I hustled with the great and ate with the vultures and snakes. My days turned to nights and my nights turned to days.

I was bringing in a lot of cash for Squalla but I wasn't doing anything with my paper except making sure my hitters were good. I knew how it was when you didn't have cash. It's not cash that's the root of evil. It's the lack of it, and I had to stay full and also keep my Young Boys full.

Being in the streets you had to move like a G and if anyone got out of line, you had to keep your foot on their neck. My soul was dark and team was strong. My mother had gotten herself together and was thinking about moving down to N.C. The streets of York had gotten really bad and it was sad to say that I had a hand in it being that way. There were a lot of territory grids that people would've like to own. I had no problem with territory because me and my homeboys went wherever we wanted. Dee and Woodz were not one of those guys. I wouldn't think Woodz to have a little hate toward me for doing my thing. I had some of the best work around and still those two either wouldn't have the cash for it or would buy from someone else. The minute they let their pride get in the way the, less cash they made. Money, on the other hand, was moving with the wave. Money had the gift of gab. Anything and everything he got his hands on he moved it. He was a trap-aholic. Neither Money, my Young Boys, nor myself were doing anything with the cash besides looking out for our families. It wan;t going to be long before my mother, stepfather, and sisters moved down to the N.C. Even though I was only eighteen, taking care of myself wouldn't be a problem with the cash I was making there. I had been spending a lot of paper on rental cars while on the other hand Squalla had been buying cars.

When you grind like I was grinding you're supposed to reap the benefits. Taking Squalla his cash, I rode by a car lot. A Mercedes caught my eyes. There was no doubt in my mind that I was going to get that car. My stepfather knew a lot about cars and it would be good to talk to him about it. My stepfather gave me some good advice. If I was going to stay in York on my own, I should be looking to get an apartment. My stepfather was right, but I wanted that Mercedes and no one was going to stop me. Before I bought the Mercedes I went home to count all the cash I had. There was more than enough cash to get the car and to get my own apartment if I wanted.

That next morning, I bought the Mercedes and felt like no one could tell me shit. No one, not even my stepfather really thought I was going to buy the car. My mother just had stepped out on the porch for her morning coffee and saw me get out the Mercedes. She was so happy when I told her I had bought it by the time I got dressed my whole family knew about it.

There was not a girl I could not get driving that car. My pussy rate was up before but ever since I'd gotten that car. I couldn't have kept them off my dick if I tried.

They say love is blind and I knew that. The more time I spent with Misha, the more I found myself liking her. She had been there for me when I had nothing and been there when I had a lot. She never changed the way she treated me. She knew if I was going to keep on the way I was going I would be one of the ones to die young.

After getting my own car, a lot of doors had opened up for me. More people were interested in getting the drugs I had and I made a lot more cash. I also had a lot more enemies. I had lost a lot of friends and they weren't even dead. Yet, I tried to be humble but with the life I was living, it made it real hard for me to be that.

My mother, stepfather and sister had moved to N.C. I was officially on my own. If I wasn't staying with one of my girls, I was staying with my aunt.

I had very bad trust issues and I didn't like banks, so I would have Squalla hold my paper, which helped me out in the long run. Money had no problem putting his cash into banks. After making a deposit, he asked me to take him to the mall to get an outfit for the night, which I had no problem doing.

Butterfly had been seeing me riding around in my Mercedes and had been telling her friends that the car was one of the girls' I was fucking, which was a lie.

I knew Misha had not liked Butterfly and today was

supposed to be all about me and Misha. So when I went to pick up Money, I brought her with me. Butterfly was standing outside, thinking I was going to be alone. I took Money to the mall and dropped him back off and took Misha home. Misha didn't want me to go anywhere, her mother nor father were home. Me and Misha had been talking for a while. We got close to fucking but it was never the right time but that day was just right. I always had a thing for dark skinned, pearly white teeth, big butt girls like Misha. All she was looking for me to say is that I wanted to be with her, that I loved her and that pussy was mine.

Misha's pussy was good but nothing could compare to Butterfly's pussy. So if I wasn't fucking Misha, I was fucking Butterfly. With me being in the streets it wasn't any problem for me to go from Butterfly's house to Misha's house. Ms. T still didn't like me but like I said with me having a car, and not just any car, it opened a lot of doors for me. As far as Ms. T knew, I had a job and was a working man. So she let me go to her house.

CHAPTER 19

One of Money's homeboys that went by the name, Nook, had just come home from a place where everyone was ice cold. The way he carried himself, I knew holding a nickel plated pistol and getting paper was not going be difficult. Before I could see what he was about, he stopped me to get a ride to one of the blocks that was known for making people show their true colors. Nook was as humble as they came, but when it came to showing his teeth, he had no problem doing so. When I did get the chance to chill with Money and Nook, there was a lot that I found out about Nook. It was a good thing to find out that he was more on the color blue than a little and so was Money. If the town could not see Money and Nook was on the color shit they were blind.

Nook had no problem doing everything solo. He was real hard with his forty-four and he followed all the rules to the game. After Money went back off to Job Core, Nook and I became closer. If there was a problem with anyone, Nook was down to ride and vice versa. After one incident I got in, niggas were comparing me to Uncle Murda. I appreciated the compliment but I know I didn't get that busy. People could not get on my level. I was living fast and thinking I was going to die young. With me being young there was a lot of older guys that could not bear to see me doing better than them. They tried to put me down anyway they could. Starting by doing little things like busting out my car windows, to try to get people to rob me. The icing on the cake was when someone tried to get me killed. I was doing a lot. Wearing all my jewelry, riding around in a Mercedes, fucking, getting top and back rubs from niggas main things. I knew I was going to pay for it and that I did.

Nook and I had taken over one block. When I was in the trap house catching paper, Nook was outside catching paper. And when I was outside, he was in the trap house catching paper. This day, things were jumping. It was the first of the month and cash was rolling in by the hundreds. I took my Mercedes to get washed and a new stereo system hookup. Squalla asked if I would go with his girl to pick up a rental car. While we were at the rental place I decided to get a rental car myself.

There was not any time to be wasted. Nook had called me to tell me the block was doing numbers. I had not bagged up my work so I took Nooks shift and went in the trap house while he went outside. The paper was coming like clockwork that I didn't have any time to bag up the work. Everything was going from the scale to their hands. My pockets were so packed that I had to take my pistol out and put it up. Every time I did decide to leave to put some cash up someone would knock on the door looking to buy some drugs.

I had called Misha to tell her to come pick up this paper. If there was anyone I could trust, it was her. She called me to tell me she was at the store waiting for me. I left the trap house to see the block full of people and I knew they were going to be people knocking on the door looking to buy some drugs. If Nook was not around they were on their way to the trap house. I got to the store to give Misha the cash. She had told me she'd just saw Nook and he told her to tell me he'd be back. He had to drop some cash off at the house. I gave Misha the cash and told her to call me as soon as she got to the house.

There were a couple of my Young Boys on the block but their ambition was nothing like mine or Nook's. When it came to trapping they made a few $100 and off they left.

Nook had just gotten back to the block. I could tell he was high on those Z bars. It was just a matter of time before he wanted to come out and I let him go in the trap house. I only had been gone for ten minutes and one of my clientele had said he just spent $300 with one of my Young Boys. If I was at the trap house I would have not missed a thing. There had been all types of people from out of town coming to buy some drugs. A lot of them were new faces. The ones I didn't know I made them show me their photo id card and made them do a hit in front of me to make sure they were not an undercover cop.

The paper was great but if at any time the police or jack boys kicked in the door there wasn't much I could do but get rid of the drugs or get to my pistol that was in the next room. I had been in the trap house all day and my instinct was telling me to get out of that house but the cash was rolling in. It was making it harder for me to leave. I would change shifts with Nook but he had gone to get another car for the week. Things would die down for ten or fifteen minutes, giving me enough time to bag up some work before getting a knock on the door. One of my clients had been spending with me all day. The only thing I didn't like was that this time she had brought someone with her and he was a control freak. The cash she went to spend, he'd made her spend more. You could clearly tell it was not his cash he was having her spend. So he didn't give two shits.

She told him she had to keep some cash for some food for her son. After hearing her say that I kind of felt bad for her and wanted to give her something on the house but as far as I knew that could've be the plan, to get me to give them something on the house. Plus everyone had the gift of gab when they wanted something. I had given her what she paid for and told them they could leave. They guy she was with was hesitant on leaving. He would get to the door and turn around as if he was about to ask me something. He didn't. He turned back around and left out the door. He was giving me a bad vibe.

I was just about to get my pistol when my phone rang and I heard the sound of my mother's voice. I hadn't talked to her in over a month. She was calling to let me know that she was on her way to York to visit for the weekend and that she wanted to see me. My mother was going to be very proud of me. My family had moved to N.C. seven months before and not once had I called them asking for any cash. I rushed my mother off the phone so I could see who was knocking at the door all crazy.

Before opening the door I looked out the window to see who it was. It was the lady and guy that had just left. There was no way they had finished the work I just had sold them. I let them in to see what was up. I opened the door to hear them talk about how I had beaten them for their paper and sold them some fake work which I knew was a lie. I had been selling the drugs all day and not once had I had someone come back saying my work was fake. They were only saying these things to scam me out of some more work. I had not realized the whole time the guy was explaining himself to me that he was planning to make his move. He had pulled out a butterfly knife that he had been hiding in his hooded jacket. I stepped back to try to avoid him from stabbing me in the neck but he still ended up stabbing me in my face. It knocked me back and over the couch. I went falling to the ground. I knew if I didn't get up fast enough that I would not make it out of the house alive. He was doing everything in his power to kill me and I was doing everything in my power to stay alive. He was a big guy and on top of that he had a knife. I was looking for anything to even the odds out. I couldn't get to my pistol that was in the next room due to him blocking the door way. He had already had stabbed me in the face and I was losing blood fast. I was feeling like I was about to pass out. He rushed me and I used everything I had in my might and landed a right hook to his jaw. He folded like a lawn chair, the knife flew behind the refrigerator and he was out cold. That still did not stop me from putting hands and feet all over him. If it wasn't for the lady coming back into the house I would have still been there fucking him up.

I walked out the house to see if I could find Nook. One of my clients had walked up to me with the looking at me like there were two UFO's behind me.

"Honey," she said. "What is wrong with your face?"

I knew he had stabbed me but when I put my hand on my face and my two fingers went in my mouth, I knew it was bad enough that I'd passed out not once but three times. The first time, the lady that told me about my face caught me and when I woke up I was in her van. I looked down. The left side of my shirt was full of blood but my main concern was to get the drugs off me. The lady that had me in her van I had only seen a few times and I knew there was a chance that if I gave her my drugs I would never see her again. I knew when she took me to the hospital that the nurse was going to take everything out my pockets so I took a chance and gave the lady my drugs.

Just before I passed out for the second time. When I did come to, I was at the hospital with nurses all around, asking me my name. I had no ID, no Driver's License, nothing except a whole lot of cash and jewelry. The nurse stitched me up and left me there. Just as she was walking out the room, the cops were walking in. From the start of the conversation they were true dick heads. They were more stuck on that maybe I did something to call for me to have a hole in the side of my face! They were being dick heads but I was being a super dick head. They tried to use reverse psychology by saying the knife that went in my face was three inches from hitting my jugular. It did not matter to me what the cops were saying because I was going to get my own revenge. They laid one of their cards down on the table beside me and walked out the door, mumbling something under their breath.

The nurse walked in the room and handed me some aspirin to take down the swelling in my face. There was a knock at the door. I thought it was the cops coming back to ask me some more questions but it was not. It was Tank and Woodz coming to pick me up. They kept asking me what happened but I didn't want to talk due to the pain in my face. My Young Boys was blowing up my phone. I answered to let them know I was alright and to meet me at the low key spot. That was all I had to say and Nook and the Young Boys were there dressed in all black with their pistols in hand. They didn't want to know what had happened. All they wanted to know was who had done it and where they could find him. But nothing would be better than getting revenge myself.

All I wanted for Nook and my Young Boys to do was find the guy and keep an eye on him for me until my mother left town. Nothing hurt me more than for me to see my mother cry from something someone did to me. This weekend was supposed to be all laughter but instead it was all cries. My mother begged me to go back with her to N.C. but I couldn't see myself doing so. Not with all the cash I was making.

As soon as my mother left, it was as if everywhere I went became my hunting grounds. I still hadn't found or seen that guy that stabbed me in the face.

I ate my competition like Bobby Fisher. If you were not with me or my team, we had a problem. I was the cold hearted, black soul with the nick name G.M.G, Getting Money Gangster. It seemed like the more enemies I had the more cash I made.

There wasn't anyone I really had to look out for. My mother, sisters, grandma, and stepfather were all staying in N.C. My cousin, Tank, stayed with his girl out of town. With that being said, it wasn't hard to win a battle when you didn't have anything to lose.

It was like having beef with a suicide bomber. I always won and I was playing the suicide bomber. Woodz and Dee were nothing like Nook or I. They never chilled as much as Nook and I did. Woodz was down bad and wanted to borrow some cash. Woodz was my homeboy, but he did dumb shit with his cash when he got it. Like putting down payments on cars and not having the money to finish the payments. When Woodz came to borrow some cash from me, I told him before borrowing paper to decide which he needed more. They say the truth hurts, and I could tell he didn't like what I'd said but he also knew I had the type of paper he was looking for and that I was not the one to play when it came to getting my cash back. Woodz took it and turned right around and bought some painkillers from one of my Young Boys.

Being in the streets, you find out about a lot of things people do in the dark. When the sun rose, I rolled my Sour up and loaded the semi up. One of my favorite games to play was hide and seek. What the streets hid, me and my team would seek. We were addicted like Pablo Doe for that paper and it was calling us.

By 10 O'clock we were drinking double cups, getting

paper cuts. Some of my team was begging to get bagged for the work we were putting in. That didn't stop us. It just slowed us down a bit. Until my niggas left the can, they're just tuna fish. We all came from the bottom so we stayed going in. We all had bling, cars, paper, and the women stayed rolling in every week. It seemed like I had something new and bad. Most of the time when they saw my Benz and saw the face on my watch, things looked up for me and my niggas. But what goes around comes back around.

***

Squalla always told me there are always people out there in those streets that aren't with the bull shit as well. He was right. There had been some boy around my age that had moved from New York to York. He was easy to recognize considering he only had one eye. He let it be known that he wasn't one to be played with. His first day in York, he shot two people for saying something about his one eye. Come to find out he had been to York over the summer time awhile back when I was locked up at my placement. He must have been the guy with the one eye that was trying to talk to Misha. She'd wrote me about him. But that did not matter to me because of something Misha said to me one day.

"Rome I love you so much," she said. "If you cut off my right arm, I'd hug you with the left one."

But instinct told me when you give a girl good dick like I was, they would say anything at that time. Don't get me wrong, I knew Misha loved me. I was about to see how much she loved me.

I was about to be gone for a while. There was something I had to do for Squalla down in Florida. And I couldn't let Misha or anyone know where I was going. Squalla would not even tell me.

He said everything I needed was down in Florida. I'd never been to Florida before so I was looking forward to going. The view was nice but the fourteen hour drive was a killer. I stopped at a hotel to get some rest for a few hours and then got back on the road.

Squalla called to give me an address to the house I was going to be staying at while I was in Florida. In the type of rental car I was in, my Florida trip might have been a drug trip. There could have been anything that I was about to bring back, if I was going to bring anything back. I pulled up in the drive way of the house that I was staying at.

Everything about the outside of the house let me know that no one had been here for a long time. I called Squalla to let him know I was out front of the house. He had told me to look inside the mailbox. That the key to the house was taped to the top of the inside of the mailbox. I started to wonder of the trip was maybe a hit to kill me. I was young scared and under control of bad people but I couldn't see Squalla putting a hit out on me when I was making him a lot of paper and I had never crossed him.

I stuck the key inside the door and opened it. I hit the light switch and to my surprise, the inside of the house was nothing like the outside of the house. The inside of the house was swank marbled floors and an all-white four piece living room set. I had walked around the house for about fifteen minutes not knowing whose house I was in.

There was not one photo or sign that anyone had stayed there for a long period of time.

Squalla called to tell me to stay at the house and that someone was on their way. I was nervous and didn't have anything to protect myself with but a knife that I'd taken from the kitchen. I looked in every room in the house and most of them were empty except one with nothing but a king size bed and a 22-inch TV. The refrigerator had a case of beer, one bottle of Hennessey, and a bottle of Grey Goose. The freezer had a pack of hotdogs and a bag of ice. There wasn't even an ice tray in the freezer. I had been on the road for fourteen hours and I was tired but I couldn't get any sleep until the person Squalla said was coming to the house arrived. I fell asleep, not realizing that Squalla was calling. I had missed two of his phone calls but I was guessing he was calling to tell me that the person was outside, waiting for me to open the door. I opened it.

A woman named Yuri was there holding a bag of groceries and a black bag. Yuri handed me the black bag and groceries and told me those were all the things I was going to need. I took the bags still unsure of what I was down in Florida to do. Yuri told me to get some sleep and that she would see me in the a.m.

I couldn't wait to see what was in the black bag. I knew it had to be something crazy because when Yuri handed it to me she had on some black gloves. Everything in the bag was right for a robbery or a hit.

That next morning, the woman came to pick me up. When I got in the car Yuri asked for the phone I'd gotten from Squalla. She handed me another phone which Squalla was on. He told me that the woman I was in the car with was going to tell me everything I needed to know. Yuri broke down everything to me that I was down there to take revenge for the death of Scrap. One of the guys that Scrap tried to kill had made it and moved down to Florida after he got out the feds. He was also one of the guys that was involved with Scrap's death but got off the murder due to the other guy taking the charge. My objective for the day was to find my way around and the fastest way back to the house.

Yuri showed me the other car I was supposed to drive back to York. Day by day, me and Yuri drove around and she gave me game on things.

It was so hot down in Florida. Ninety percent of the cars had dark tints on the windows so it was hard to see our face. The only time I got out of the car was to go in the house that I was staying at.

The more days I was in the woman's presence the more Yuri showed that she liked me. Yuri was in her mid-thirties but had a body like a twenty year old. I could tell Yuri was from Brooklyn from her attitude and accent. I knew this was not her first time doing something like this before.

She showed me the guys face and told me everything about him. I knew the time he had to be at work, the time he got off work, I even knew the side girl he would go see on his break from work.

The month and half I'd been in Florida I hadn't done anything for fun. It was all business. It was a Saturday night and we were supposed to see what club the guy was going to be at for the night. But there had been a killing and they hadn't found the guys that did it. The cops were out heavy and Yuri didn't want the chance of getting pulled over and the cops asking for my ID. She didn't want anyone to know that I had ever been in Florida. So that day, Yuri stayed at the house with me. She had no kids, no job, and no husband to go home to. She had no responsibilities so she stayed with me. I hadn't eaten a home cooked meal or had any pussy in over a month. I played with my dick the whole time I'd been in Florida and if I wasn't eating out, I was making me something to eat in the microwave. So when Yuri looked in the fridge and saw I hadn't been eating all the things that I couldn't put in the microwave or heat up, she cooked a nice big meal. There was not a table for me and Yuri to sit at so we sat on the floor of the bedroom with the lights out and the TV on. We ate, talked, and got to know one another. Yuri was sweet but also about her business. She said that she'd be going back to New York the next week. She had just come down to Florida to show me around and point out the guy that killed her cousin, Scrap.

After eating, she washed the dishes and told me to get the black bag. I had looked in it once, when I first got it and hadn't touched it since. I took out everything that was in the black bag and laid it out on the floor. Two black 38 revolvers, one black bullet proof vest, a pair of gloves, one light, lighter fluid, a pair of black boots, and a one piece Dickey shirt.

Yuri drew a time line for me on a piece of paper and told me to do everything just as she had it written down. I had a lot to think about. Like if things didn't go right, I was going to end up in jail for a lifetime or die. Scrap was like a father to me and I wanted to kill the guy that had something to do with his death. I desired him to die by my hands. And next week, it was on.

Yuri brought two cups, a bottle of liquor, and a case of beer.

"We can relax for the night, and take some weight off our shoulders," she said to me.

I drank two beers and was about to be on my third one when Yuri called out the bathroom door for me to bring her a shot of liquor and a beer. I knocked on the bathroom door to give Yuri the beer and shot of liquor, Yuri told me to come in.

I wasn't expecting for Yuri to be standing in the shower with the shower curtain wide open with nothing but tits and pussy showing. I didn't want to turn my head. Yuri didn't budge, the only thing she said was, "You can come in. Don't act like you never seen pussy and tits before!"

I walked in, sat the drinks on the sink and walked back out. *When she comes out I'm going to try and hit that!*

It was fifteen minutes before Yuri was calling me back in the bathroom, but this time, she just wanted me to wash her back. I slid some little comments to see what she would let me get away with and she shot back with, "Boy you would not know what to do with this."

By this time, I'd seen every part of Yuri's body. There was no need for her to put any clothes on. She grabbed her things and walked to the bedroom ass naked. If Yuri was going to give me some pussy, I had to take a shower. I had a little smile on me. When I got out the shower, Yuri had two candles lit. She still didn't have anything on but a robe. I looked at her and she looked at me and said, "There is no need to drag it out."

She handed me a box of Magnum condoms. I took a shot of liquor to give me a little bit more courage, which I needed the way Yuri was talking. She was acting like my dick wasn't going to do shit for that fat ass and fat pussy. Don't get me wrong, Yuri knew what she was doing but she was running when I put my big black man dingo in her guts. That pussy was good but her head was even crazier. She could suck a bullet out a 357 with the safety on!

After we got done, Yuri went outside to the car to get something. I wasn't expecting to see a board game in her hand. She asked me to get six candles and meet her in the next room. I had no idea what she had in mind to do. Yuri asked me to put a candle in every corner of the room, give her one, and keep one for myself. I realized that we were not about to play a game, but talk to the devil.

The board game was an Ouija board. Yuri thought that if Scrap wanted me to kill the guy he would let me know. Yuri left the room. I had no idea on what I was supposed to do. All Yuri said was to talk to the board as if Scrap was in the room. I did just that, thinking nothing was going to happen. There wasn't a window open and the door to the room was closed. I put my hands on the board and asked one question. "Should I go through with it?"

All the candles in the room went out besides one. It was giving me just enough light to see the board. It said yes.

Right then and there' I knew I'd taken a slice of the devil's pie. My body was ice cold and all I could think about was killing something. Yuri had left the house. She left a phone and note, telling me to do whatever the Ouija board said to.

***

The week had come and gone, I had gone over every detail to make sure I did the job right. It was easier than I thought. As soon as the fuck boy came out his house, I'd cruised by and give him all 12 slugs.

Before his body hit the ground, I was gone. I switched cars and back to York I went. I didn't know if he lived or died. I was not staying around to find out. I turned a fourteen hour ride into a ten hour, not getting any sleep. If I didn't need to put gas in the car, I would not had stopped. I got back to York and went straight to Squalla's house. I didn't know how cold hearted Squalla was until I walked in the house to him pistol whipping his son for taking one of his pistols and selling it. Squalla was colder than the Russian mob.

Besides him pistol whipping his son, he was happy to see me. He had a $3000 and a different rental car waiting for me. I could not wait to get up with Nook and my Young Boys, but I really just wanted to get some rest. I would have thought with me being gone for a month, Misha would have something to say, and she did. The next morning, she let me have it. She wouldn't let me go anywhere until I explained to her where I was at for a month.

After telling her a lie about me going down south to see my mother, she let up on me. Misha thought that I wasn't being myself since I was back. She wanted to ride with me everywhere which I had no problem with. She also told me that my homeboy, Nook was running crazy, getting in all types of shit. He'd even gotten locked up and was out on bail. I had to go checkup on my home boy. Knowing him like a book, he would either be at his house or on the block.

My phone was off for a month. All it took was for one person to see I was back in town and it was as if I'd never left. A couple of people had made a home for themselves and Misha was with the one eyed dude who was one of them. He and a few of his homeboys had taken over one of the blocks.

When I pulled on the block he tried to be disrespectful by trying to talk to Misha right in front of me. He saw the way I was looking, let him know I was about violence. He knew I wasn't talking just to hear myself speak. He grinded and walked off.

Misha knew I wasn't one to get disrespected. My mind was formed by what it was taking in and it was taking in a lot of violence. All my mind was thinking about was dropping Misha off and coming back and blowing out his other eye. Good thing I saw my homeboy, Nook. We had a lot of catching up to do but the day was all about Misha.

I called two of my Young Boys, one my driver and the other my shooter. As long as Misha was with me she didn't mind my Young Boys chauffeuring us around. It was getting late in the day and Misha wanted me to herself, which was understandable being that I was gone for a while. I knew she wanted to get dicked down, but I wasn't going to let anything stop me from making my cash.

The longer I stayed out the madder Misha got and the

longer I stayed out the more things I saw, like Nook talking to the one eyed boy I'd had words with earlier that day. They were talking like they'd known one another all their lives. I had to do my homework on One Eye. He was building a team fast and the odds were starting to be in his favor.

Misha had reached her boiling point and wanted me to take her home. I had to take in consideration that she was with me all day doing the things I wanted and not once had I asked her what she wanted to do. One thing for sure was that she wanted to fuck bad. She didn't know I had the whole day planned out. All I really wanted to do was make sure that things were in order, which I did, drop some work to my Young Boys and make sure they were straight, and to catch all the paper I could before 9 O'clock. Then I wanted to spend the rest of the night with her. It was eight forty-five and I'd just made it to the liquor store before it closed.

Misha wanted me to get her a bottle for her and her friends. She was under the assumption that I was going to drop her off and go about my business, but she was wrong. We got to her mother's house where her friends were on their way to. Misha reached over to give me a kiss but I smiled and got out the car.

She got out the car, looked across the street, and said, "First you take off for a month without telling me, and then when I try to give you a kiss you get out the car! What's wrong with you?"

I grabbed my bottle, locked the car door, and told her to come here and said, "I'll chill with you for the rest of the night."

I gave her a big wet kiss on the lips just as her friends were walking up. One of her friends yelled out to Misha, "Girl I told you he loved you!"

That made me assume that Misha must have been talking about me, telling her friends that I didn't love her. Misha grabbed me by the hand and took me and her friends in her mother's house. The night was like any other night. Her friends were doing one another's hair and getting tipsy before they went out. One of Misha's friends that I always thought liked me offered me a hit of her blunt. Living in the moment, I hit the blunt. That took Misha by surprise when she saw me hit the blunt. If looks could kill I would have been dead. The look Misha was giving me, I don't know if it was because I was smoking or because I put my lips on her friends blunt. Misha never said anything and continued to help with her friend's hair. It was about nine thirty and Misha's friends wanted to make it to the party. I had told Misha I was done for the night but one of my big spenders had called me. Good thing Misha's friends asked me to drop them off. I knew Misha wasn't going to let me take her friends anywhere without her being with me. I dropped them off and went and dropped some work off to the big spender and drove back to Misha's house. We sat outside drinking and talking. She asked me if I wanted to go in to watch a movie. I said yes, knowing her real true intentions were to make love.

The movie wasn't on for five minutes and we were making love. Afterward, we cuddled until we went to sleep. For some reason, I could not sleep. Satan woke me up. Every time I closed my eyes, I would see demons. I did not know if it had anything to do with playing with the Ouija board, but all I could see were images of corpses. I did not get any sleep until the sun came up.

Weeks went by and I had started sleeping in the day and being awake all night. I usually would have been asleep in the day from being up all night, but one of my big spenders had $400 that he owed me and I knew if I hadn't gotten up and got it, that there was a chance he would have spent it. I hadn't been getting the rental cars, so I was driving my Benz.

One Eye had been seeing me a lot now that I was back in town. I could tell he couldn't stand me and could not wait to start something. That morning was just the time. I usually would take my P89 but I decided to take my 38.

As soon as I pulled up to the block where my spender was with my $400, I saw One Eye looking mad. My spender gave me my paper and I gave him some work and told him to call me when he was done.

I drove back to Misha's and lay up until the night but that did not work. Misha woke me up to tell me someone was calling my phone. It was my spender and he needed some more work. She did not make sense. I'd just dropped him off a $400 pack and he was done? I decided to wake up and take this time to see how things were going for myself. My spender told me that he was one of the only ones up there with work besides the boy with the one eye but he had run out. While me and my spender were talking, One Eye was walking toward us with his hand in his hoodie. The last experience I had with someone with their hand in their hoodie, I ended up getting stabbed in my mouth. Instead of

One Eye asking me for some work he tried to demand me and my spender to get off the block. I told him I was not going anywhere. I heard the sound of the gun cock I put my hand in my back pocket on my 38, my spender took off. Before I knew it, One Eye and I were exchanging gun fire. I had let off about three to four shots and One Eye let off about seven or eight shots.

God had to be on my side. One Eye and I were about 7 feet from one another and neither he nor I had hit one another. I let off my last two shots just to keep him behind the car, giving me enough time to take off. I got back to Misha's house with my heart racing. She already knew what was going on from one of her friends. I couldn't put Misha in danger so I got my things and left. I knew One Eye wouldn't do anything to Misha but if he caught me it would be a different story.

I called Nook and my Young Boys to tell them what had went on. Nook and my Young Boys wanted to move right then, which wouldn't be a good move, knowing people knew we had just had a shootout. Squalla hooked me up with all types of things to get the job done right but he did something even better. He had someone do it for me. Squalla had invested a lot into me and did not want anything to happen to me. I had gotten a bad name. Word on the streets was that One Eye had run me out of town. In a way he did, but little did he know, I would get the last laugh.

Squalla would have his girl ride around to show her what One Eye looked like. Every time I saw him, I just wanted to get out the car and blow his head off because it was not just any beef. If I wanted One Eye gone, I had to do it right. The element of surprise was the best way to get someone. Just when they thought it was all over. You give them everything they've been asking for and I did just that.

Months went by Squalla had told me the best times to get One Eye was now that One Eye had got shot in the leg. Squalla called someone to come pick me up. I had never seen the guy before and the vibe he gave me was that he'd downed someone before. He handed me a bullet proof vest and a sawed off shot gun. He must have been following One Eye for weeks, maybe months. He drove right to where One Eye was staying. He never said a thing to me, besides don't miss. I wanted to still get One Eye but months went by and that fire that was inside of me had died down. The guy that I was in the truck with saw it all in me that I really didn't want to kill One Eye. I still was unsure if the guy down in Florida died or not. I knew I'd shot him the fuck up but didn't know if he died. With this twelve gauge shot gun at close range there was a one out of ten chance One Eye was going to live. It seemed like we were out front of One Eye house for hours waiting for him to come out which was a good thing. It gave me some time to ask myself if I really wanted to take the boy's life?

No, but I had to let my presence be known. One Eye walked out the house on his crutch, looked around, and began to walk down the stairs. The devil was on one side of me, saying blow his head off his shoulders, and an angel was on the other side, saying don't do it. I jumped out and aimed the shot gun right in his face and I just could not get myself to pull the trigger. One Eye was gave me a look like he knew he was going to die. He opened his mouth to say something but words wouldn't come out. I hopped in the truck and told the guy to pull off. He looked over at me and told me for not pulling the trigger, I was going to pay, and may be with my life.

Squalla wasn't too fine with me having his homeboy come all the way from New York to help me put in some work just for me not to do it. I really did not care how Squalla was feeling. I was going to have to live with One Eye on my conscience and I could not live with that.

The streets heard everything and the word on the streets was that I pulled a shot gun out on One Eye but never used it. They thought I'd become soft ever since I'd gotten back. Even some of my Young Boys were losing respect for me. The only one who seemed to understand was Misha. She told me things I never heard come from any of my girl I'd talked to. I told Misha that I loved her and she was right when she replied back with, "Until you love yourself enough to change, you can't possibly love me."

She was right, I didn't care if I lived or died. All I wanted was paper and now that I had that I was looking for something else, and that was love. But all the dirt I had done in York made it hard to do romantic things with Misha. I could not bear something happening to Misha over something I'd done.

Everyone got their turn in the streets and I had mine. There was different type of breed of niggas in the streets. They did not care about making paper. All they cared about was shooting and killing one another and the drugs they were on made it worse.

I tried to change for myself and for Misha. Everything with Misha began to change. When I wasn't with her she thought I was with some other girl. Besides things were good between Misha and I. One day when I had planned, to take her out I took her to get her hair done and I went to get my haircut. I knew it would be awhile until Misha got done so I went and chilled with one of the homeboys, who happened to have his girl and her friend with him.

I thought I would have some time to chill before I went to pick up Misha but I was wrong. Misha had been done and decided to walk home. On her way home she saw me, my homeboy, and the two girls. Looking from the outside, it would have appeared that I was talking to the other girl, even though I was not. Misha wasn't trying to hear me. She went off on me and the two girls. Sartly, Misha saw some boy walking down the block and put her arm around him. I went from 0-100. I blacked out and before I knew it, Misha was on the ground and the guy she'd put her arm around was running up the block. Misha was bleeding from her mouth. Misha walked home and I walked back down the block thinking nothing of it.

When a car came speeding down the block, two guys hopped out asking if I was Rome and if I'd put hands on their cousin. It was two on one and they still could not fuck with me. I had no problem fighting and I could tell I still had it.

They hopped back in the car and took off. I tried to walk off when my knee buckled. I didn't know what Misha's cousin's intentions were until the next time they saw me. I made it to the block to get one of my pistols but my homeboy didn't have any shells in the gun. From the corner of my eyes, I saw someone pop out of the alley and open fire on me and my homeboy. Hitting my homeboy in the shoulder we hugged the ground until the gunshots stopped. Misha's cousin had taken it from a fight to guns. My homeboy was okay from the gun shot and I had been laying low until my leg got better from the fight I'd had with Misha's cousins. I had been falling back from all the bullshit but this was the icing on the cake. I'd just let One Eye get away with shooting at me and I was not going to let Misha's cousins slide.

My Young Boys gave them hell for three weeks straight until they called it quits. All my team had gotten into something with someone and that week, it happened to be Nook. He always took care of things on his own but I could tell he needed me. We took no time taking care of his situation or any situation for the most part. The only thing with Nook was he began popping Z bars more and more and ended up having a shootout with the police. They ended up catching him and gave him ten to twenty years up state.

Losing Nook, I was trying to stay away from beefs. I wasn't resting right. I was all alone in the streets. The only friends I had were a .40 caliber, 357, Mac 90, and 1911 Cult 45, but that did not matter. When God calls for you, you're going. With me alone in the streets, one or two things were bound to happen. I either was going to end up killing someone or getting killed.

CHAPTER 20

Ever since the beef between One Eye and Misha's cousins, I had a feeling they were plotting to gang up on me kill me. I did what any smart man would. I got the fuck from out of that town. I left my little cousin one of my pistols, kept two, sold the rest and went down to N.C. for a while.

It was good to be around my mother, sisters and stepfather. The only problem I was having was going from living one way and running the streets while looking back over my shoulder to getting the rest I needed, living with my mother. Eventually, I got tired doing the same old things every day. I didn't know anyone and the people I did meet would have taken me down the path of using drugs.

I had met a couple of girls but they either had too many kids or were really not my cup of tea. Every day, I fought with myself not to go back to York, PA. If it wasn't for my stepfather getting me a job under the table, I would have gone back to York.

There wasn't anything I needed to spend my cash on besides helping out around the house. So my paper was stacking up. I kept in touch with my little cousin while I was down south. He let me know things were the same; people getting shot and killed. He also let me know that every time Misha saw him, she would ask about me and would give him a number for me to call.

The last time I had talked to Misha was right after I and her cousin's had beef. My pride got in the way for two days, the third day I called her not, knowing what to say. Good thing she was the one to do all the talking. It was a shock when she said she wanted to visit me. I thought she was just saying that because she hadn't not seen me in a while but it was more of a shock when my stepfather and cousin drove to York to look at a car my cousin was thinking about buying.

Misha had no idea that I was going to be in York. I called her and told her that I would come get her to take her back with me to North Carolina. She told me that she'd be ready. Misha had no idea that I was already in York. I called her to tell her that I'd be in York in a couple of hours to get her but what Misha didn't know was that I had been outside of her dad's house for over 20 minutes.

I knew that her cousin died the beef but I wasn't going to take any chances. My cousin didn't like the car so he decided to go back to N.C. that night. I called to let Misha know that I was outside. She thought I was lying but that didn't stop her from running down the stairs to find out. She opened the door and I stood outside. The last time I'd seen that look on Misha's face was the first time that I saw her when her cousin Woodz brought her to my house.

Misha gave me a hug and kiss. I told her that I could not

stay for long. I was waiting for Misha to say, "Okay, call me to let me know you got back safe." But those were not the words that came out of Misha mouth. She told me to come help her bring down her things. I still wasn't going to believe her until she got to N.C. Misha was either crazy or crazy in love to go 600 miles away from home with me after the situation between her cousin and I. But that wasn't the only thing that surprised me. Misha had plans on staying down south and starting a family with me. Misha truly loved me but the thought of having beef with her cousin was making it hard for me to show her the love back.

After a while of being around her, the signs started to show. I would say things to her that would have her walk out of the house in the middle of the night and when she would come back she'd be cold as an ice cube. One thing I would not do is put my hands on her. I put Misha through a lot but not once did she ask to go back to York. I never took her anywhere or did anything for her. She was just there for me to have someone to fuck on. I was cold hearted but not that cold hearted to keep putting her through the bullshit. I decided to take her back to York. She was happy to be back but not happy that I'd stayed and started doing me. I did things a lot different back in York. Like, making paper on the low. Misha was the only one who truly knew I was making paper. It had been 2 months since we had been back and I only fucked Misha about 6 times. Now she was coming out with she was pregnant, which I didn't believe her. She wasn't showing any signs but then again it was only 4 months. Even if Misha was telling the truth, I didn't want it to be another situation like Butterfly and I had. If Misha was pregnant, she was not showing it at 4 months or having any signs. I was convinced Misha was lying. I sat her down to have a conversation about the baby. She tried to blame it on me and said due to the stress that she had lost the baby. It couldn't have been my luck that Misha lost the baby to stress. I would have been upset but I was not believing that. Just the thought of me and Misha having a child together ran across my mind a lot.

A month later, Misha did end up getting pregnant but not by me. It hurt to see Misha carrying someone else's child when she'd lost ours. That still didn't stop me from trying to do everything to help her out. But Misha being Misha, out off the respect she had for her baby's dad, 90% of the time she would not even say hi to me. The only thing that kept my mind off Misha was the street life. She was the only real reason that I'd stayed in York and didn't go back to N.C.

My aunt Rob did not mind me staying with her until I got my shit together and found a crib. The only thing that made me do was spend more cash on things I did not need or care about. Knowing that I had somewhere to rest my head at the end of the night, I did not care how I spent my cash. I became real reckless and the more I made the more I spent. I sold every type of drug and when there was someone getting in the way of me making it, I robbed them, not caring if I lived or died. I didn't know why I was feeling the way I was. I did not care about anyone but my family. But all that was about to change.

On my way to take care of this nigga who had been

running his mouth that I robbed, I ran across this cute faced brown eyed girl but with a smart mouth. She was cursing me and my homeboy out because of how fast we were going and could have hit her and her son, considering that she was pushing in a stroller. A truck pulled out in front of me and the homeboy and a car was behind us, stopping us from going anywhere. The girl and her son walked past, still running off at the mouth. I was already pissed off that this truck was in front of us and that he was stopping me from taking care of my business, and on top of it this girl was standing beside the car talking shit. I rolled down the window to give her a piece of my mind but the words I wanted to say came out a lot differently than what I had in mind to say. Instead of cursing her out, I apologized for almost hitting her and her son. She looked at me and rolled her pretty brown eyes. I still couldn't get myself to curse her out, maybe because she had her son that looked like he was only about 3 or 4 years old. I got out the car to say something to the truck driver and to see why he was taking so long to move his truck. The truck driver just got back in the truck and was about to move. I got back in the car.

My homeboy looked at me. "You got out the car and did not try to get her number?"

I wanted to get to my business that I had to take care of done. But being a guy, I told my homeboy to pull beside her. I rolled down the window to get her number. She looked at me and kept smiling but this time when she smiled I knew I had a chance to bag her. I wrote my name and number down on a piece of paper, got out the car, and handed it to her. At first she did not take it but on the second try she did. I told her to call me.

I got back in the car saying to myself that she was not going to call me and if she didn,'t fuck it. Me and my homeboy rode and took care of that little problem and afterward, we chilled with some girls. I had forgotten all about the girl I had given my number to the day before, until she called me saying she thought I had given her a fake number.

I had no idea who it was. I was in so much of a rush to take care of that business that I did not get her name. I had a hard time remembering who it was until she explained how I knew her. She told me her name was Natasha aka Tash. At first, I thought she was a jump off on how happy she was to know that I gave her my real number. Tash and I talked off and on, on the phone for a week. She seemed to know a lot about me and I was dying to find out. Tash had set up a time for me to come see her at her dad's house. I was expecting for Tash dad to be there and he was and he also knew me and had been feeding Tash her info but that was not all how Tash knew me. She also knew my sister Quesh and had gone to school with me and my sister. That's how she knew I was lying when I told her that I was from York. That first date Tash set for us was nice. She was a very sweet girl and I couldn't wait to see her again.

Tash called to see how I was doing and would I be able to see her again the next day. The next day, I had called Tash to let her know that I was on my way to her dad's house to see her but Tash asked me to meet her at the park that was up the block from her dad's house.

I had a lot of foes that stayed on that side of town so not

bringing my pistol was not an option. I met Tash at the park. There was a basketball game going on and there were a lot of people there. It may have been a coincidence that four of my foes where there together or Tash had set me up.

I pulled my pistol out ready to open fire and they did the same. I didn't open fire due to so many people being at the basketball game and I'm guessing they were thinking the same thing. There would be another time to see one another. They walked one way and I walked the other. I had not realized that Tash was still walking two feet behind me, if she did set me up, she would have caught some shells from them and me if we had opened fire. If she did set me up she was not that crazy to take me back to her dad's house where her and her son rest their head.

It was my second day seeing Tash and she'd almost seen me put in some work. If the things her dad and family said did not convince her to not talk to me, this would for sure be all the reason for Tash not to talk to me. I stayed at Tash's house for twenty minutes. I thought that would be the last time I talked to Tash but it seemed like she called me more.

Tash was a good girl looking for an authentic nigga. It was a little hard to spend time with Tash when she had her son, Nell with her. Thanks to God I never ran across any of my enemies when I was with them. There were a lot of times I was spending with Tash and her son, Nell. When Nell would go asleep Tash and I would kiss. It was going on a month and I still hadn't got that pussy.

I got close, but her son came in wanting to see a movie. If I was not at my aunt's house, I was with Tash at her dad's house. She seemed like the only one I could trust and feel comfortable around until I met Bel.

Bel was something I had never been with. She was Puerto Rican, slim like Tash, but nothing the same. I had met Bel three weeks after meeting Tash. Bel had been parked in front of the barber shop, waiting on her boyfriend to get done getting his haircut. I said something to her, thinking she was looking to buy some weed.. The next time I saw Bel, she had been looking to buy some weed for her ex-boyfriend. I didn't understand why she was still buying weed for her ex-boyfriend but I did not really care who she was buying it for as long as she came with the paper.

By this time, Tash knew that I was in the drug game from different women calling my phone. She understood that most likely nine out of ten times it had to do with some cash. Besides, Tash and I was just friends, so if I had been talking to someone besides her there was not much she could say. One day out the blue, Bel called me, not for some weed but to talk to me. I really didn't want to go unless it had something to do with cash but there could have been something she really had to tell me. Bel did not come across to me to be a girl to set people up to get robbed but I was not going to take that chance. I told Bel that I had to get dressed and I'd call her as soon as I got done.

My true motive was to call my cousin, 10x, to meet me on the block, just in case it was a setup for me to get robbed. 10x was a lot like me. I gave him one pistol and told him to stand in the alley across the street. I called Bel and told her that I was on the block that she could come see me. Bel pulled up from the jump. I could tell something was up with her. She had dried tears on her face. I asked her what was wrong. She started her truck up and was about to pull off. I stopped her and told her we could stay here and talk. I really wasn't paying any attention to what she was saying due to me looking in the side mirror thinking at any time some guy was going to run up to the truck to rob me. I did not want my cousin to just be sitting in the alley for forty-five minutes so I told Bel that I'd be back that I was going to run into the store across the street to get something to drink. I got out the truck saying to myself if it was a robbery they would do it now that I was out of Bel's truck but nothing happened.

I got to the store and called my cousin to tell him that all Bel wanted was to tell me how her and her ex-boyfriend had a big fight and she was never going to get back with him.

That the fight started over me because she said if she would talk to another guy then that guy would be me.

I told my cousin that I was going to go back to the truck to see if anything would happen, but if nothing popped off in ten minutes, I was going to have her pull off and he could go home. I got back to the truck, handed Bel a bottle of 7 Up and told her that we could drive around if she didn't mind. We did just that.

I could tell that she was interested in getting to know me but the pain that I'd endured with Butterfly and Misha, made it hard to let anyone get to know me. I already had let Tash get to know a little about me. The way Bel would look at me seemed like she was looking into my soul. I had never come across a girl that looked at me the way Bel did.

Bel had thanked me for putting a smile on her face. She said she would not mind returning the favor. Bel had dropped me off around the corner from 10x's house.

I gave my cousin the whole run down on what was said between me and Bel. In the mix of talking, Tash called to see if I was going to come over. I really did not feel like going on the other side of town to see Tash when all my paper was on my side of town. If it was not for someone calling wanting an 8 ball, I would have never gone to see Tash. I'd been running all day. I was tired and Tash knew it. She had grabbed a blanket and put it on the floor for Lil Nell so he could watch his cartoons. I couldn't help it before I knew it I was out. Every time my phone would go off Tash would wake me up it would be some more paper. So I would wait 'til Tash's father would go to the store or upstairs and I would go out the back door to catch my paper around the corner. And then go back to Tash's house.

Tash's son had fallen asleep. She took him upstairs to put him in his bed. Tash gave me that look like if we were going to do something, we had to do it right then, while her dad was at the store. We were just about to do it but we stopped when we heard her son coming down the stairs. Tash and I didn't have five minutes to ourselves but that would not matter because 10x had called and told me something had went down, and that I had to go to the crib.

I dropped everything to go see what the fuck was happening. I did not have a car and I needed to get to my cousin fast. The only one who came to mind was Bel. I know she would not mind coming to get me to take me to my cousin's house. Bel came right away to pick me up. I got to my cousin's house to find out that it was a joke. Nothing had gone on. He'd just wanted me to head to his house because my homeboy, Money, was back in town. I was mad and happy at the same time.

Money had been home but was staying at a halfway house thirty minutes away and wanted to see me before he had to go back. I busted it up with Money until his ride came to get him. I could tell by the way he was talking that he was going to get right back in the drug game.

Tash called to see if things were alright and said she would see me tomorrow. While Tash was going to bed, my night was just about to begin. My phone went off all day but around 11 O'clock to the next morning it really was popping. It was a little hard to get around being that I'd sold my Benz before I went down to N.C. and if I wanted another car I had to play the night shift. I was done for the night and decided to take my ass to my aunt's house to get some sleep. But like I said if I wanted another Benz, I had to get all the paper I could. I got like three hours of sleep and got up to take a shower and got dressed, then it was back to the block I went. I could tell it was going be a nice day.

It was 7 O'clock and the sun was beaming. Tash called me around 9 O'clock to say good morning, thinking I was sleep. She had not known, I'd been up for two hours already. I asked what she was doing. She said that her dad had woken her up to tell her that he was taking Nell with him to get the car inspected and now she was up and could not go back to sleep so she was going take a shower.

I told her to call me when she get done. Shit I already knew what Tash was trying to say. The next call I got came from one of my clientele. I had them take me to the corner from Tash dad's house. As soon as I got dropped off around the corner from Tash's dad's house, Tash was calling me. I asked where her stepmom was at. She told me she gone with her dad.

I told Tash to open the back door. She did not believe that I was out back of her house. She opened the door, still wet from getting out the shower. At first, she seemed a little upset that I got to her dad's house that fast. She thought that I had stayed the night at another girls house because I had showered got dressed and made it to her house all before she got out the shower. She really did not believe me that I had been up since 7 O'clock and already was outside and got a ride over. I'd be damn if I explained myself to her. I was seconds from leaving her house. She got her shit together fast and asked if I wanted something to eat. She cooked but that was after I busted her ass. I couldn't count how many times she told me she loved me. I beat the breaks off that pussy. I don't know if I should have done that. What Tash did not know was that her dad had gotten a tune up because he had planned to take her, Nell, and his wife on a vacation. I didn't get to see Tash before she left. We talked on the phone but what was a nigga supposed to do when a girl gives him some pussy and the next day goes on a vacation.

When Tash came back her true feelings started to show. She found out where my aunt stayed and would pop up asking my aunt where I was at. Calling my phone and hanging up for no good reason. Tash was turning me off or maybe it was that Bel had my attention and I could not see that I had a diamond but had chosen glass. Tash was a gorgeous girl yet I could tell her baby daddy had put her self-esteem down and I built it back up. The same with Bel. The only thing about Bel was she knew about Tash but Tash had no Idea about Bel. It was hard to stop seeing Bel when she was doing everything without me saying anything. Bel and I could communicate without saying a thing to one another. I was falling for Bel and had been putting Tash off. I barely answered Tash's phone calls and when I did, it was to get some pussy or some rest while I was on that side of town. I was playing ping pong with Tash and Bel.

When Bel would go to visit her family in Puerto Rico I would spend time with Tash, and when Bel would come back I'd spend time with her. Someone's heart was going to get hurt and it was not going to be mine or was it?

There had been a double homicide. A guy and girl had gotten killed three weeks ago and the cops still had not made any arrests.

I had been driving to get my paper and on the way there, I got pulled over. The cops had found a 357 two shot Dellinger. They booked the shit out of me. I sat in the back of a cop car on my way to York County Prison. There was no one I could call to bail me out. I don't even think anyone knew that I was in jail. I did not know anyone's number by heart, so I sat in jail until my court date. I was not expecting any mail but Tash was the first one to write. She had not talked to me in a couple days and decided to call

York County Prison to see if they had picked me up. Tash did not know why I was booked and was not concerned about it. She just wanted to know that I was alright. The next week, she came up to see me and wanted to know if I wished to be with her. I had no one to ride with me, so I said yes.

Tash told me she'd gotten in touch with my aunt and let her know that I was in jail. So, I thought the next visit would be my aunt or Tash but never in a hundred years would I have thought that it would be Bel.

She'd ran across my aunt who told her about my situation. Bel really showed me that she had my back. She wrote, came to see me, put paper on the phone for me to call and she made it to my court dates. Tash, on the other hand, just wrote me from time to time.

The six months that I was locked up, Bel was there for me the most. I knew that there was a good chance that I would beat the charges, but if not, I knew I had Bel and Tash to ride my time out with me.

I ended up beating my charge on a technicality. The officer had no reason on pulling me over. I had not broken any laws.

Bel and my aunt were the only ones there at my court date. They were both supposed to pick me up when I was released, but Bel was the only one that was waiting on me. She was showing me that she truly cared for me. But my heart had been broken so many times, it was going to take a lot more from Bel for me to make her my girl and cut off Tash.

Bel had dropped me off at my aunt's house to get

dressed. As soon as I got done, Bel was calling my phone.

"I've made plans to take you out for some food," she said.

If there was any girl I wanted to be my baby momma, it was Bel. I had never been treated like Bel was treated me, and it did not stop there. She stayed with me at my aunt's house until the next morning. As soon as Bel left, I hit the block but not for long.

Tash pulled up on me, she had just left my aunt's looking for me. I could not keep Tash on the block being that Bel stayed right around the corner.

When I got in the car, Tash did not have much to say. But she really did not have to, I knew the oldiess' language, and that was body language. She did not seem too happy to see me but that did not matter. I could not see myself being with Tash for too long. I needed someone, besides myself, to motivate me.

While I was with Tash, Bel called me. She said she had something else in mind for us to do for that night.

I did not like the vibe Tash was giving me, so I told her to drop me off at my aunt's house.

After Tash was gone, I called Bel to come to pick me up. Bel's plan was to take me to the movies but that never happened. We ended up having sex in her truck and then went to her mother's house to take a shower. After we got out the shower, Bel dropped me off so she could pick up her mother.

***

My mother and stepfather came to York to get me. My stepfather had a job already lined up for me.

I was starting to realize there was no reason for me to stay in York, besides Bel. If it was not for Bel going back to Puerto Rico, I would have never left. She was only going to be there for 2 months and was mad that I was leaving. She even tried to get me to go with her but I could not get myself to go.

I made a deal with Bel, that if she came to N.C. to see me when she got back from Puerto Rico, that I'd take a vacation there with her. But when Bel got back, she had someone else on her mind besides me. She'd gotten back with her ex-boyfriend. That did not stop her from calling my mother when I was at work to see how I was doing.

I really was beginning to miss Bel and Tash. All I did was work or sleep. And it never failed, everywhere I went there was someone looking to buy some type of drugs and the company my mother kept was showing signs of using drugs. I did not know if my mother had slipped and gone back to using. She did not know, but I loved her so much I'd take someone's life for her.

When I would get off work, she would be across the street with some white people that all looked like paper.

"How long has Momma been over there?" I asked my sister.

"All day," she had replied.

***

I finally had a moment to meet the people across the street. The first thing I saw was my mother in a car full of people. My blood was boiling.

My mother, some lady, and some guy got out the car. I looked in the car to see if I noticed anything out of the ordinary but the only thing I saw was a case of beer. My mother tried to introduce me to her friends but I was not trying to get to know them and my mother knew it.

"What are you doing over here?" I asked.

"Nothing. We just got back from getting some beer," she said.

I asked where my stepfather was and my mother said that he'd gone to the store to get something to eat for that night. My mother was giving me a vibe that she was doing something she had no business doing.

If my sister had not called me, to come to the house because someone was on the phone for me, I would have shot that old guy that was looking at me all crazy. I said something smart, hoping he would say something so I could beat the shit down his leg, but he didn't say shit. He just walked in the house.

I walked across the street to see who was on the phone for me. I thought it was Bel but it was Tash, crying her eyes out. She told me she loved and missed me. However, I had heard that so many times that it went in one ear and out the other. A lot of things are there one day and gone the next. I deeply believed that Bel and Tash were those things of the past.

**

Things around me started to change fast. My mother started to have more people come to the house that I did not approve of. My sisters were getting older. One of them had been sneaking out the house to go see some boy when I was at work. Another of my sisters had been getting smart and talking back to my mother, while the other played peacemaker and stayed to herself. Lastly, my stepfather had found another job so he was never home.

My family did not feel like a family. We all were doing our own lil thing. It took for something bad to happen for my family to come together. My sister had snuck out the house one night and had not made it home the next morning. What made it even worse was that there had been breaking news of a girl that had been killed like a mile away from where we lived. I'd never seen my mother so down and depressed. She was not sleeping, all she did was crying. I had taken a couple days off work to help find my sister. We got news from someone that they had seen my sister riding around with some boy. They knew where to find them but there was no need because the boy she had taken off with brought her home. Good thing he drove off before I could get to his car because something bad would have happened to him.

I could tell my mother wanted to say something to my sister but did not, she was just happy that my sister was home.

***

For a few weeks, the house was quiet. My father had taken my sister to fill out an application for the army.

My sister was a very smart girl. She just made the wrong decisions. I think that enlisting in the army saved her life. Shortly after she joined, she started talking to some guy who later became her husband. The wedding was nice besides one lil thing; my mother being late to her own daughter's wedding. My mother only cared about herself. How could she not be there on time? That was the last straw for me. I knew if I stayed with my mother any longer, I would end up killing someone.

I told my sisters that I was going back to York. They understood that I was doing my best to change my life but it was hard being that my mother was not in the right state of mind. I loved my mother but I had to show her love from a distance. Things would have been a lot better for me if I went back to York to stay with Tash. I just had to keep the same frame of mind, a job, and stay out of trouble.

It was not just my mother that had me thinking about going back to York. Tash had my mind on starting a family. I could tell myself that I was not in love with Tash but my heart said otherwise. I could not stop thinking about Tash, no matter how hard I tried.

CHAPTER 21

Tash got an apartment a week before I went back to York. It was an okay apartment but nothing I could see us staying in for long. With the little cash that I'd saved up from the job I had down in N.C. and Tash staying right around the corner from the block I used to run, it was going to be hard not to get back in the drug game. When Tash was at work, I would stay in the house looking in the newspaper for a job. When I was not doing that I would call my lil cousin to come over and play the PS3. I tried to do any and everything to not go back to the street life.

The way Tash and I were fucking, I was for sure she was going to get pregnant.

There had been some shootings that did not have anything to do with me. But the life I used to live had made Tash's mother think me or my homeboys had something to do with it. Tash's mother pleaded with us to move in with Tash's sister on the other side of town. My first thought was no, but I knew staying on that side of town was going to get me into some shit. Plus, it was not all about me. Tash had a son that I needed to think about as well. So Tash and

I decided to move in with her sister.

Tash's sister was a workaholic and never home. Tash had a nine-five job and Nell was either with his dad or grandma. So a lot of times I had the house all to myself.

I didn't do anything but sleep. Every once in a while my homeboy, Money, would pick me up to go with him to make a few runs. Even he could not believe that I was out the drug game and was turning into a family man. I knew at any given time I could get anything from Money.

***

It never failed that every time I went to the store, someone would ask me if I had anything for sale. Nell and Tash's birthday was right around the corner. I wanted to do something nice for them. I decided to sell an ounce of weed to finance a party for them. All I had to do was call Money, and that's what I did. Money was there in no time with an ounce of weed that smelled like a pound. The smell was so strong that I tried to cover it up by putting it in the trash can. Money left to go see his girl and I took a shower before Tash got off work.

I waited to get a phone call from the guy that wanted the weed. He called but had already got the weed from someone else. So, I was stuck with an ounce of weed in Tash's sister house. I hadn't noticed that Tash's sister had taken off work that day. She found the weed in the trash can. As soon as I got out the shower, she let me know she had found it and that I needed to get it out her house. I thought Tash's sister was going to tell Tash when she got home that she had found my weed but Tash's sister never said a thing. I tried to give it back to Money, but he told me that I could do what I wanted to do with it. Before Tash got off of work, I ran to the store to get some incense to get rid of the weed smell that was in the room.

I went to the store with the weed on me. It smelled like I'd just smoked. Damn near everyone I walked by smelled it, even the guy that worked at the store smelled it. I got the incense and left the store.

On my way back to Tash sister's house, some girls stopped me.

"Do you have any weed on you?" one of them asked.

I knew they did not have the cash to buy the whole thing but when one of the girls offered fifty dollars, I could not let the money pass by me. I eyed out an eighth and handed it to her. She gave me her number, telling me to call her anytime if I wanted to chill. I took it but before I got to Tash's sister's I deleted the number. I had never taken a number and not used it.

Could I be in love and not realize it? Only time would tell, I thought to myself.

***

I got to the house just in time to see Tash pulling up. I ran in the house, lit the incense, and went downstairs to help Tash with her things. I could tell Tash was drained from work. She did not even feel like cooking but she had to, it was her night to cook. I would not have had a problem cooking, I just did not know how.

Tash and her sister were about to get into it over Tash not cooking on her night. I defused the situation by ordering whatever they wanted to eat. I could understand why they were both mad. They'd both worked their ass off.

While they waited for the food to come, I ran Tash a nice hot bath while she put her things away. Tash's sister wrote her boyfriend that was incarcerated. I went and sat on the porch, waiting on the food and to get my thoughts together. I don't know if it was me maturing, but I was looking to do something with my life other than shooting, robbing, and selling drugs. It even felt odd having that ounce of weed on me.

The food came. I took Tash's sister her food and made a plate for Nell and Tash. Nell was playing a video game, mad that he couldn't get to the next level.

I went to the bathroom to take Tash her food. Tash was so tired that she'd fallen asleep in the tub. I walked in the bathroom just in the nick of time to turn off the water before it overflowed. Tash took a few bites of the food and asked me to put it on the sink. I took my clothes off and got in the tub with her. She didn't have to ask me to do anything, I already knew what she wanted. I lathered the wash rag and started washing her body. Before I could re-lather the rag, Tash was out cold.

There had been plenty of times I took a bath with a girl but something about Tash was different I felt at peace just being with her. I sat in the tub, massaging her and kissing her neck while she was asleep.

Glancing over at the ounce of weed sticking halfway out my pocket, I told myself after I got rid of that ounce I was done selling drugs. I was in love with Tash and I wanted to be a family man.

If it was not for Tash's sister needing to use the bathroom, Tash and I would have sat in the tub until we grew old. We rinsed off and went to the room. It felt like an ice box in the room. Nell had been playing with the AC and turned it on max. Tash had been so pissed from all the other bullshit that had been going on that day that she was going to take it out on Nell. If it was not for me telling Nell to go upstairs to his room, Tash would have jumped all over him. Tash asked me to massage her feet, which I had no problem doing. That foot rub, turned into a back rub, then a body rub, and ended with me eating her pussy. She went right to sleep.

I had planned on going out but had fell asleep myself. When we did wake up, it was the next morning and almost time for Tash to go to work. The way I'd eaten her pussy the night before had put all smiles on her face before she went to sleep, so why not wake her up by doing the same.

I ate Tash's pussy so well she had a hard time getting out of bed. She almost called off work. But I needed her to go to work so I could get the weed out the house. Even the weed being in a zip lock bag could not keep the smell from getting out. Tash had begun to ask what the sour funk she was smelling was. Tash's sister knocked on the door to tell her that she was taking Nell to his grandma's house and then off to work.

Tash finally got the strength to get out of bed and went to take a shower, taking my phone with her thinking she was going to find something in it. Little did she know, I'd been faithful to her.

I changed for Tash and for myself. Tash got out the shower, got dressed, gave me a kiss, and went off to work. I wasted no time in taking my shower and getting dressed.

Money was on his way to pick me up. He wanted me to go with him to a couple girls' house to keep them company while he took some photos. It was hard not to talk to some of the girls that were there, especially when they changed into their lingerie but I wasn't going to mix business with pleasure.

Money took some photos of the girls, they paid him, and we left. Money wanted me to go with him out of town but my plan was to get this weed off and I was not going anywhere without doing so. Money dropped me off back at Tash's sister's house. I was about to play with fire.

Bel had seen me get out the car with Money and decided to come back around the block to see if she could catch me before I went into the house. I had not seen Bel in a long time. The last time I had, she was telling me how much she loved me.

Bel asked if I was doing anything that night but all I could think about was Tash and picking her up from work. I wasn't going to tell Bel that though. I knew she was still in love with me and just to be in my presence she would do anything. I knew that she'd help me though if I gave her time. I told her that we couldn't do anything until I got the weed off me and just like that she was calling me to tell me that her cousin wanted to buy some weed.

Bel brought the cash but said her cousin wanted to buy the whole ounce. I wanted $500 for it but seeing that I'd sold some earlier to that girl, I took $450. I gave Bel $25 for helping me get it off. Bel took the weed to her cousin then wanted to chill with me.

Bel was a little upset that I'd lied to her about chilling

once I got the weed off me.

I was proud of myself that I hadn't tried to fuck or get some head from Bel.

I knew it was real. I was turning into a family man.

I took my ass in the house just in time to meet Tash's sister. Out of the $425 I made from the weed, I gave Tash's sister $25. She agreed to take me to Tash's job so I could surprise her.

***

Tash had just called my phone to see what I was doing when we pulled into the parking lot. She hadn't realized I was in her sister's car across the parking lot looking at her. When I told her I was outside, it was like telling her the sky was green.

She finally walked out and saw me standing in the waiting room with a bag of food and her favorite soda. I loved the way Tash would smile when she saw me. It put a warm feeling in my body that I'd had never felt before. When I was with Tash, time seemed to fly by quicker.

Tash had a twenty-five minute break and it seemed to only last five minutes. Tash's sister called to see if I was ready so she could stop by the store before it closed. I kissed Tash on those sexy ass lips of hers and told her that I would be back to pick her up.

I got back to the car to hear Tash's sister going off on her boyfriend. She hung up the phone, looked at me and said, "Rome I hope you don't think that I'm crazy. I just been going thru some things with work and my boyfriend."

"I understand," I said. Really, in the back of mind I was thinking that her worst day was my best day, but I kept it to myself. "I'm going to ride with you when you come to get Tash later."

We went to the store, then back to the house. It seemed like time couldn't move fast enough. I went to sleep until Tash's sister woke me so we could pick up Tash. We got to Tash's job and she was standing outside with her things.

She got in the car, took a deep breath, and said, "I couldn't wait to get off work and see you."

We got back to Tash's sister's house and cops were all over the place. Someone had gotten shot. Good thing I was with Tash's sister, or she would have thought I had something to do with it.

Money had called to see if I was okay after he heard about the shooting. After getting off the phone with Money, I went to see what Tash was doing. She had gotten our things together for a bath.

"Tonight, it's my turn to please you," she said.

Before we could get in the tub, my phone went off. Not thinking, I told Tash to answer it while I got the shampoo.

The look on Tash's face when I got back to the bathroom let me know that something was wrong. Tash didn't beat around the bush. She said Bel had called to see if I was okay. "She said she'd heard someone got shot."

I don't know if Bel hadn't realized that I didn't answer or if she did and just wanted to get Tash jealous. Whatever it was, I still had to explain to Tash how Bel got my new number, which meant I had to tell her about the weed.

I broke everything down to Tash. Even about how her sister had found the weed in the trash can. Tash was a little upset, but still wanted to treat me like I'd treated her the night before with a body bath and some good top. It seemed like that little argument Tash and I had, had made the sex better. I don't know if she was scratching my back because she was mad or because I was giving her this big long black dick, maybe it was both. One thing I do know is I put her ass to sleep. I couldn't talk though, my ass went right out too.

When I did wake up, Tash was walking in the room with a plate of food but I wanted some more of that pussy instead!

After I'd worked up an appetite, I was ready to eat. I scarfed down that food and turned on the TV to catch the 11 o'clock news. I wanted to see what was up with the shooting that had happened the night before.

I glanced over at Tash and noticed her stomach seemed a little bigger than usual. I didn't know if it was from the food or because she might have been pregnant. She noticed the same thing, looking down at her smock and over at me to see if I'd noticed too. I loved Tash and wouldn't have minded her having my child.

Tash went on to get ready for work and I went back to sleep. Tash woke me up a little bit later to let me know she loved me and was off to work. After Tash left, I lay there wondering if Tash was pregnant or not. I had to get my priorities straight. I'd never had a problem selling drugs. That came easy. But it wasn't the life I wanted to live.

Mark 8:36 - "For what shall it profit a man if he shall gain the whole world and lose his own soul."

Thanks to Tash, I had realize I could be a family man. But first I had to make sure that's what I really wanted to be.

***

Sitting around was not my thing. No jobs were calling me back. I didn't want to be around any of my old friends. I barely wanted to go outside. I just wanted to be in Tash presence. I didn't know how I'd let myself get to this point. I just hoped Tash wouldn't turn out like any of my ex's.

***

It was Thursday night and there was nothing to do but wait for Tash to get off work. She walked in the door, put her things down, and got right to cooking for Nell's party that she was going to throw for him the next day.

Even though I did not know how to cook, I helped out as much as I could. By the time we got done with everything it was about two a.m. Everyone was asleep besides Tash and I. We took our shower and went to bed.

Tash had called off from work so she could be home for Nell's party, but her morning was not going well. Nell's dad had plans on taking him out of town all week. That wouldn't have been a problem with Tash if Nell's dad would have said that before she made all that food. Good thing Nell did not want to go with his dad.

It only was about 11 o'clock and people were already showing up for Nell's party. Tash, nor myself had gotten dressed and I still needed to get something for Nell.

Money called to see what I was doing for the night.

"Spending it with my step son. It's his birthday," I said. "Would you mind picking me up in 20 minutes and taking me to the mall?"

Money agreed.

I was in and out of the shower and dressed in 15 minutes. Money came to pick me up we went to the mall. I got Nell a game and a pair of shoes.

Money dropped me back off at the house. There was some guy standing on the porch, looking at me really funny. I knew it was Nell's birthday and a lot of his family was going to be stopping by, but the guy was looking at me like he had a problem with me. If it was not for Nell coming out and calling the man, "Dad" I would have never known that was Nell's father. I gave Nell his birthday gift and went upstairs to see what Tash was doing.

Tash had just gotten out the shower and was getting dressed.

I stayed in the room for most of the party unless Tash called me downstairs to show me off to her family members I hadn't met. A lot of Tash's family I had seen around before. Even one of her female cousins who used to buy weed from me and also liked me was there.

Nell's party had come and gone. His father had picked him up for the night and Tash's sister went to the club so Tash and I had the house all to ourselves.

Tash didn't usually drink, but that night I got her to drink with me. We sat on the porch, drinking and talking about our future. It got a little cold out so we decided to go in and watch a movie. That never happened.

We went straight to the bedroom and got it in. Tash and I made love for hours. So long in fact, that Tash's sister got back from the club around three in the morning and walked in the room on us. Good thing the lights were off or Tash' sister would have seen my, "Black Mamba". Tash did not like that her sister walked in the room without knocking. On our way to the bathroom to take a shower, Tash said something about it to her. She then turned on me and asked me if I did something with her sister while she was at work. I knew it just was the liquor talking, besides I would never do something like that.

After we got out the shower, we went to bed. Tash had never held me the way she held me that night.

The next day I got up a little earlier than usual. Money wanted me to go with him to move something into his new apartment. After that, we went to one of his girls house's. It seemed like when a female knows that a guy is in a relationship they try harder to get with the guy. I told Money that he had to drop me back off at the house before it got too late. Tash was blowing my phone up. I had been gone all day on her day off work.

As soon as I got to the house Tash cursed me out. She was not with me being out all day. Tash had put me on lockdown for a week. She didn't want me to go anywhere. All we did that week was fuck. I had to get out the house before I went crazy.

***

It was Halloween and Tash wanted me to take Nell and her Trick or Treating. But Money wanted me to go out with him to take a shot or two for his birthday.

I had not had a night out with my homeboy in a while. Plus, my life was about the change come the following Monday. I had a job interview that I had to be at.

Tash was getting ready for the night. I went with Money to stop by his house and grab one of his CD's that he'd just recorded. Money had told me that a couple people he was cool with were coming to the bar.

The bar we usually went to was quiet, but being that it was Halloween, there was a lot of people there. And a lot of them were my ex-girls. I was only supposed to be there for a couple minutes, but I was having so much fun I lost track of time. I still had plenty of time to take Tash and Nell Trick or Treating. I still wanted to stop by the house to check up on them and let Tash know I'd be back in an hour to take them out.

I had changed a lot, so for me to go back to the house and let Tash know that I was going to be out for one more hour had shown it. Tash understood and I went back to the bar.

When I got there, it seemed like the party had moved outside the bar until I saw a lot of commotion. A fight had broken out and before the night was over, my homeboy Money lost his life. I never got to take Tash and Nell Trick or Treating and the cops were looking for me for questioning.

In one night, my whole life changed. I still couldn't believe that my homeboy, Money, was dead until the next morning. After seeing his face all over the news, I knew it was real then. Word got out fast that the cops were looking for me.

Tash's sister tried to get me to go down to talk to the cops but I lived by a code I never broke. And since I wasn't going to break it, Tash's sister said I couldn't stay in her house.

CHAPTER 22

The way I lived, no one would've believe that I didn't have anything to do with that shit that popped off the night Money died. Just when my life changed, I ended up getting into some bullshit that had nothing to do with me and what made it even worse, was that Tash was pregnant.

Karma came around and bit me in the ass. A lot of people in my position would have turned themselves in to the cops. Like I said though, I lived by a code and I was going to die by it. I couldn't go out of town to my mother's house because I knew that would be the first place the cops would look. I had no plans on selling no drugs and the only people who would let me stay at their house were ones who wanted drugs or cash.

So, there was only one option, to sell drugs. Being on the run with Tash being pregnant, I'd be damned if I was not going to do everything in my power to make sure Tash had everything she needed for the baby.

Everything I did was a green light. There was not a doubt in my mind that the baby was mine.

It seemed liked there was more stress on Tash.

Whenever me and Tash did spend time together, I did everything I could to make her happy. It did not matter how bad my day was going, when I got around Tash, my attitude changed. But when I was not around Tash, I took my anger out on everyone around me. Some nights I couldn't sleep, just thinking about Tash and the baby, other nights, I cried. The pain I had in my heart from not being there the way Tash would of liked, turned my heart black.

I had been going through so much, from being on the run for my own homeboy's murder, dealing with beef, getting in a shootout because pussy ass niggas tried to rob me, to bouncing from house to house.

Just when I thought my luck couldn't get any worse, it did.

Tash called to let me know she was going to the hospital to see what the gender of our baby was. When she got there she called to tell me that she wanted to talk to me about something in person.

At first, I thought the cops had gotten to her and tried to get her to get me up to the hospital for a set up, but I was willing to take that chance just to make sure Tash and the baby were alright.

Everything at the hospital seemed normal. I got three rooms from Tash's when one of the nurses that worked at the hospital started flirting with me, telling me how cute I was. The nurse asked who I was there to see. When I told her, a sick look came over her face. She told me what room Tash was in and continued doing her rounds.

The door to Tash's room was closed. My heart was racing. I put my hand on the door handle, thinking as soon as I entered the room the cops were going to surround me like pit bulls. But the only person that was in the room was Tash with her big belly. She didn't look happy to see me. I walked over, kissed her and then kissed her on the stomach.

"What's wrong?" I asked her.

She sat up, looked me in the eyes and a tear rolled down her face. "Rome you gave me a Sexually Transmitted Disease, a fuckin STD!"

There was nothing I could say. I'd had a lot unprotected sex with other girls. The bad thing was I'd given Tash an STD, but the good thing was the baby was okay and that the STD was curable.

The nurse that had been doing rounds before made her way back to Tash's room and gave her some pills. She told Tash she could go.

Tash didn't feel like waiting for her sister to come pick her up. It was a nice day out and the hospital was not that far from where I was staying at. I would have thought Tash wouldn't have wanted anything to do with me for the day, but no. She wanted to spend time together and come up with some names for the baby girl we were going to have.

Tash didn't say anything to me until about half way to the house. Tash was mad. I'm guessing so was the baby cause every 3-5 minutes Tash would get cramps. I tried to take her mind off the fact that I'd given her an STD and came up with some girls' names. That put the icing on the cake for a while until we got to where I was staying.

There were a lot of females there. Tash had been to the house before. She'd met some of the females but the amount there that day must have just made the fire burn hotter.

It was like I could read Tash's mind.

when I got her upstairs she asked, "Which one of them bitches was you fucking that gave you that STD?"

"None of them," I said.

I couldn't even leave the room without Tash calling one of the girls in and asking them if we'd fucked. Tash was pregnant but all the bitches in the house didn't have a problem putting their hands or feet on a pregnant girl. Not that I would've let that go down. But I also didn't need to get into anything and end up getting kicked out the house.

Tash had fallen asleep while I was rubbing her belly. Her mother had been calling her phone the whole time. I did not want Tash to leave but if Tash's mother had any thought in her mind that Tash was with me, she would have the cops track her phone. I did not need the cops running in the house, looking for me. I woke Tash up and told her that I'd called a cab and it would be here in a few minutes to take her home. Even though I'd given Tash an STD, she didn't want to leave my side. But she understood that she had to go.

Tash gave me half the bottle of pills to get rid of the STD and I gave her some cash to get home. She got in the cab and went home. Soon as she got to the house, she called told me to be safe that her sister had had the cops at her house. The rest of the day I didn't want to be bothered.

***

Tears came trembling out my eyes due to the pain in my heart. My life was a big mixed up puzzle. I was going through a lot, more than ever before. I was doing a lot more drinking. My life was mixed with drunk words and sober thoughts.

Tash and my child needed me to be strong. There was no time to be crying over spilled milk. I had to deal with the circumstances. I was moving real crazy, not giving two shits about anyone except Tash, Nell, my child, and my cousin, 10x.

People were starting to say that I was out of my mind but they did not know what was going on in my mind. I was feeling like the man upstairs was trying to teach me a lesson from all the wrong I was doing in my life. Every day it got harder and harder for me. It seemed like the cops were roaming around every one of my hideouts. I started to do a lot of late night posting, back and forth from one hideout to another. I felt like I had a better chance on not getting caught by the cops if I stayed outside the hideouts. I was fast on my feet and knew York like the back of my hand. I wanted to leave and go out of town but I knew at any given time Tash could give birth to our child and I was not going to miss that for the world! I had to find the best way to stay out on the street until Tash had the baby. Then I would turn myself in with a lawyer. But until that day, I needed to find a secure place to stay.

All my other hideouts were getting too hot for me to rest my head at. All it took was for me to come across the right person. I had been hearing about some girl that went by the name, "Chocolate" who'd just had moved back to York. They said she was one out of the top five baddest dark skinned girls in town. Apparently, she was getting paper and didn't mind going in a bitch or niggas mouth. I had never seen Chocolate before and did not really care to. I had bigger things to be worrying about, like myself, Tash, our child, and where I was going to be resting my head. After Nook went to jail and Money died, I had no friends and the only one I truly trusted was my little cousin, Lox. But I did not want to have him around me like that. I still had a lot of enemies and didn't want anything to happen to him for something I did.

For a week straight, I stayed at one of the traps, taking a shower, changing clothes, and to get at least an hour of rest, then headed back on the streets.

I covered up a lot of my insincerity with exotic fashion but the thought of not being there for my family always lingered, it did not matter what I did. The only time I felt happy was when Tash was in my arms. I needed to find a new road to follow. One that was strong, not old and hollow. I had no friends so that just meant more paper for me. Everyone else I chilled with was just in my life for material things. They thought they were using me, not knowing I was using them.

My heart was cold again. People had started calling me by my old name, GMG, Getting Money Gangster. I was closed lipped. I did not do a lot of talking, I let my action speak for themselves.

One of my associates that I would let hold one of my pistols to move some of my drugs would always have my paper and make some for himself. He would always spend his paper on bottles, rentals, cars, getting fly, and going clubbing. Which I didn't mind. I knew he would always ask me to let him hold some drugs so he could make some paper for himself. With me being on the run, that stopped me from going outside as much.

It was a Friday when he had stopped by the trap I was staying at to get some drugs. I had just dropped Tash off $450 dollars and re-upped, so I had plenty of drugs for him to move. I could tell he was relying on me to give him some drugs. He needed the cash. He had already got a rental, new outfit, and a bottle for the night. He was down to his last $100. I looked out for him because I knew he would not play with my paper and in a way, I needed him to fuck up so he would always be in my pocket. Anytime I needed to go somewhere, I knew I could call him to let me hold the rental car.

It was about twelve-thirty. I had been in the trap house all day, making paper and talking to Tash. Her hormones was jumping off the wall. We had not fucked since she'd found out that I gave her a STD. It was going on a month and I had been taking these pills every day of the week to make sure I got rid of it. As bad as Tash wanted some dick, it was just as bad as I wanted some pussy.

Tash told me the cops had been in an unmarked car across the street from her mother's house earlier that day. But being that it was after midnight on a Friday night, I knew the cops would not be there for too long.

I called the youngin' and told him to let me hold the rental car for an hour. Good thing he wasn't that far from where I was. I just had to walk to the building where the party was.

I finally got to see Chocolate. She was a bad ass dark skinned girl. I looked around the room to see if I could find my youngin'. Chocolate and I made eye contact for a moment until my youngin' came from out the back, hooked up with two girls. He handed me a Corona and the keys to the rental car. I left, going right to Tash's house.

***

Tash and I talked on the phone until I got there. I could hear her mother asking her why she was still up.

Tash's mother asked Tash to go over to her sister's house and put the clothes in the dryer that she'd forgotten about. That was all I needed to hear. I drove around to the back of Tash's sister house and waited for Tash to call me to let me know that if it was safe to come in the house.

Tash and I knew we had to be quiet. Soon as I touched Tash's pussy, that thing got crazy wet. I bended that pregnant ass over and fucked the shit out of her. It did not take long for her or I to get our shit off. I knew it would only be a matter of time 'til Tash's mother decided to come check up on Tash. We stood in the doorway kissing and talking until we saw Tash's mother coming across the street. I gave Tash some cash and a kiss and left out the back door.

It was about 2 a.m. and my youngin' had been texting me to bring the car back. When I got there, he was standing outside with the two girls from the party, and Chocolate. I figured they were waiting for me to get back with the car so my youngin' could take them to round the block. There were too many police out for me to be riding around with them plus, Tash was texting me to call her. If she would have heard the girls in the background she would have had a fit. I told my youngin' to drop me off at the trap house that I was staying at. My youngin' had my paper from the drugs I'd given him earlier that day. I didn't like doing business around people I didn't know so I told him to give me my paper he owed me and come see me in the morning to get some more drugs. The whole ride, Chocolate was all in my face.

I never said a thing to her, even when she tried to start a conversation. I was too focused on trying to come up with a lie to tell Tash about why I hadn't called.

I could tell Chocolate was used to guys being all over her so when I was not giving her any of my attention, she started to come out of her mouth a little sideways. Whatever she was saying went in one ear and out the other.

Youngin' dropped me off, I went in the house, closed the door, and called Tash. We talked until we fell asleep. It seemed like I had only gotten about forty-five minutes of sleep before it was the next morning.

My youngin' was calling to let me know he was about to stop by to pick up the drugs. Good thing my youngin' did call and get me up. I was missing paper.

I brushed my teeth and headed outside, almost forgetting that my youngin' was on his way. I walked to the store to get some breakfast before starting my day.

Seeing people eating with their family made me wonder if I would ever get to live a life like them?

I didn't have time to get my food before Youngin' was calling me, telling to come out front. He said he couldn't wait to tell me about the night he'd had with the two girls after dropping off Chocolate.

Youngin' went on and on about how Chocolate was

talking shit on me. For Chocolate to still be talking about me after he dropped me off, I knew I could pull her. What really was on my mind though, was making some cash.

My youngin' drove me around all day until I ran out of work. The only thing I still had was some weed. Chocolate had called my youngin' to get some sour but when she saw me in the car she cursed him out for bringing me to her house. What Chocolate didn't know was I was the one with the weed that she was looking to buy.

Chocolate wasn't trying to buy the sour off of anyone except me because everyone that sold her sour never had the real thing. She know If she didn't get it off me right then and there that there'd be a good chance she wouldn't find it. Chocolate grabbed the rest of the sour I had and wanted to buy some more. She gave me her number to call her when I re-upped.

My youngin' had to make a run all the way to the other side of town. I didn't want to go with him and the way Chocolate smiled at me, I knew I could get her to let me stay at her house 'til my youngin' got back.

Chocolate was smart. "You can stay here," she said.

As soon as my youngin' left, Chocolate's whole attitude changed. She began to be super nice to me, telling me how sorry she was for getting smart. She said she'd just been going through some things with her ex-boyfriend after running over his bike with her truck. She said she'd have to get a new truck and pay for his bike.

The whole time Chocolate was talking, I was texting Tash to find out the best time to stop by to give her some paper.

My youngin' got back and Chocolate asked him to take her to get her rental car. I had no drugs or weapons on me so I decided to ride with them to the rental place. When we got to the rental car place, Chocolate got the car and wanted me to ride with her back to York.

My youngin' followed in his rental behind us. Tash had texted me to let me know that I could stop by the house to give her the cash. I would have told Chocolate to pullover so I could get in the car with my youngin' but I needed to spend all the time I could with her. She had a nice crib that was in the cut. I asked Chocolate if she could take me to drop off some cash to Tash. When I got back in the car, Chocolate asked why I didn't have a car with all the cash I was making. I could not explain, instead I asked her to drop me off at the trap house that I was staying at. I let her know that I'd give her a call when I re-upped.

***

I bagged up some more work and took a shower and got dressed. Chocolate was the first person I called. I had to get a hold of her and show some signs that I was interested in her. Seeing that she had just stopped talking to her ex-boyfriend, she was very vulnerable.

All Chocolate really wanted was someone to talk to that would listen, and not try to get in her pants. When she came to pick me up, I told her that even though I didn't know her, that if she needed to talk about anything I was just a phone call away.

I knew by saying that she would ask about me and my baby momma. I told Chocolate that I was very in love with my baby momma and that she was staying with her mother for now. But that we weren't living together because her mother did not like me selling drugs.

Chocolate opened up to me more. "You're very mature for your age," she said. "If you ever need me to take you to get anything for your child, I'll do it. "

I had Chocolate right where I wanted her. She bought some more weed and dropped me off at my aunt's house. I wanted to give her some time to think about what I was saying, plus I didn't want to be up her ass all day like most of the other guys.

***

I had to do some more homework on Chocolate. Her name was good in the streets and a lot of people knew her. While I was doing my homework, Chocolate was doing her own homework on me. She had found out that I went by Rome and GMG. There was an after hour spot where Chocolate wanted me to stop by. There were some people that she knew that were looking to buy some weed.

Chocolate knew that I had no transportation to get over there so she came to pick me up. I couldn't lie, Chocolate was already a cute woman but the shit she was wearing made her look even more attractive. Without a doubt in my mind, Chocolate was one of the 100 baddest women in town.

She took me to the after hour spot. I made a $100 then asked her to drop me back off. Chocolate couldn't understand why I wanted to leave so soon when I was interacting with everyone and having fun. I was usually really quiet when I was around Chocolate. So she had a hard time trying to figure me out.

I was fucking the shit out of Chocolate's brain and I wasn't going to stop until I got everything I wanted out of her. All I had to do was be patient. Two hours went by and Chocolate was calling me. Not to buy some more weed, but for me to chill with her. I could tell she was drunk. Her words were slurred and all she kept saying was that shots were on her. Out of all the guys there, she decided to call me.

I wasn't for the dumb shit or feeling too well. After I turned down the offer, she got quiet. She then said some people were looking to buy some sour. She knew that would get me to come out.

I told her to pick me up but to come by herself. I called Youngin' to see why Chocolate was calling me instead of him to get the weed. My youngin' explained that Chocolate had been talking his ear off about me to him. Saying how cute I was, that I was a quiet guy, and that I was all about my business. Before I could get off the phone, Chocolate was calling me on the other end. I told Youngin' that I would be at the after spot in a little. I grabbed my pistol and got in the car with Chocolate. I told her that I'd changed my mind. I'd take her up on that offer to chill.

I did not want to keep being seen with Chocolate. She was the center of attention and I didn't need that, so I let her walk in first.

I sat outside for about five minutes and then went in. A couple of girls and guys there that had bought some sour off of me earlier that evening, came straight up to me to buy some more. Just as they'd ordered, youngin' walked up to me. I let him catch that paper while I went and sat at the bar. I could see Chocolate having a conversation with some of her home girls. Chocolate and four of her home girls walked over to where I was sitting. They all bought drinks and went back to the dance floor. Chocolate bought me a Corona and a double shot of Hennessy and the same for herself. We talked for a while.

Things were going alright until my youngin' told me that he was about to go get his pistol because some guy had beat him for the sour.

There were too many people in the club to get the guy right then and there, plus I did not want anything to happen.

"Do you want something else to drink?"

"No, thank you," I said to her.

"Can I take you home," she asked.

"I'm, good. I'm going to have Youngin' drop me off," I said.

Chocolate had no idea what was going on. Me and my youngin' left. He took me to the crib so I could grab my Mac 11 and we drove back to the after hour spot. Everyone had left, including the guy that beat my youngin' for the weed. It wasn't that much of a loss. It was more of the principle that had me and my youngin' mad.

It was about three something in the morning and we knew we would not find the guy. There was no need to be riding around with a Mac 11 in the car, so I had my Youngin take me back to the crib.

On our way there, I'll be damned if my youngin' didn't see the guy that beat him for the sour. He was with a few of his friends outside a building, chilling on the porch smoking our shit. My youngin' told me which one did it and parked on the side of the building.

I didn't care how many there were, I knew they weren't going to try anything with me holding this gun. I hit the corner with the Mac 11 in my hand, telling everyone not to move.

I knew there were a couple of females outside with them and I was for sure, it was Misha and her cousins. I could not do anything to the guys. Especially after the way Misha was screaming and yelling out my name. The only thing I could do was get a good look at every one of their faces.

I made the guy that took my youngin's sour empty his pockets. "Karma is a bitch!" I said before running away and getting in the car.

I came up a $300 profit, plus the sour. Good thing I told my youngin' I would take care of the guy. Knowing him, he would have done more than rob the guy back.

When I got back to the car, I could tell from the look in his eyes that he wanted to still do something to the guy himself. I told him to go straight home after dropping me off and to come get me in the morning.

I got in the house and turned my phone back on. A message popped up from Chocolate, seeing if I'd made it home and to say goodnight. I thought about calling but I just left a text, letting her know I made it home safely and to call me when she got up.

***

The next morning, it was raining heavily. There was a knock on the door and at the same time, my phone was ringing. I opened the door, Chocolate was standing in the doorway. I was not expecting to see her. She was supposed to call me when she got up, not stop by. Since she was already there, I asked her to take me to get some things for the baby.

I wouldn't have even known that Chocolate had kids. Not one, not two, not three, not four, but SIX KIDS until we got in Wal-Mart and she started buying things for them.

I asked where her kids were, but she didn't want to talk about it and changed the subject. She really wanted to know if I was in a relationship with my baby momma or just there for our child. I knew that my chance to get in with Chocolate. I told her what she wanted to hear. That conversation went from her asking was I in a relationship to Chocolate asking me if I wanted to stay at her house. Her friends had given her the whole run down on me being on the run and staying from place to place.

Chocolate took me to drop off the things I got Tash at her sister's house. I could not stay long at Tash's sister's house but I explained that the girl in the car that I was with was going to let me stay at her house for a while. Tash understood that I had to do everything I could to not get caught.

Chocolate called my phone and told me to get out of Tash's sister's house. She said she'd just saw two undercover cops ride by. I didn't want to go out the front door, so I told Chocolate to come around back to get me. I made it out of the house just in time.

If Chocolate was not there, I would have been sitting in jail. That opened my eyes a whole lot. I had to get shit done and fast. I told Chocolate to stop by the trap house so I could get my things. That same night, I moved in with

Chocolate. The first two nights I slept on the couch, trying to hold back from sleeping with her.

Every night she wore less and less. It was about to be a week and all I did was stay in the house, counting my paper and bagging up some more work for my youngin' to move.

Chocolate would get dressed to go out. I knew Chocolate had someone she was fucking. I didn't care but one thing I would give to her was she would never bring anyone to the house while I was there. As far as I knew, no one knew that I was staying with Chocolate. Everything was going really well.

***

I was restless and wasn't getting sleep. The paper was rolling in and I had not seen one cop by the house. I knew that no one had knowledge of me staying with Chocolate.

I took a chance and went to the bar to check things out. Everyone in the bar that knew me and had not seen me in a while and had thought I moved out of town.

I wanted some pussy badly but I could not go to see Tash. The cops were over there looking for me. There were too many cops out that night for me to be out.

Chocolate did not want anyone to know she knew me. So she texted me and told me that I should go to her house and that she would do the rest of my running around for me.

I listened to Chocolate. Too many police were out for my liking, I could just tell my youngin' to pick up the paper people owed me.

The cops must have gotten word that I was at the bar. As soon as I left, I saw one of my aunts talking to an undercover cop. Something more important than me must have been happening cause the undercover cop turned his lights on and took off.

When my aunt turned around and saw me, her eyes lit up. Before I knew it, I was all over her like a pit bull and she was on the ground with a bloody lip.

I took off and did not stop running until I got to Chocolate's house. I went in, closed the door and turned off all the lights. I ran some bath water, grabbed my 12 gauge shotgun, my pistol and took them in the bathroom with me. I sat in the tub to gather my thoughts. I was losing my mind.

***

Chocolate had come in the house calling my name.

"I'm in the bathroom," I said.

"Is it alright if she comes in," she asked.

"It's cool," I said, thinking she had to use the bathroom or get something. She really wanted was to tell me that the cops were looking for me because I had beaten my aunt up. She told me if I wanted to continue to stay at her house that I couldn't go outside for a while and that she would do all my running for me. I thought she was just talking until someone called with a $300 order. I gave Chocolate the work and my phone. She left, got the $300, and come back to the house.

Chocolate was about her business. Anything I needed, she did, not asking for a penny from me. The next night, I gave everything that I had to Chocolate so she could move it for me while she was out.

Before 2:30 a.m., Chocolate moved everything. She had

all my paper and wanted to know if I had any more drugs.

"No," I told her.

"Have you eaten?" she asked.

"No," I said. She came home with some food and every single dollar of mine.

I had to do something nice for Chocolate. I could not get out to get her anything and she did not want to take the paper I was offering her.

"If you want to do something nice for me'" she said. Help me cook a nice meal and watch a movie with me.

I did not know how to cook, so I helped by cutting vegetables and getting things ready. We cooked the food.

Chocolate jumped in the shower while I setup the DVD player. I was going to check on the food and make sure the it wasn't burning when Chocolate called me in the bathroom to wash her back.

I hadn't gotten any pussy in over 3 weeks. So, soon as I saw Chocolate, my dick got rock hard. I washed her back and got the fuck from out of there.

Tash texted my phone while I was checking on the food. She told me she loved me and to be safe. She said the cops had stopped by her mother's house to see when they'd last saw me.

I lost all my appetite. Chocolate had gotten out the shower, fixed our plates, and made us something to drink. She could tell that something was on my mind. She thought I didn't like the food. I told her that the food was good but that I was thinking about Tash and my child. Chocolate sat her plate down, walked over to the couch where I was sitting and said, "Rome, Do you know why I let you stay at my house?"

"Because you like me," I said.

She smiled and said, "That's got something to do with it. But the real reason is, you're not like the other guys," she said. "I could tell you used to be in the streets heavy. But I also know that you love your girl and child. You're not just in the drug game to get rental cars, go out with your friend, and spend cash on bullshit.

"A lot of the cash you make you either have me get something for your child or to take you to drop some cash off to your girl. That's why I let you stay at my house. You're not just looking for a place to stay. I know if it comes down to it, you would stay anywhere as long as your girl and child are ok."

I couldn't say anything. Chocolate was right about everything. I just couldn't understand if she would be nice to me and help me, why didn't I see any of her kids? Not even a photo.

Just as I was thinking about all that, Chocolate came back with a box full of photos of six of her kids. Photo after photo, she shared a little story with me for each. We had gone through about 100 photos and I could tell it was getting to her. Shit, it was getting to me too. The more I looked at her kids' photos, the more I thought about how my little girl was going to turn out.

The liquor wasn't making things any better. A tear rolled down Chocolate's face and then a tear rolled down mine. Before we knew it, we were holding one another, crying our pain away. Something popped on the TV that made us both smile. Chocolate wiped my tears away and I did the same for her. Then, our lips made contact.

I woke up to Chocolate sleeping beside me naked. Multiple condom wrappers laid on the side of the bed. I'd fucked up and slept with Chocolate. I just knew it would turn out to be a big mistake.

I went to jump in the shower and when I got out, Chocolate was looking in my phone. The whole time I'd stayed with her, she'd never said a thing about making me a key to her crib or gone through my phone, as far as I knew anyway.

She jumped in the shower and left the bathroom door and shower curtain open. I had to go downstairs to get the rest of my paper that the youngin' had.

Chocolate hopped out the shower ass naked and asked me where I was going. I told her that I was going downstairs to get the paper my youngin' had for me. She wrapped a towel around her and watched me out the window the whole time until I got to the car.

So many things were running through my mind. I got back into the crib and put on some music. I soon got back to business, bagging work and counting paper.

All six of my phones were going off. I even had Chocolate's phone was doing numbers. There probably wasn't a drug I didn't have. But if I didn't have something, Chocolate would get it for me.

Chocolate was going out but something was telling me not to put all my eggs in one basket. I had gotten back in touch with Sayna. She would move some of my drugs for me but not as fast as Chocolate would.

***

It was going to be a big night. At noon, a lot of people were going to get their checks. I needed everyone that I trusted to move my drugs. Chocolate had already left and my youngin' was on his way to come get the drugs I had for him. I couldn't stay in the house much longer.

I figured Chocolate would be gone for the whole night so I thought about staying at Sayna's. That way, in the a.m. I could stop by Tash's house to see her and drop some paper off. But that plan didn't work. Sayna had too many of her family members over and Chocolate had called to let me know she was on her way back to the house. I left Sayna some work and told Chocolate to come get me before she went back to the crib.

I got in the car and Chocolate was pissed I had left the house. I wasn't trying to hear that. I told Chocolate to take me to drop some paper at Tash's.

She looked at me. "That GMG true side that my friends told me about is showing," she said.

I didn't say anything to Chocolate. I texted Tash and told her that I'd be there in a few to drop off some paper.

The way Chocolate was driving, I knew she was pissed off. I would have cursed her out but that wouldn't have been a smart move on my behalf, considering I had all my cash and things at her crib.

As soon as we got back to her house, I gave Chocolate a piece of my mind. She tried to make it seem like I wasn't thinking straight. She thought continuously going out and dropping cash off to my baby momma's wasn't smart. I knew I took a big chance on getting caught by the cops. As much as I tried to make it seem like I wasn't in the wrong, in all reality, Chocolate was right.

"It doesn't matter what you say," she said. "You're smarter than that. I'm just trying to look out for you, I love you."

I knew I wasn't tripping. Chocolate had just said she loved me. There was no need for me to say it back. She already knew I was in love with my baby momma.

So I made her say it twice just so I'd know if she for real.

There was no way that Chocolate really loved me. "We don't know one another like that," I said to her.

Chocolate cooked and made our plates. She put on a movie and I sat on one end of the couch with her on the other. She played with her phone the whole time, not saying a thing. It was getting to me. "What are you doing?" I asked.

"Come sit next to me. I have something I want you to see," Chocolate said.

Chocolate had put on her Facebook page that she was in a relationship with an amazing guy. She said she'd realized she was in love and if she could've she would put the name of that person out.

Clearly Chocolate was talking about me. I used that to my advantage and had Chocolate doing everything I could think of to make me some paper. She started to show her ass when I told her that Tash had my daughter. Chocolate was pissed off. There was a lot Chocolate could've done, like tell me to get out her crib but she didn't.

Chocolate took me to see my daughter one day. I had a bad feeling that the cops would be somewhere by Tash's mother's house. Chocolate drove by the house and just like I'd thought, the cops were there. All I wanted to do was to see my daughter and it seemed that was not going to happen that night. If it was not one thing it was another.

***

Satan loves to divide a family and he was working hard on mine. Things seemed like they were only going to get worse, not just for them but for me. The only way I could get my mind off my daughter and Tash was by drinking away my pain. I couldn't count how many times I tried to sneak and see my daughter and Tash. Every time, the cops would be parked on Tash's block. If I didn't take my ass in the house I might not have ever seen my daughter.

I couldn't sleep and there was too much paper calling my phone for me to go in. I stayed out all night, doing everything I could to avoid the police.

Chocolate asked me to come to the after hour spot to take my mind off not seeing my child. The after hour spot was full of people, outside and inside. While everyone was having a good time enjoying themselves, I was sitting at the bar feeling down. I drank so much that I dropped my pistol not once but twice. Chocolate knew that it was time for me to take it in. I made a few more sales and told Chocolate that I was leaving. She told me to hold up 'til her homegirl got back with her phone and then we could leave. I was drunk but not too drunk to notice that there were three guys watching my every move. I'd seen them around the hood before and they were known to be jack boys. All three of them left before Chocolate and I did.

There were two more sells I had to take care of before

Chocolate and I went to the crib. It was 4:40 a.m. and I was waiting for a guy to come buy the rest of my drugs.

I was getting really tired and so was Chocolate. I started the car and began to drive off. Someone sitting in their car in front of me flashed their headlights. I'd seen the car before but was too drunk to remember if it was one of my clients' or not. I pulled over and saw that it was one of my clients, but the way he was acting made me think he was setting me up.

Chocolate hit the horn to get my attention. I turned around to see what she wanted. Chocolate was yelling something and pointing. I turned around to see three guys running in my direction with their pistols out. My client grabbed my arm, trying to hold me from running anywhere. The three guys were getting closer and closer. I pulled out and let off five shots at the three guns and one at my client's car. The sound of my .45 was like a bomb had gone off.

Two of the guys ran behind a church and the other guy continued to run toward me. I let off some more shots his way. He got the memo that I was not playing and ran behind the church where the other guys were waiting. I ran to the car, got in, and told Chocolate to keep her head down until we got somewhere safe. I drove to Chocolate's house and got my box of ammo. Chocolate was now begging me not to go anywhere else.

My adrenaline was rushing. I could not believe someone had tried to rob me. Chocolate and I sat in the house for an hour until one of her home girls called.

She told Chocolate that someone had been shooting and

some guy was dead in the middle of the street. Chocolate looked at me as if life had left her. Chocolate hung up with her home girl, letting her know she'd call her back when she was out of the shower.

Chocolate looked at me and said, "Rome they're saying someone is laying in the street dead!"

Did I kill one of those guys, I thought to myself. I was for sure I hadn't hit any of them, not the way they'd run off. *Maybe there was another shooting.*

Chocolate turned on the TV to see if anything was on the news about the shooting. There was, and someone did get killed around the corner from where the shooting took place.

After Chocolate finished cooking, we ate and went to sleep.

For some reason, I was having cold sweats and seeing ghost. I had to wake up. I did not know if I was having cold sweats because I almost got robbed or because of the shootout. It could have been all the liquor I had drank. Whatever it was, something wrong with me. Even Chocolate could see something was different with me. Chocolate and I did not feel secure staying in the house. We got dressed and went out, being on point more than ever before. We stopped at Chocolate's friend's house to find out the word on the street. Chocolate's friend told us that the guy that got killed was still in the middle of the street. Chocolate, her friend, and I walked up the block to see the body. There were a whole lot of people around, along with the police. They had the block taped off with yellow tape. Chocolate saw the body first, then I. It felt like the devil was trying to pull me down to hell. Every step I took felt like I was walking in quicksand. I could not believe it, my client was laying there in a pool of blood with my casings trailing up the block like discarded pistachio shells.

Chocolate looked at me and said, "Let's Go!"

We got the fuck from over there, trying not to seem suspicious. We left and went back to Chocolate's house.

With our eyes stuck on the news, it put me at ease to see that they still did not have any leads on the homicide. Chocolate was too scared to hang out with her friends or stay in the house alone. I knew my homeboy's grandma, Mrs. Fish, would let us stay at her house as long as I looked out and gave her some paper.

Chocolate and I packed a few things and went to stay at Mrs. Fish's house. There were so many cops out I could not count how many times they got behind us. One wrong move from Chocolate and they would have been on our ass, but she kept it cool until we got to Mrs. Fish's house. Chocolate could not wait to get out the car and go in the house. I took my chance and went to see my daughter. It was just a big enough window for me to see her before Tash's mother got back to the house. Tash brought my daughter Zamora downstairs. She was so beautiful. Seeing my child for the first time made me feel like the heavens had opened up. I wanted to hold her so badly, it was killing me.

Tash dad came in the front door and I had to rush through the back. He saw me and tried to stop me but by the time he got to the back door I was gone in the wind.

I was playing it close to close. I drove back to Mrs. Fish's, walked in the house and saw Chocolate's eyes still glued on the news. I knew if I did not get Chocolate from in front of that TV, she might do something crazy like call the cops on me. I took her upstairs and fucked the shit out of her. I felt bad about fucking another woman while the one I loved was home taking care of our daughter all alone. The more I thought about my daughter, the weaker I got. I did not want to eat, fuck, sleep, or get paper. My daughter was becoming my kryptonite.

A week went by and they still did not know who'd killed my client. Just when I thought I was going to get away with a homicide, my face was all over the news. I was wanted for questioning.

Mrs. Fish saw my face all over the news and asked me and Chocolate to leave her house. Back to Chocolate's house we went, knowing I could not stay there for too long. Every one of her friends knew I fucked with Chocolate. All day, they would call and text Chocolate, telling her I was all over the news.

I had to gather all my paper from everyone that owed me and sell my pistol. One of Chocolate's friends was about to stop by the house to see her because she had not seen her in a while. That gave me some time to go out and get my paper. I was only out of the house a few minutes before the cops were behind me, trying to pull me over. I lost them. Good thing I had a spot to hide the car. Unfortunately, that left me on foot with a pocket full of cash and a pistol. I hid out.

Something was telling me I would not make it. The next

morning, I went to take Tash some cash and let her and my daughter Zamora know that I loved them. The door to her sister's house was open. I saw Tash sitting there holding my daughter, not thinking I walked in. When Tash's sister saw me she ran to the kitchen and grabbed a knife. I did not understand why Tash's sister was going off the way she was. It hit me, she'd seen my face on the news for a killing and she did not know what my intentions were. For all she knew, I was there to kill Tash, our baby and everyone in the house. I gave Tash all the cash I had on me and left before I had to put hands on Tash's sister.

I went back to Chocolate's house. She was sitting in the living room in her bra and panties with the TV and lights off, drinking a glass of wine. I sat by Chocolate and told her I was tired of running from the cops and living the life I was living.

That night I had a feeling that I would not see another week on the streets. I fucked Chocolate like that would be the last time fucking her. After I put her to sleep, I lay there looking out the window at a star. It was the brightest star I had ever seen.

Chocolate rolled over to me. "Is everything alright?"

"Before anything happens to me, I want to pray and ask God to forgive me for all my sins."

After we prayed, Chocolate and I lay there before having sex again and going to sleep. We were awakened by six heavily armed U.S. Marshals standing in our bedroom with guns drawn.

"Are you Jerome Dickson," they asked me. The marshals were more nervous than I was. I could tell they wondering why it was taking me so long to pull back the cover until they saw I and Chocolate were bare naked. They put me in handcuffs, put some basketball shorts on me, and told Chocolate to cover up with the blanket. They looked around the room for a pistol, not finding a thing but Chocolate's V bag, five cell phones, and some cash. They walked me downstairs and put me in the back of one of their unmarked cop cars. In a way, I was kind of happy that it was almost over but also so sad that I would not be able to be the father I always wanted to be to my daughter. After eight months, Chocolate could not take the pressure from the detectives and told on me for the murder. I was sentenced to twenty to forty years for all 3 charges, the murder, the shootout and the incident that happened with my homeboy, Money, dying. I was young, naïve, and wanted the right things for the wrong reasons. I reaped everything that I sowed…

THE END

We Realize the grass is not always greener on the other side. We don't see what we have or how good we have it, until It's all gone. If only I knew back then the things I know now.

Everything that we do, Good or Bad in life is up to us. We have a tendency to blame others for the life we have lived. But the only one to truly, fully blame is our self.

KJV Galations 6:7-8

Be not deceived; God is not mocked: For whatsoever a man soweth, that shall he also reap. For he that soweth to his flesh shall of the flesh reap corruption but he that soweth to the spirit shall of the spirit reap life everlasting.

We Reap What We Sow

For information about my book, "You Reap What You Sow" go to Rome D. Dickson at facebook.com.

To order please go to Amazon.com, Create space, Barnes and Noble, and Books a Million.

Made in the USA
Middletown, DE
13 May 2022

65737468R00186